To Nancy:
May you change the world more than the world changes you!

SABAN AND THE ANCIENT

Book One of "The Transformation"

by

Danté A. Amodeo

Danté Amodeo
10/07

Cover Design by Laura Schulhauser, civictekxx@yahoo.com

ISBN: 0-9777290-8-7

Published and distributed by:
High-Pitched Hum Publishing
321 15th Street North
Jacksonville Beach, FL 32250

www.highpitchedhum.net

High-Pitched Hum
Publishing

DEDICATION

To my father, who passed away just a few weeks before the final edits were completed: we both thought you would make it a little while longer, but things don't always work out. Still, you knew the book was "in the system," ready to be printed, and I'm glad that made you happy.

For the rest of the world: now I know why authors always seem to thank their families first. Despite my best efforts to steal time only from my slumber, this effort inevitably worked its way into many Saturdays and weeknights and early mornings, not just 10pm to 2am. To my wife, Deborah, who allowed me to leave for hours at a time, and to my wonderful daughters, Kathryn and Janae, who continued to laugh and dance in my absences, I am eternally grateful.

Then there were others who helped along the way: Susan Tyler, who encouraged me to finish the story after reading the first five chapters of a horribly rough draft; Kate Kirk, who was the first to read the whole thing, poor dear; Andrew Burt's Critters at www.critters.org, who critiqued chapter after chapter. And still others (forgive me if I forgot someone) who gave me encouragement or valuable feedback: Matt and Jessica Amodeo, Finnis Beattie, Michael Berry, Jenna Bowen, Rose Britton, Michelle Burdick, Skyla Dawn Cameron, "Tonito" Cinca, Rosalie Cullen, Emmett Grandy, Beth Harmon, Susan Laurence, Mary Neville, Paul Poirrier, Shannon Stanley, Ryan Summers, Steve Tamburrino, and Cathy Wagner. And thanks to John Kunkel, who threw his support behind me at a critical juncture.

Finally, I would like to thank my publisher, Bill Reynolds, and my final editor, Dr. Dana Thomas, who worked more quickly and thoroughly on the last draft than I would have hoped for. If you see a bit of clever editing, that's her. If you see a mistake, it's probably because I ignored her advice. But that's a writer for you.

Why are you still reading this? Go…shoo! You're running late for the prologue, and the adventure is about to start without you…

SABAN AND THE ANCIENT

Book One of "The Transformation"

by
Danté A. Amodeo

PROLOGUE

Whatever else might happen tonight, unruly hair would not be an option. Fax pulled every strand of her strawberry blond curls into a tight, efficient bun but decided to keep the helmet off a few minutes more. Once again, she went through her mental checklist of personal items so she could easily reach anything she might need: gum, mirror, nylon cord, truncheon, ammo—everything a girl needed for an evening out. Not surprisingly, nothing had changed in the few minutes since she had entered the transport.

The small cargo plane she and her companions occupied was almost freezing, and the roaring vibration of the engines washed over everything around them. At 13,000 feet, the interior wouldn't have been warm on the best of days, and, as it was, winter was approaching. The faint scent of diesel completed the cruel ambiance, though it occurred to her things could be worse. They could be in one of those professional sky-diving planes with no side door.

Instead, they were in an aircraft where part of the tail would soon open like the rear gate of a pick-up truck. This plane wasn't meant for passenger comfort, rather for moving its payload from point A to point B.

And dropping it.

That payload was six young adults, each one dressed in sky-blue fatigues designed for warmth and camouflage against the blustery heavens. Their uniforms were offset by deep-blue boots, utility belts and cloth-swathed neoKevlar helmets. Peeking out from each helmet was a set of night-vision goggles, and each person clutched a curiously-shaped firearm that looked like a cross between a paintball gun and a rifle. Except for size, the numbers emblazoned on their shoulders were the only way to tell them apart—unless the headgear wasn't being worn, which was the case with Fax and her brother.

Fax and Franklin sat beside each other so they wouldn't have to speak too loudly. For the millionth time, she resisted the urge to move his long and wild hair out of his eyes. Instead, she made note to address it with him later. Best not to push over small matters too soon.

"It's going to be dusk by the time we get there," Fax said, trying hard to sound casual.

"I hope not, I've only done one other night jump."

Oh, splendid. "You're joking, right?"

"What do you think?" he said, smiling. "The qualifying jump for Alpha team is still a night drop, with full combat load. There's no other way I would have been allowed to join."

"Did you repack your chute like I told you?"

"Why would I?" he replied. "I saw you packing mine when I showed up. Who's more exacting about this stuff than you?"

"You're not going to start with me, are you?"

"Hey, truce, remember? Yes, I repacked it. You're not starting with me either, are you?"

A crackle of electricity broke up the all-pervasive noise from the motors, and a voice came over the loudspeaker situated in the rear of the plane. "Sixty…" it began in a voice that sounded to her ears like a slow, slow baritone.

"I'm glad we get to wear these new armored outfits," Franklin said, tapping the plate beneath the "A19" patch on his uniform's shoulder. "But they chafe the heck out of me."

"Better than being chafed by some random projectile." Fax had a similar patch, an "A47," on her own shoulder. "They'd like to think we're going to be in and out without a problem, but I have a feeling there's going to be trouble." Others thought her cynical, but Fax considered herself to be a realist.

"It's a shame you're such a pessimist," Franklin said, as if reading her mind.

He could not, but they were twins. Even when they disagreed, which was more often than she liked, they always seemed to know what the other was thinking.

"What's a shame is that Demo can't wear the body armor," Fax observed with a nod toward the largest by far of the six passengers.

"He's too heavy to jump with it. Even without it, he's almost too heavy. You're clear on what we have to do?"

"Hit the ground about eighteen-forty hours, local time. Head to the security shack, eliminate any opposition," Franklin recited with exaggerated boredom. "Then you and I do a sweep of the campus perimeter, take out any stragglers and meet at the target for further orders from Demo—or our mysterious 'Alpha T-com,' whoever he or she is." Franklin waved his hand and switched topics abruptly. "Okay, why do you think the identity of our Alpha T-Com is pass-coded?"

"So whatever agent is embedded won't blow his or her cover unless they have to. I've narrowed it to a handful of people, but we both know who it probably is."

"Do you think any of these guys know who it is?"

Fax shrugged. "I'm sure I have no idea."

"What? The all-knowing Fax has no idea!" he said. "You do know the rest of our team, don't you? I read their dossiers, but I was counting on you for introductions."

"…minutes…" came from the loudspeaker in the same deep, molasses-like pitch.

"Of course I know them. Demo and I have worked together for months, and you should remember Spar from our days in training." Spar, a petite Asian girl with close-cropped hair, was snuggled like a kitten next to Demo. "The others are—"

"I was kidding. I know all their names, and I remember Spar from training, years ago."

"She and Demo…" Fax said, "they're like us, you know."

"Irish?"

"Siblings, stupid. And Talents."

"I know. I was kidding. I told you I read up."

"I hate these codenames."

"I know. You didn't have to be 'Fax.' You could have been—"

"Don't you say it." Fax was nervous despite trying not to be and fought down the persistent urge to repack her ammo cartridges and a dozen other little things that might not be perfect. *How can he be so calm?* Sitting still was killing her. "Spar has a great reputation," she said, immediately irritated with herself for nervous talking.

"Just what I like—a girl with a reputation."

"Stop that," she said. His smug expression irritated her further. "You promised you'd get serious if Demo allowed you on the team. Why did you want to be a field agent, anyway?"

"…until…" continued the loudspeaker.

"I'll be good, Sis," Franklin said with a smoothness that inspired no confidence. "I was just tired of being a bean counter." He paused, then said in a serious tone, "No, that's not it. I just…I didn't want you to be by yourself if anything…if you ran into…you know. Saban. This could be a long mission—"

"Oh, please." She cut him off. "I don't need a babysitter, because I am quite over all of that. It's ancient history. No pun intended," she added.

"None heard. But I'm not trying to be your babysitter. I'm trying to be your brother," he said with surprising intensity. "I've missed you, and I want to be there for you."

Maybe he's growing up, after all. It was about time. They were almost twenty-one. She put her hand on top of his and gave it a little squeeze, sighing wearily.

Sometimes she wondered if she would always have to keep an eye on him. It was sweet he wanted to reciprocate, but really, it meant more work for her. He could barely care for himself. How could he look out for her?

No. She resolved to make this work. He passed all his tests and earned his spot on the team. They had finally reconciled. And since he wanted them to be closer, she would make it happen. She would watch over him. And woe be unto anyone who gave him trouble. Except for her, of course.

"What will we do, if…if…you know?"

"We'll do what we're paid to do," she said, more coldly than she intended. "Dead friendships are not a factor. It's 'mission first'—first, last and always."

"Right," Franklin said. "No, you're not tightly coiled at all."

"You said you weren't starting with me."

"…drop," the loudspeaker finished.

Fax forced herself to decelerate as much as she could and glanced up at the loudspeaker, marveling at how she and her brother could have a complete conversation in seconds. And the fact that they were getting faster made her uneasy in a way few things could.

What are our limits? Where will this end? Franklin seemed to be in love with every aspect of their new life.

She was not. Their organization, the Ancient, was highly structured—wonderful. Each field agent was required to take a codename—irksome, but tolerable. Their talents, however, were not exciting, or even comforting. To Fax, they were bizarre and frightening. In her eyes, coloring inside the lines was a perpetual goal, and their talents put them forever outside the box. Couldn't he see that?

"I wasn't trying to start…" Franklin said, then stopped himself, sighed and leaned his head back. "Forget it. Wake me in an hour."

Fax knew her brother would not go to sleep. She closed her eyes as well but kept her hand on top of his.

PART ONE:

The First Evening, When the Pieces were Gathered to One Place

CHAPTER 1: The End of a Perfect Day

Mirrors always held a split-second of shock and recognition for Saban, as if his appearance were so dull, even he couldn't remember what he looked like. Brown hair, brown eyes, medium build—*nothing to see here, folks. Move along.* He knew he wasn't particularly handsome but not so bad he frightened small children, either.

He stared at himself for another minute, motionless—*I don't think she cares, anyway*—then exited the bathroom and continued down the wide, echoing corridor of Quinlan Hall to the sturdy double doors. He took a deep breath and stepped into the cool October air.

The sun hung low enough in the sky to be just under the approaching clouds and marked the end of a perfect day near the end of a perfect week. Freshman year of college was supposed to be hard (even harder since half his classes were sophomore level), but the philosophy exam he had just aced was the last of four midterms, and he was feeling better about life than he had in months, perhaps years.

"Out of the way, dork!"

Saban barely sidestepped a trio of hulking upperclassmen as they ran past him. He watched them race down the sidewalk to the parking lot, knowing they had most likely forgotten he was ever in their way.

A handful of his classmates were milling around after the test, but none of them seemed to notice him either. He had no problem with that. He enjoyed the company of others but did not go out of his way to attract attention. The perpetual anonymity that came with being nondescript was one thing he could usually count on. Usually, but not always.

"You wanna get something to eat?" said a distinctly Southern voice to his right. Mikey was a large fellow with a black crew-cut and an inch-long soul patch under his lip. Unlike Saban, who was taking this class a year early, Mikey was probably taking it a year late. Or perhaps for a second time. Saban had considered it rude to ask.

In his head, Saban used to call him "Massive Mikey"—an easy trick to remember names. But they had been study partners for over a month, and the nickname was no longer necessary. It was just Mikey now. "No, thanks, I'm waiting for someone. Are you always hungry?"

"Pretty much. I have reverse bulimia," Mikey said. "Are you going to any of the little parties on campus? I think most people have left for break."

"No, I have—"

"Wait, wait, lemme guess. You got some work to do. M-Suck."

"Hilarious. That's M-Sec. Millennial Security."

"I know, I know. When don't you do stuff for them? They're always—"

"They're always paying my bills—since high school. Four years, almost."

"Four years!" Mikey dug through his satchel and pulled out a candy bar as they talked. "I thought you were like only eighteen or nineteen."

"Nineteen," Saban said, nodding his head. "I graduated, uhm, early. And the first good job I got was with this security company. Then I sort of...moved up...into management. And they sent me here." *Which was mostly true.* Saban was careful not to break eye contact with Mikey as he talked. "You know how it goes."

"Uh-huh. You gotta get the degree to back up the position." They let a few of their classmates pass between them. "So other than work, what 'cha doing over break?"

"That really depends on my boss. I've had my phone off for the past few hours."

Mikey glared at him. "Other. Than. Work."

"Oh. Not work. Well then, nothing much. Same old. You?"

"Same old." Mikey turned to leave. "Tell her I said 'hey.'"

"Her? What makes you think I'm waiting for a girl?"

"Not *a* girl. *The* girl. I got eyes, man," Mikey said, pointing to his own as he walked away. "Give her a kiss for me. Later."

"I haven't even given her a kiss for *me*, yet," Saban replied louder than he intended. He looked around. If anyone was listening, there was no indication in the expressions of the few people nearby. As usual.

Still, he gave several half-hearted and unnoticed hand waves to the last dispersing members of his class, all of whom were heading toward student parking. He followed them for a time, keeping an eye on his surroundings. Even with fall in the air, the scent of dogwood and pine hung heavy, and the occasional oversized pinecone made for great sport, as they littered the ground like prickly footballs. He kicked a few simply for fun, enjoying a stolen moment or two free from all responsibilities, then made his way along the meandering sidewalk to the front of the campus library.

The library, easily the largest building on campus, was flanked on both sides by enormous elms. Anyone could see it was three stories high. It was also two stories deep, a fact Saban discovered after wearying the librarian with polite but constant requests for archived volumes. And it had to be at least a century old, like several other buildings on campus—*and perhaps a few of the instructors,* Saban thought with a mental smirk. But even on a campus as venerable as Dauphin Hill College, this building was in its own class.

Ah, the library! He resisted the temptation to enter. Anyway, the facility was closing early today. He sat down on the top step of the library's main entrance and looked out at the large athletics field in front of it. A recent spate of thunderstorms had left the playing field in a not-so-playable condition.

Not that Saban would ever play on it. John kept him way too busy for sports, even if he were interested. Of course, the whole "college" thing had been John's idea to begin with, and John had said he should enjoy himself. Maybe he should ask John if he could…

No, that would be selfish. Nothing needed to change. His grades were top notch, his research for John had been completed. And then there was the girl…

He looked around. *Man, where is she? Where's Margo?*

Margo was the third person of his and Mikey's little study group. She was also the first person to finish the mid-term test they had just taken. Margo wasn't merely smart—she was captain of the soccer team. Whatever she did, she liked to finish first, and she had little patience for those who did not mirror her own personal drive.

She would often tease Saban that he could answer "continued on back of paper" for a true-false question. But the simple truth was that Saban's world was full of paragraphs and parenthetical comments, while Margo was all bullet points.

In a rare display of compromise, she had let him choose their meeting place for a final farewell before the long weekend. He chose the library. It was his favorite place to be, but additionally it was…

Ah. The doors were opening behind him. *Margo must have—*

He knew something was wrong before he was shoved from the stoop and onto the grass. He was able to recover his balance before he went face-first into the soggy field—that would have been just plain nasty—and landed unsteadily on his feet. When he turned around, he saw one of his classmates on the ground nearby. *Why is everyone in such a rush all the time?* Saban waited for the apology he felt sure would be forthcoming, but as soon as the classmate drew a breath, Saban knew he wasn't going to get one. Far from it.

"Hey! Look at my jeans!" Sure enough, the rugged-looking blonde—whom Margo would call a "doof," which was what she called everyone who made fools of themselves—had big grass stains on both knees of his blue jeans. "Why don't you watch where you're going!"

"Uhm…I wasn't moving. You ran into me."

"Now you've made me late, squirt, and you're gonna be a pain about it, too?" The doof wasn't as big as Mikey, but he was certainly bigger than Saban. Was Mikey still nearby? Probably not.

This was trouble Saban did not need. He took a step backward. "Look, it was an accident. I'm not trying to start anything."

The doof wasn't calming down and took a step forward, saying nothing.

"Don't be lame," Saban said. "You're not really going to beat me up over this, are you?" *Oops. Probably shouldn't have used the "L" word. Stupid mouth.*

"Wasn't going to," his classmate said, smiling with menace. "But what a great idea." He took another step forward and pulled his fist back.

Saban had to stop this before it got out of control. He changed the modulation in his voice and repeated his question. This time, however, the question was more like a statement and carried an indefinable heft. "You're not really going to beat me up over this. Are you?"

The doof froze as his eyebrows knotted. He seemed to be concentrating, listening.

"I don't think you're mad at me," Saban continued. "You're mad because you're late. Aren't you getting later every second you waste here?" *C'mon, buy it, buy it...*

The doof brought his fist down to his side. "You're right." He picked up his few textbooks that had fallen in the collision and began walking away. "Maybe I'll find time to pound on you after the break," he said as he headed toward the parking lot.

Always something to look forward to in college. Chances were, though, the guy would forget about Saban by tomorrow. But it was a good thing the skirmish stopped before it began. Saban knew that if the doof had really gotten angry, no amount of his special "spin" would have prevented a fight from starting. And that would have been no fun at all. Saban hated fights. Fortunately, those days seemed to be over. Usually.

Saban gathered his own textbooks, which thankfully weren't too dirty, and resumed his Margo-watch on the steps of the library, nine feet away from the doors this time. Besides the library being his favorite place, it was located at almost the exact center of the campus. From here, his line of sight could move around most of this tiny college like the hands of a clock. Saban looked up from where he was sitting and began a visual sweep of the campus.

At the ten o'clock position and one hundred yards away was the president's house, well-preserved despite its age. Known as "Mayberry Manor" by students and staff alike, it was the kind of rustic white-washed house one would expect to find on a century-old university. The Manor's front porch was enclosed by a heavily repainted handrail that nearly hid two cozy rocking chairs. Between them sat a small wooden table that no doubt had hosted a thousand glasses of sweet tea.

In front of the Manor, a small cul-de-sac emptied into a narrow road lined with moss-laden elms. The graveled one-lane edged from the Manor to the far corner of the campus, running ten o'clock to two o'clock. The drive was one of two entrances to the college from the main road, and each entrance was lined with alternating elms and dogwoods that swayed in quiet anticipation of imminent rainfall.

The campus was separated from the main road by a fourteen-foot tall stone barrier. The "Great Wall," as it was called, was a yard wide and surrounded the entire campus, except in three places: the two entrances off the main road, about three hundred yards apart, and one entrance toward the rear of the campus.

Between the front entrances, a smattering of student dorms extended parallel to the road and past the library. Though unseen from this vantage, directly behind the library were the recreation rooms, cafeteria and radio station. And to Saban's left were the computer and science labs, which brought him back to the president's house, completing the sweep.

Where is she? He loved the smell of impending rain, but he was going to get soaked if she didn't hurry. She lived on campus, which was fine for her, but his Volkswagen was all the way in the rear parking lot. A stiff wind would soon blow those distant rain clouds right over him.

He looked overhead at the clear but dimming sky, and toward the looming clouds westward, trying to figure out what time it was. Somewhere up there was a plane—he could hear it—but it was too high to see. "Six-twenty-five," he guessed aloud.

He looked down at his watch. It was six-thirty. The doors to the library would be locked any minute. It occurred to him he should turn his cell phone on and check messages, but John was the only person who might call, and in Saban's estimation, John could handle things better than he could any day of the week.

"Hi, sweetie!" Margo hurried out from the library, narrowly avoiding the heavy double doors as they locked shut behind her. She moved with a grace that spoke of professional training, though her build was more swimmer than dancer. "I wasn't sure if you could resist the lure of the written word, so I figured I better camp inside, in case I needed to play 'Girl Speed-Bump' and slow you down. Do you still want to swing by that party? I'm not leaving for home until tomorrow."

"You know I might have run over you anyway if the new book on—"

"You wouldn't really have run me down, would you?" Margo pouted.

"Uhm, no! No, I was just…" Saban reddened a bit.

"Doof," she laughed, pushing his shoulder. "You're so easy to fluster!"

"I hate it when you do that." He pretended irritation and looked her over, as he had done many times, for ever-more-complex reasons.

Margo was all around impressive, and he had never needed any clever tricks to remember her name. She was smart. She was funny. With shoulder-length dark brown hair and hazel eyes, she stood an inch or two shorter than Saban, but gave the impression of being much taller. He liked the way her shoulders were always back, never stooped.

He also liked the way she dressed with counter-culture modesty. With her figure, she could make burlap a hot fashion if she wished, but she mostly wore tee-shirts and blue jeans. And not those low-cut jeans that make every girl unappealing as soon as they bent over (*crack babies*, Saban often called them). Her clothes actually clothed her, and though he would love to see "more" of her, the mystery was…alluring. He was always amazed at how most girls could not understand this simple principle. They were constantly pulling up their jeans and pulling down their undersized shirts. *Why wear something that's not comfortable?* He would never understand popular fashion.

He was glad she seemed sane in that respect, though she was still a girl—no sense in trying to figure out how she would react to what he was about to say. "Listen," he began, "I know you pride yourself in being unpredictable…"

"Oh, I like to think I'm very predictable, at least to other women. But there's only so much accuracy in prediction—like the weather." She dazzled him with another smile.

She's trying to play me, he thought with mild annoyance. Darned if he wasn't kind of liking it, anyway. "…and I know you love to interrupt me—"

"—because you pause too much—"

"—because I actually think before I let the word-things come out of my mouth, unlike some people…" He waited for her next interruption. She stayed quiet, smiling. "But I was wondering if maybe you would…if you would like to be…uhm, believe it or not, English is my first language."

"Get to the point, Saban." She made a series of rolling gestures with her hands.

How can someone so nice be so confrontational all the time? He was reminded of watching her play soccer. On the field, she was a bruiser. Margo could take a hit and give a few in return. *Put her in a dress, though, and she's all woman. Girl. Whatever.*

Concentrate! Okay, immediate objective: say what I came to say. "What I'm trying to say is…I love our little study group—you, me, Mikey. I really enjoy your company. And I would love to hang out with you more, you know, just you and me. But there is this problem with the timing."

"Problem? Are you terminally ill?" she said in mock seriousness. "How long do you have?"

"Gee, whiz! Could you stop for a second?" Saban leaned back and looked up at the sky, as if for some sort of guidance. He made a mental note of a small flock of impossibly high, oddly-shaped birds. "I'm trying to talk to you. This is important!"

Margo settled down, a twinge of guilt in her eyes. "I'm sorry, Saban, really. I'm just giddy from mid-terms being over. Say what you want. As long as you promise to never say 'gee whiz' again."

He took a deep breath. "Look, I like you, no lie. But I have these goals I need to accomplish, and finishing classes is only one of them. I can't afford to…it wouldn't be fair—to you—if we started going out and you always came in second or third place, priority-wise."

"Saban, you can't be breaking up with me. We're not dating. I don't even know if I would go out with you."

"I know we're not dating. I'm not…wait, why wouldn't you go out with me?" He didn't know whether to be relieved or hurt.

"Well…" She stepped back and surveyed him. "Don't you do security stuff? You're a little scrawny to be a guard. I hate to say it, but I probably weigh more than you do."

"Never said I was a guard. And have you ever heard of isometrics?" he said defensively. "I have muscles like you wouldn't believe! And I'm at least two inches taller than you."

"Inch and a half. And you don't have to prove the other statement to me. Please, do not. Plus, you're a loner. I don't think I've ever seen you talk to anyone but me and Mikey. I'm not a psych major, but you may have…" she whispered in a conspiratorial tone, "…issues."

"Issues?" Saban looked skyward again in agitation, noting the birds were closer than before and unsure if they really looked like birds. "Margo, this isn't…what I wanted to say is I really can't…*date you*, date you…but I wouldn't mind, sort of, being in the same place as you while we both eat. Or hang out. Or something." *Sad, very sad.*

Faintly, he heard the engine of the librarian's car pulling out from the parking lot on the far side of the building. *At least some things happen like clockwork.* "You know, I can usually speak better than this, but then you send me on these tangents…"

"I know," she said. "I'm just having some fun throwing you off your game. But am I wrong in summarizing your proposition as officially asking to not go out with me?"

"Uhm…yeah." Saban tried to look earnest. "Look, this wouldn't even be an issue if I couldn't foresee your becoming, uhm, important to me." *Maybe it's already too late.* "But I'm trying to juggle a lot of things right now, and I like you too much, as a friend, to let you become another thing to juggle. I have a lot of responsibilities, and I don't want to start something I'm just not free to pursue."

"This is so unusual—a boy who fears commitment," Margo said with teasing weightiness.

"Think of it as a vote of confidence for friendship. Yay, friendship!" he chorused unconvincingly. He was really making a mess of this.

"Saban, I like you too; you know I do. You're the first guy I've met here who doesn't look at me like you're trying to figure out what color my underwear is. And you can make me laugh when I'm in a bad mood."

"Purple. With polka dots."

"See? And Mikey is cool, too, but he's different. Safe. And you—I used to think you were boring, and you still are a little…"

"Thanks a lot."

"Get over yourself. Anyway, you're more calm than boring, but maybe…maybe not-so-safe. I can't figure you out. But after getting to know you for the past two months, I at least consider you my friend."

"You do?"

"And if you think our grades would be hurt by serious dating, I'm not going to argue with you. I kind of feel the same way."

"You do?" he repeated, blinking back his surprise.

"Yes," she said, "I do." She leaned into him a bit then purred "I do" in a way that made him feel more nervous than assured. "Besides," she said, abruptly pulling back, "I'm not sure I'm ready to bring down my dating stock as a sophomore girl seeing a freshman boy, even a freshman placed in sophomore classes."

He laughed. "You are a funny girl, who I suspect takes some funny medications. And someday…someday…" Saban looked up into the darkening sky. "Something's wrong."

The birds Saban had been too distracted to watch were coming into view, and they weren't birds. They were people—six gliding parachutes, each with a person in sky-blue camouflage underneath. *M-Sec?*

From this distance, it appeared each person was holding an odd-looking stick, but he knew they weren't sticks. *Not M-Sec. They're wearing Ancient gear. This can't be good. Why are they here?* He began to consider his few options.

CHAPTER 2: Evasive Actions

What exactly are they holding? Margo wondered. She watched three of the para-gliders heading straight for the open field in front of them, while the other three were moving toward the parking lot behind the library. The troopers' legs moved methodically—not quite peddling air, not quite flailing. They were somehow controlling their descent and direction by foot straps, which left their hands free to hold whatever it was they were holding.

From their rate of descent, Margo figured they had about a minute before they would touch down. "Uhm, Mar?" she heard Saban say.

Margo took a step backward toward the entrance to the library. "What's going on? ROTC exercises?"

Saban continued to look up, mesmerized. "Maybe," he said in a far off voice. "Why don't you go on to the party? I can ask them when they land."

"Saban, it's a post nine-eleven world," she said. "I think we both need to be gone. Gimme your books." He dutifully handed his books to her. She tossed them into her backpack and threw the whole thing next to the stairs as something small exploded on the steps near them. She looked up and saw several of the stick-like weapons aimed directly at them.

Guns, she thought with alarm. *Help me, God, those are guns!* Another projectile shattered at Margo's feet. "Back into the library!"

"Mar," Saban began, "I don't think…"

They retreated a few steps, but the doors were locked. She took his hand and pulled him to one side. They leapt off the steps and moved under the trees next to the library, temporarily concealed by the thinning leaves.

"We have to move!" She tried to gauge the limits of his somewhat meager frame.

"Where to?"

"Closest exit. How fast can you run?"

"Fast enough. This way." He motioned toward the president's house.

"Wrong direction. We'll cut across the field to the road," Margo responded. "Try to keep up." She started to pull Saban behind her.

"No." Saban refused to move and actually jerked Margo backward before she could venture from under the trees. "We're too exposed when we cross the field. No cover. We need to cut up to Mayberry Manor. The tree canopy will hide us all the way to the main road."

What is his malfunction? Margo weighed the fact that he was sturdier than he looked with her aggravation at being countermanded.

"You know I'm right," he insisted. "Come on!"

They ran off the sidewalk, spattering mud with every footfall, up between the computer lab and the biology building. Margo noticed Saban trying to match her step for step. He could not, but he was able to stay close behind her, which was kind of impressive to her.

Once past the chemistry lab, they sprinted behind the Manor, over to its far side. With the Great Wall on their left, they walked quickly past a locked storage shed on the right that jutted out from the base of the Manor, then made their way up to the building's front corner. The trek was quite a distance, and Margo was surprised that Saban was not short of breath at all.

Crouching next to the Manor, with the porch and handrail just above their heads, they could see the whole playing field and the front of the library where they had been standing. Hopefully, it would be a straight shot down the road and off campus.

She looked across the field, trying to sift through things, make connections, find the players—like soccer, but with "sudden death" acquiring a sinister significance.

She heard a quiet beep and found Saban had turned on his cell, a combination phone and web device. He was apparently absorbed by whatever it was trying to display.

"Pay attention!" she whispered. "I counted six coming down. Now I only see two." *Doof! Get your head in the game.*

He stashed the device in his pocket. "Where did they go?"

"How should I know?" She watched two of the blue-clad commandos gathering up the remains of the gliding parachutes and stashing them next to the library. "They must have taken cover while you were blocking my view and playing with your cell. If I hadn't moved us, those guys would have landed on our heads."

"I was not…you didn't…. I was trying to see if I could find some information that might help us!" he fairly shouted as a whisper. "And who made you the boss?"

"I did. Are you using your cell to call the police?"

"Uhm...I can't. It's out of service."

"Then you need to put your toys away and focus on keeping up with me!" Margo was only half-joking. She watched the two commandos vanish behind the computer labs, moving swiftly—very swiftly—in the direction of the campus security building. *Who are these people? And how fast can I get us away from here?*

"I was thinking," Saban said, his expression sober. "Before they fired a shot, you got rid of our books so we could run faster. How did you know to do that?"

"I didn't," she said quickly. "I just made a decision and went with it. One of us had to. That's what leaders do. They lead. And before you argue, I've watched you in the cafeteria, staring at two desserts for a month trying to figure out which one you want. Decision making: not your strong suit."

"You've just never seen me make important decisions," Saban grumbled, retreating a few steps to the stone barrier behind them. "Maybe we can get away over this wall?"

"Depends. It's fourteen feet high. Are either of us seven feet tall?" She stopped to mull it over, concentrating deeply.

She had a simple idea, but it was going to require an awful lot of trust. And she did trust Saban, though she hadn't known him for very long. How would he react? Given the circumstances, she supposed it didn't matter. If the choice was being looked at like a mutant or saving her friend's life, there was really no choice at all. "Listen," she said, "how good are you at keeping secrets?"

"I can keep a secret."

"Really?"

"Really. Trust me on this."

"Then let me try something. Give me some space, and freak not." Margo crouched into a deep knee bend, then jumped straight up with her hands above her head, trying to grab the top of the wall. She was about three feet short. *C'mon, girl, push it.* She tried again. Two-and-a-half feet short. *Stop holding back, for once!* One more time, still about a foot short. She looked up at the wall. "I might be able to push you up far enough to climb over. You can call for help."

Saban was staring at her, an astonished smile on his face.

"What?" she demanded. "I play soccer. My legs are…are really strong!"

"Bull! Mar, that was almost a six foot standing jump. You're, like, Buffy!" He was smiling broadly now.

She hadn't let her guard down in so long, she couldn't remember any of her old excuses as to why she was so strong. Truthfully, she didn't know why herself. But at least he wasn't running away from her. Given how horrible it had been the last time she cut loose in public, Saban's reaction was a welcome surprise.

She blushed and smiled. "I'm not all that. It's no big deal." Then the smile faded as she came back to reality. "I still couldn't get over. So let me push you up."

"Wait, wait. I was thinking you should go. Why would you stay here?"

"Because I can take care of myself better than you can. And it'll be all I can do to get you up that wall. I'll only make you fall if you try to pull me up. I'll stay. You go."

"No. You probably run faster than me, too," he said. "You could find help sooner."

"Forget it," Margo replied in a tone that left little room for discussion. As they talked, Margo scanned the field. "If you're not going, we stay together. If there's any trouble, let me handle it. Besides, what if more of them are stationed outside the walls?"

"Hmm…okay, we stay together and try to figure the best way to get out of here." He pointed down the field at two commandos that were a ways from the closest entrance. "They're back, fanned out to the road. We should…oh, no. Is that Mikey?"

Mikey was on the far side of the campus, jogging through the arches that covered the campus entrances and moving fast for a man as big as he was. From this distance, it appeared he had a burger in one hand and a take-out bag in the other.

A wide ring of thick shrubs surrounded the bases of the trees closest to the campus entrance and most people walked around them, but Mikey veered off the road and onto a small shortcut to the playing field, a narrow path in the thick underbrush Margo knew well. He came through it so quickly that he was on top of the gunmen before either party could stop.

"C'mon!" said Margo, "We have to help—"

"Shhh! Be quiet. It's too late."

From across the field, they could see Mikey stop short in front of the gunmen. One of them motioned with his weapon as Mikey just stood there. The gunman moved forward a bit, into the illumination of the street light, motioning again.

Margo and Saban got a good look at the gunmen. They were dressed identically in sky-blue jumpsuits, with deep blue boots and blue gloves. Their heads were wrapped in swaths of cloth, with only a large set of goggles appearing from underneath. Margo squinted; each had a number of some sort on his shoulders, perhaps a seventeen or a forty-seven. And there might be a letter next to the number. She was too far away to be sure.

She watched the gunmen motion Mikey to lie down. Margo gasped as Mikey charged. He tackled one assailant to the ground, but the other spun away in an instant. When the gunman regained his footing, his weapon was trained directly at Mikey's back. The gunman retreated a few steps; the muzzle flashed soundlessly, and Mikey went limp.

Mikey's arm sailed through the air like a dying windmill as he was rolled off the downed gunman. Together, with his partner, they dragged Mikey's inert body into the thick underbrush around the trees. Only the upper torsos of the gunmen were visible until they re-emerged from the shrubbery. Then they each put a hand to their right ear, as if listening to something. As one, they moved toward the main road, past the dorms and out of sight, accelerating at an inhuman speed.

"Okay, listen," Saban began. "We have to...." He turned to Margo.

Her eyes were tearing up.

"Mar," he said to her, "there was nothing we could do. You have to pull it together."

"I'm not 'not together.' I'll get us out of here. I'm just..." *Our friend is dead!* She looked away from Saban, her head spinning. "I'm just trying to grieve for a second. Is that okay? Can I just grieve?" Yet the tears in her eyes would not quite overflow. *What's wrong with me?* Maybe she would cry when they were out of danger. "Where the heck is campus security?"

"I don't know," Saban said. "But that 'grieving' stuff may be premature. I don't think he's dead."

Margo looked up. "What?"

"I don't think he's dead."

Margo considered this as she wiped her eyes with her sleeve and sniffed. "We need to help him."

"Right," replied Saban after a reflective moment or two. "But we need to be quiet, and we need to be quick. It's gonna be okay." He paused and smiled reassuringly. "I have an idea how to do this, of course, but..." He finished with deliberate slowness, "Let's not waste time arguing. How would you like to proceed? Boss?"

She sniffed again and smiled back at him, gave him her thoughts for half a minute, and together, they agreed on a plan of action.

Margo and Saban stayed close together as they methodically moved from tree to tree, careful not to walk on the noisy gravel between the road and the dirt. Go, go, go—stop. Go, go, go—stop. As they moved, the light mist that arrived with the clouds turned into a soft drizzle. It took almost half an hour to work all the way down the road, as they scanned between each stop for any sign of the shooters.

Finally, Mikey was within their immediate view. They moved out from under the trees, dropping to their hands and knees, and kept going. All their running and ducking had made each of them grimy, but they abandoned all hope of staying dry or clean as they crawled through the last few feet of underbrush and muck to get to their friend.

Mikey was lying on his stomach. They knelt next to him as Saban examined the hole in Mikey's shirt, then tore the shirt open. The fabric was stained with blood, a patch several inches wide, but very little anywhere else. Saban wiped his hand on one of the few remaining clean parts of his own shirt, examined the wound and pointed—the injury was superficial. Margo spotted a small, half-crushed glass ampule about an inch long and half as wide.

Saban plucked the remains from Mikey's back. "Help me turn him over," he said.

Margo grabbed hold of one of Mikey's shoulders and pulled him over by herself.

Dirt and grass covered most of Mikey's face, but his open eyes gleamed in the light of the rising moon. Margo touched his neck, then leaned over his mouth with one ear and listened. "He *is* alive!" she exclaimed. "How did you know?"

"Well, first of all," Saban said, counting on his fingers, "the two guys—I'm assuming they're guys—tried to get him to lie down. If they were, y'know, Weapons of Mikey Destruction, they would have just shot him. We didn't hear the shot; therefore, they have silencers, so noise couldn't have been a restraining factor. Then, when the one guy actually did shoot him, he backed off before he fired. If they were real bullets, he probably would have stood still or moved in closer. Anyway, these look like mercy bullets. Non-lethal."

"Wha?"

"I've read about them. They contain a paralytic agent, a sedative and a coagulant. At close range, they can still do some physical damage, so when that guy backed off, I think he was trying *not* to hurt Mikey. Also, the muzzle flash was too dim. The propellant can't be excessive, or else the ampules shatter when fired."

Margo stared at her skinny, filth-covered companion. "How do you…?"

"Well," said Saban meekly, "I read a lot. I was always getting sick as a kid, and there isn't much else to do when you're always laid up in a hospital, getting tested for something no one can find. So…I used to read a lot. Still do." He raised his head up for a moment, just barely over the top of the shrubbery and looked across the field.

She did the same, but there was no one in sight. Margo resumed kneeling, speechless.

"Like you said, it's no big deal." Saban seemed embarrassed.

"Wow. Who would have known you could be so…so versatile? I guess I'm doing a little of that freaking out thing right now. So these guys," she said, getting serious again, "they dress the same, probably have radio headsets, fall out of the sky on cue…."

"Like the flying Elvises," he said.

"I'm sure that's funny to you, but I have no idea what you mean. What can you tell me that's useful?" She made several of the rolling, get-to-the-point gestures with her hand that conversations with Saban often demanded.

"Okay, the good news is I don't think they want to kill anyone. The bad news? These guys are professionals. Mercenaries or something."

"You think?"

"Hey, you asked!"

Be nice. He's trying to help. "Sorry. Uhm, like I said, freaking out a little. So, Mikey's going to be alright?"

"I think he'll be fine. But we need to get off this campus, away from them."

"Agreed. Let's go." She stood and looked around.

"Let me check his pulse one more time," Saban said, still bent over Mikey.

She barely heard the sounds of gruff conversation in the distance. More men were approaching, coming from the direction of the entrance, on the other side of the shrub line.

Saban doesn't hear them yet. Oh God, help us! What do I do now?

An idea flashed through her mind, and for Margo, thought and action usually traveled together. She launched herself into the mire of the field, grabbing Saban's collar as she sailed over him. He hit the ground face first and slid several feet, coming to rest next to her.

"Gross! What did you do that for? Man!"

Margo had to make him instantly understand. She watched him shake the mud out of his hair, and when he opened his eyes, she let him see something on her face that very few people had ever seen: fear.

Her eyes were as wide as she could make them. She had one finger extended to his lips as she motioned with her head toward the advancing voices behind them. Saban looked over his shoulder.

What looked like four soldiers were approaching from the road. They were dressed in camouflage. Their faces were painted with olive-themed greasepaint, from the thick black lines under their eyes to their clean-shaven chins, except for one man with a bushy black beard and a cammo bandana.

None wore headgear, except for Bandana-man, which told Margo they weren't U.S. military, but they weren't part of the blue team, either. And they carried themselves much differently. The blue team was trying not to be seen; their body language was obvious.

These guys? They didn't care. They were looking for trouble. They *were* trouble.

"No, no, no…." she heard a soft voice saying. It was Saban's voice.

CHAPTER 3: Being an Impact Player

Since the beginning of the semester, Margo had been continually bothered by a feeling of disconnect. Her highs felt like they could be higher, her lows were never really that low. At times, it felt like she was looking at her life from a distance, but she couldn't seem to muster the desire for further introspection.

Moments ago, when she thought Mikey was dead, she almost had to force herself to cry. And even now, she was only scared. Not terrified, but thoroughly scared. *How am I going to get us out of this?* She looked at Saban.

He was peering intently at her face, and mouthed three silent words: "Play dead. Wait." Then he plopped his head on the ground, limp, but maintained eye contact. At least he understood what she was trying to do.

She did the same, with a soft "sploosh" as her head hit the moist ground. She slowly, slowly closed her eyes. She hated waiting. Hated it.

How was this happening?

This morning she had woken up thinking mostly about mid-terms and going home for a few days to see her little sister and parents. Instead, she was sprawled out cheek-to-mud on the very same field where she averaged better than a goal per game for her team.

Soccer was wonderful because it was like a quick game of body-chess: you see the board, move the players, overcome defenses—score! She had always been naturally athletic (even before her extra strength had begun to manifest), and fell in love with the sport almost as soon as she set foot on campus. With a modest amount of work, she made the team, much to the chagrin of her parents.

They had never wanted her to draw attention to herself. And she had always tried to respect their wishes, but she was a natural leader—in sports, in her classes, everywhere. She shied away from student government (it seemed almost unfair to compete), but on the soccer field she truly came alive, holding back nothing. Well, almost nothing.

She always had to hold back a little; her life was an exercise in restraint. "Slow down; pace yourself!" "Don't make the other kids feel bad." Some of her instructors' admonitions still echoed like tired mantras. "Precision, not power!" She first heard that one when she was eight. At the time, she handled it as well as any child could.

As she entered her teens, her tutors were occasionally more than she could bear. Her parents would comfort her, caution her, and try to help her understand. "You're a special girl. Your time will come. But for now, just wait…."

So Margo had waited. And waited. When her strength and speed skyrocketed a few years ago, restraint was so ingrained, she barely noticed the changes.

But after she arrived at college and made the team, she realized how weary she had become of always being less than she was. She was making friends easily and having the time of her life. Her only regret was in showing so much moderation that she was considered only an average player.

She could hardly stand warming the bench, but that perspective changed in an afternoon.

Last year, a week before their first game, the team had been scrimmaging all afternoon, and the score was tied. As usual, because she was only average, she was watching. And waiting, instead of playing. The pressure to make a difference began to build in her like a steel spring.

Finally, the coach let her in. Whatever self-discipline she had was left on the bench.

She was everywhere, up and down the field. She couldn't help herself. She delighted in the stunned looks of her opponents, moving around them like they were in slow motion, asking her body for one hundred percent, and getting more. She didn't notice the stunned expressions of her own teammates.

About midfield, an opposing player managed to boot the ball toward their goal. Margo would have none of that. She ran down the ball before it had gone ten yards, pivoting directly between the ball and the receiving player and kicked it with all her strength.

The clothesline shot sailed perfectly between the heads of all the players. Even the goalie had no time to react. The ball went directly into the net on the far side of the field. Margo threw her hands into the air exultant. She looked around to bask in the astonishment of her foes, the adulation of her allies. Her opponents were indeed shocked. Yes!

But so were her teammates. No one shouted. No one said a word. She felt like she had done something…shameful. Something very wrong.

Then the coach shouted for joy, the spell was broken, and the botoxian demeanor of her peers changed into expressions of amazement. "Wow!" "Incredible!" "How did you do that?"

At the time, she told them it was a one-in-a-million shot, and over the course of the season, she proved it. She allowed herself to be the best on the team, but not by much. And she never forgot those initial reactions: apprehension, horror. *And this from people who like me.* Her parents had been right. Who would have known?

When she returned to school two months ago for her sophomore year, she felt more comfortable with herself. Or perhaps she simply did not question herself as much. She still had a few friends from her freshman year, but she had nothing to prove to them or anyone. She was okay with not being at the center of things. Life was easier for her to be…less.

She just wasn't sure less "what."

It wasn't like she felt entitled to lead. If someone else could do the job better, she would gladly step out of the way. She was sure of it. There just wasn't anyone else. There was never anyone else.

Still, she never stopped wishing she could find something—or someone—with whom she could just be herself. And she tried not to remember the one soaring moment where she really cut loose. She wasn't sad about it. Just kind of resigned.

Then she met Saban. He was so quiet, almost invisible. In fact, he might never have registered on her guy-dar at all, but an old friend of her father's told her to "keep an eye out for a chap named

Saban Smith." She remembered watching him the very first day of classes but had held off introducing herself.

First, she had observed him for a day or two. Though he apparently lived off campus, he spent a lot off time at the library and a lot of time just…walking around. He was careful to stay out of people's way. When someone was in his path, he would move aside, let them pass, and then continue on his way like he was marking something along the ground. He seemed a little strange, but Margo could not find any fault with that.

There was something else, however, when he wasn't busy trying to fade into the background—something about him that made him look like he really needed a hug. Or a body guard. After two weeks, she decided to bump into him after class. She believed that real women make their own "accidents." They hit it off right away. She had no desire to be close to anyone, but their friendship had been so easy, so natural. So unlikely.

After all, she was a year ahead of him: they shouldn't have been in the same class. And he was introverted. She was not, and had to stop herself from dominating every discussion. She was athletic. He was kind of puny, but in a cute sort of way.

But one thing they had in common was that both of them were smart. In fact, he was at the top of all his classes, just like she was. She had yet to find a topic he wasn't well informed about, except maybe women, which she was not above exploiting.

And that brought them to this afternoon. When he asked her to meet him before the long weekend, she was unsure what he had in mind. She had hoped he wasn't going to ask her to "go steady" or anything juvenile. For one thing, she had very clear standards as to what sort of guy she would date. For another…well, she still couldn't get over her feelings of needing to protect him. Fine for a friendship. Bad for a relationship. Unequally yoked and all that, in more ways than one.

But tonight, Saban had surprised her with his decisiveness. She surprised herself by trusting him. He might have run away when he saw how freakish she was, but he didn't. In fact, it was kind of weird how well he took it all in stride.

She heard the sounds of conversation moving toward them, and that snapped her back to the present. Her hair was matted with grass and mud. Her clothes were soaked and disgusting, and her underwear was riding up. To make matters worse, the temperature was dropping, and the light rain began to get heavier. She tried to open one eye.

"Make sure you two update me when you find it," one of them was saying. "And if you see anyone labeled 'Alpha T-Com,' do not engage!"

"Copy that," came the distant reply. "We'll find it, Mr. Ford."

"Meanwhile," said the man named Ford, "let's see what we have here. Three kids, already out of the picture. You think they're dead, Rambeau?"

Margo heard the soft thud of something hard making contact with something soft. *I think he just kicked Mikey. Poor Mikey...*

"No doubt, mon cap-i-tan." Rambeau spoke with a thick accent somewhere between a Mississippi drawl and a Cajun twang. "What kids in der right mind would be layin' in da mud? Well, I say we shoot each of 'um once just to make sure."

Her heart pounded in her ears. There had to be a way to get her and Saban out of this! He was depending on her; she was sure of it. She just had to wait for her chance. *Lord, help me be patient.* She focused her attention on the conversation of the mercs.

"For the last time, Rambo, this is not a 'search and destroy.' I don't know who did this, but we are not, I repeat, not authorized to go lethal against non-combatants. I can't believe you're still on this team."

"Well, you sign the paychecks, Ford. So I guess yuh *can* believe it after all. And for the last time, it's 'Ram-beau,' not 'Rambo.'" The two mercs walked past Mikey and stood at Saban and Margo's feet.

"Listen, Rambutt. I don't have any problems dropping a foreign Ops member if we run into them. I couldn't care less. But these Alpha-whatevers weren't supposed to be here. We don't know their origin, their training, or their parameters. All we know is their target. If we want our team hired again, we acquire the target first, and we do not make headlines with civilian body counts."

Margo heard "Rambutt" spit something into the mud near her face, splattering on her nose. It smelled like tobacco. *Ew-ww!*

Then he said, "But all we got is these cockamamie goofy-guns. So you don't mind if I drop one or two of 'em, right?"

"Using these weapons was part of the contract. If you weren't so good with demolitions, I would have fired you a long time ago."

"Cuz if they're in the way," Rambeau continued, "I got a pistol that says they get dropped for real. Any of these so-called civilians start to look like a threat, yuh know what they're gonna git? A bullet! Just like these kids."

"Rambeau." Ford's casual tone did not change, but there was a hint of violence and crunching bones in the way he said that one word. "No one else wanted you as a partner because they're all scared of you. All of them but me. You settle down, or you and I are going to have… a problem."

Margo shuddered to think how Ford solved his problems, but she guessed Rambeau knew well enough. She would have sworn she heard Rambeau gulp, but all he said was, "Now, now, there ain't no need for none o' that. I'm just sayin' I'm prepared to make an impact in this here mission. Cuz you just don't know who's bringin' what to the table." He spit again, the tobacco juice hitting Margo's ear.

Double-ewww! Margo was listening hard. *Maybe Saban and I can sneak off if these men walk away. Are they going to walk away? Are they going to check to see if we're dead?*

"Actually, I'm not sure they're dead," Ford said, as if on cue. "Check out the back of the incredible bulk, there. You can see a wound, but not much blood. I'm guessing a mercy bullet. Odd, his shirt is ripped open…."

Uh-oh.

Two large jump boots suddenly appeared at her left shoulder, blocking any view she might have of Saban. She closed the one eye she had open.

"Ah'm getting a creepy feeling here, and I don't like 'creepy.' Ah say we shoot 'em all and let the top spooks sort 'em out."

"Calm down, I said." She felt a boot at her other shoulder. They were practically standing on top of her. "Kick her over; see if the entry-point is on her front. I can't believe two kids would just lay there while we talk." Ford paused.

"And?"

"We may need to wipe them just to be sure," Ford said.

Ford sounded sad in the same way one might feel if the meatloaf had been ruined. Margo was initially taken aback by Rambeau's fervor, but she decided Ford's coldness made him the deadlier of the pair.

Her adrenaline was pumping, and her body felt like she was under a sun lamp. This is it. Fight or flight. If she was going down, as they say, she would go down swinging. In a moment, she would fight with all her strength. She would not hold back.

"Wipe 'em?" Rambeau had not calmed down at all. "Is dat all you can say?"

"Rambeau…"

She could hear his voice moving as he backed up. More scenarios raced through her mind. *If Saban can distract them for a moment, I might be able to get to my feet; we might have a chance. How much can he help? Maybe he can tackle one of them or something. No, he would never do that; it's all on me.*

In five…four…

"Why you gonna take a chance? You crazy, Ford!" Rambeau said. "I'm not wiping anything! If it's breathing, I'm gonna kill it!"

Three…two…

She had to get her bearings, if only for a moment. If she could just catch Saban's eyes one last time. She tried opening one of her eyes, the one closest to the ground, without making the other eye flinch.

But Saban was gone.

"That's enough," Saban said from above her head. She raised her head out of the mud to look up at the three of them.

Saban was standing within arm's length of Rambeau. He and Ford must have been concentrating on her so hard, Saban had stood up without them noticing. *How did he do that?* He was standing with his fists at his sides, and his muddy face fierce with anger

She had never seen him so furious. Only then did she realize what was going on. *He's trying to protect me! Me!* She struggled to get to her feet, but kept her attention on him so she could try to get him out of harm's way. In her mind, she put together a hasty plan of attack, but what unfolded next caused her to rethink…everything.

Saban kicked his leg up into Rambeau's outstretched hand, the one that was holding his rifle. The rifle and its strap went sailing up into the air, faintly flashing moonlight as it twirled. Saban moved under it and took to one knee, delivering two well-placed jabs into the agent's breadbasket. And one more, lower, with dramatic effect.

Ford was trying to get his weapon up to fire a shot, but Saban had placed himself so Rambeau was between him and Ford.

As Rambeau doubled over, Saban brought his knee up into the man's face. Rambeau cried out in pain and fell backward, while Saban took two small steps forward and thrust his hand straight up. Into his hand fell the spinning weapon.

Ford had taken a sideways stance and was bringing his rifle to bear on Saban, but Saban was still on the go. He swung Rambeau's rifle by its barrel, like a baseball bat, while assuming a low crouch. In the time it took Ford to adjust his aim, Saban had smacked the rifle into the backs of Ford's knees. They buckled and Ford fell backward, with Rambeau's rifle wedged between the backs of his thighs and his calves. Saban released his grasp and let Ford fall away from him, returning his attention to Rambeau.

Rambeau was flat on his back and trying to get up, but one hand was stuck in the mud while the other grasped a mangled nose from which blood flowed freely. His face was mottled in pain and anger. Mostly anger, though Margo couldn't get a clear view of his face because it was covered with camouflage greasepaint and blood. Saban had gotten him good.

The same thick mud holding Rambeau and Margo didn't seem to be affecting Saban. As Rambeau struggled to rise, Saban fell backward with all his weight onto the enraged merc. Saban tilted his head back once to make sure he was on target then slammed his elbow with devastating force into the side of Rambeau's face. "The atomic elbow," she thought she heard Saban proclaim under his breath.

With Saban on top of him, Rambeau fell like a chopped tree back into the muck, downed but not out. Margo heard him cursing groggily. So did Saban. He gave the battered agent an almost clinical look, then subsequently reared up and pounded his elbow again into Rambeau's face. Then a third time. And that was enough.

By now, Margo was on her feet, but unsure what to do. She wanted to help, but Saban and Rambeau were between her and Ford, who was rising with a weapon in each hand.

Saban jerked his body away from the unconscious Rambeau. He threw his feet up in a reverse somersault that had him heels over head and standing a moment later. Ford seemed momentarily confused at the prospect of having two rifles, like he couldn't decide if he should use them both or throw one away to use the other.

He fumbled too long. Saban took three steps and leapt at the agent's midsection, hitting him like a human javelin, shoulder to stomach. Ford was knocked down yet again, and the two started to grapple, twisting and spinning on the ground. Margo saw Ford and Saban launch a blur of punches, blocks and counterpunches as they rolled around. By the time they stopped, Ford was face down with his head wedged against a tree root. Saban sat on his back, holding both of the agent's wrists and looking like a kid riding the merry-go-round outside a grocery store.

He glanced at her and grinned. "Wanna turn?"

Margo stared at him and finally understood what her teammates had felt after her cross field shot into the goal. A little awe. A little fear. And a whole lot of what-just-happened? The burning sensation Margo had briefly felt was gone, replaced by confusion.

Saban called over to her. "Hey, duck down so no one can see us. I think we need to get some answers. And Mister Ford here is gonna give them to us." Saban was winding Ford's wrists into the rifle strap.

As grateful as she was for not being dead, this was simply too much. "Hello, time-out!" Margo said, unable to contain herself. "Answers? Why do you want to ask questions? Why don't you want to tie them up, run away and call the police?" Her voice started to rise. "What's wrong with you? I only have one question for you: who—"

"Wait to ask that question, okay?" Saban interrupted. "I'm your friend. I'm not sure what's going on here. I intend to find out. Just wait."

Oooh, I hate waiting.

Margo's expression did not change, but a growing sense of dread began to overwhelm her innate confidence, and it did so with a clarity that cut through the detachedness that had been plaguing her. Her patience with the unknown was wearing thin. She would go along as far as she could, and clearly Saban could take care of himself better than she previously thought. But if things got much crazier, she would have to take charge, for both their sakes.

CHAPTER 4: Mind Tricks

Saban brushed wet and dirty hair from his eyes and adjusted his position on top of Ford while keeping a firm grasp on the rifle strap that kept the man's wrists bound. Saban's heart was racing, and his mind was whirling faster. Alpha team and some weird cammo-team. Mercy bullets and mercenaries. He had barely gotten over "there's something about Margo" when suddenly he had been fighting for his life. *And I won! How cool is that?* All the training John had put him through actually paid off.

Margo was kneeling beside them, her eyes dark and accusing. Saban needed time to organize his thoughts, but it didn't look like Margo was going to give him any. *Is she going to lose it? No, not yet.* Immediate objective: keep her calm.

"Mar. Anyone else would have run away screaming, but you didn't. I don't know why you and I happen to be so capable, and honestly, this is the strangest night of my life. But if I had to pick someone to go through this with me, you're at the top of a short list."

Her eyes softened as she brushed a muddy strand of hair off her face, her fingers leaving small tracks of dirt across her cheek. "Why don't we just leave? Let the police handle this?"

"Do you see any police around? I want to, believe me. But what do you think will happen after I roll off Mr. Ford, here?" Ford started to say something, and Saban bent lower, changed the modulation of his voice and whispered into his ear, "You should be quiet now."

Margo seemed to have forgotten Saban was sitting on a live person. "Can't you just…you know…." She punched a fist into her other hand, then nodded at Ford.

"No. I'm not going to just beat someone unconscious. I did what I had to do with Rambeau. It's not like I practice taking on bad guys every day at work. Every other day, at the most." He grinned. "Besides, I hate violence."

"You do? But…but…you're so good at it."

"I wasn't always. Anyway, fighting is a last resort—it makes people look at you funny." Attracting attention was exactly what John had wanted Saban not to do. Not until the U-crystal was safely away. If he had known Alpha was coming for it, he would have arranged to be somewhere else. He would rather not run into any of them, and one or two in particular.

Secondary objectives: move the very headstrong Margo to a safe place. Keep from blowing his cover as a student. Try not to get shot by Alpha team or Ford's team.

This was all good to list, except these were not grocery items he could simply check off. He had no idea what to do next, and he still had no the time to see if John had posted any information for him on the web.

Too many factors and not enough information. He didn't want to do it in front of Margo, but he was going to have to spin some information out of Ford.

And before he did anything else, he needed to make sure he and Margo were on the same page. If they worked as a team, it would be easier to get themselves, or at least her, out of danger. "Listen, Mar. There are at least two more people on Ford's team—the cammo guys, who may start capping people at the first sign of trouble. And there's still the six Alph…I mean, the blue-teamers who may not want to kill anyone, but are no less dangerous. If we leave to call the cops, there's no telling how long they'll take to get here. No one's going to get hurt if I can do anything about it."

His words came out a little over-dramatic, but they had the intended effect. From the maternal way he had seen Margo treat younger classmates, he knew she carried a tremendous sense of responsibility.

She considered his words. "What do you want to do?"

She's in. That's cool and...kind of weird. He couldn't decide which, but he did know one thing: he really liked this girl. *Woman. Whatever.*

"Option one: you go call the police," he said. *That would put her out of danger.* "I'll stay here and do what I can."

"We've been through that. I'm not letting you out of my sight." She began to stand up.

Man, she's stubborn. "Option two," he said, grabbing her by the hand and pulling her down, "don't get us killed." He resigned himself to the fact that she would not leave him until she felt *he* was out of danger. Ironic or moronic, and again, he could not decide which. "Stay down below the level of these bushes. If you pop up like that again, someone's going to play whack-a-mole with your head, bullet style, unless these people are friends of yours."

"No," she said. "They're not friends of mine. Sorry."

"Okay, then. I need you to tie up Rambutt. Take off his bootlaces and knot them together. Use them to tie his hands behind his back, but make sure you run the bootlaces under his belt, too. Then check to see if he has a two-way radio. Clean out his pockets. See if he has any duct tape. Be thorough, but work fast. I don't know how long he's going to be out."

"I'm on it. Ugh! I feel so disgusting." She crawled over to Rambeau and began to unlace his boots.

Saban would not have much time to spin Ford. Once he saw Margo was out of earshot, he said to his captive, "Okay, we need to talk." Saban paused and chose his words carefully, in a soft and deliberate manner. The modulation and tone of his voice also changed, as he had practiced many times. "Mr. Ford, I am only a kid. I don't think it would hurt anybody for you to tell me some of what you know. I am just a kid. Just a kid. Mr. Ford, since there is nothing I can do, would you tell me how many members are on your ops team?" Saban held his breath and waited.

Ford's head moved up a bit, then rested back on the root. He sighed and said, "Ah, what could it hurt? You're just a kid. There's ten of us. Me, Rambeau, my two science guys, and two more at each entrance."

Only ten? That shouldn't be too much for Alpha to take care of on their own. If they're careful. "That's very interesting. What are you here for?" Saban requested as casually as he could.

"Some kind of fancy crystal," Ford said without hesitation. "Supposedly there are only three in the world, and we have one in a sub-sonic transceiver. If we get within fifty feet of another, we'll know."

How could they know about the U-crystal? I only figured out where it was yesterday. "That's fascinating. You know so much. Do you have the sensing device?"

"I'm the team leader. I'm not the science guy," Ford replied.

"Of course not, you're much too valuable as a team leader," Saban stated without a hint of sarcasm. "What if I wanted to be a team leader someday? What sort of things would I need to know?"

"Well, 'demolitions' is always good," Ford began helpfully, "though a knowledge of—"

Oops, bad phrasing. He only goes where he's led, duh! "I meant this mission. What were the main obstacles?"

"Well, you can't prepare for everything, but we had some good luck. Our employer intercepted a transmission from some other team calling themselves 'Alpha.' They weren't planning on coming for the crystal until tomorrow, so we came here tonight. I think Alpha showed up early, too. The fat kid over there was 'mercy-ed' by a pro."

"Mikey's not...." Saban was surprised he was offended. His life as a student was fake, but the relationships he had inadvertently formed were not. *But that's not bad—is it? I suck so badly at so many parts of this job. John really picked the wrong person.* Saban continued as steadily as he could. "So where is the crystal now?"

"Don't know. But I've been listening to reports while we've been talking. I am the team leader, after all."

Damn it! I didn't even think to check them for headsets.

"They're getting conflicting readings," Ford continued, "near the library and some house with rocking chairs, about one hundred yards away."

He must mean Mayberry Manor. Oh, crap, they might be near enough to see us! Saban tried to look down the field but could not raise his head quite high enough without getting off Ford. He hoped the five of them were still well hidden behind the thick underbrush.

Margo, grimy and dripping wet, had finished her tasks and was crawling back to them. She was trying to get Saban's attention, but as filthy as she was, it was hard to see her. Funny, their deplorable condition made them better camouflaged than the mercenaries.

"Hey!" she whispered urgently. "Hey! They have headsets!"

"Uhm, thanks. Hold on." He put his finger to his lips and turned back to Ford. Nothing to do now but finish up with Ford and hope he could talk his way out of it with Margo. "Two more questions. I'm only curious. Were you prepped to lookout for anything...unusual?"

"Kid, this whole thing stinks of unusual. If you knew how much we were paid for this one night, you would cry. And that transmitter-thing. Irreplaceable. I can tell you this, though. We were told to steer clear of Alpha's field leader, no matter what. He's supposed to be badder than Leroy Brown. The funny thing is, based on the radio chatter we're picking up, not only is he not with them, but I don't think they've ever met him. Or her," Ford added, casting a quick glance at Margo.

"So the blue team, the Alphas…you think their team leader is a man who may not be here." Saban tried to clarify how much Ford knew.

"I'm assuming it's a man. You never know. They kept calling him the 'Alpha T-Com,' whatever that means."

"Mister Ford, you've been very helpful. I only have one more question: who do you work for?" He held his breath again.

Agent Ford grimaced slightly. "I wish I could tell you, kid."

"You don't know?"

"Of course I know, kid. What am I, stupid?"

Saban let that one pass.

"I mean I can't tell you. Everyone gets beaten once in a while. It won't cost me much. But if I say anything about my up-line, I'll never work again. Or worse."

There was no sense in trying to push—it would most likely go nowhere. He had hit the limit of what he could influence Ford to do or reveal.

And Margo was still listening.

"Okay. You should stop talking now," Saban said with a slight crack in his voice. "*And don't move around too much*." He looked over at Margo, who bore an expression of disbelief. "What?" he said sharply.

"Uhm, I hate to ask this, but do you two know each other or something? What were you doing?" Margo asked tentatively.

"Help me tie him up first." They took off Ford's laces and secured him like Rambeau. Margo was careful not to get too close to Saban, though. They finished and crawled a few feet away, still in the brush but out of earshot.

"Okay, what kind of mojo were you doing over there?" Margo was a little wild-eyed again. "Shouldn't your nose be bleeding or something?"

"That's just in the movies. It's kind of a…a form of verbal hypnosis." *Close enough to the truth.* Saban spoke quickly, hoping she wouldn't question. "You use the same phrases over and over to create a perception in the person's head, and then you sort of ask questions from that perspective. But it's not like 'subliminal man.' I can't make someone walk into traffic. Or violate their core values. I guess one of Ford's is client confidentiality."

Even if she accepted his talents the way he had accepted hers, he knew her well enough to know he had just opened a huge can of worms.

"This raises all kinds of philosophical problems for me—" Margo began promptly.

"Which we can discuss at a time when we're not up to our necks in weirdness, other than the weirdness that is you and me." There was a practical part of him that hoped she could get past this, and another part—a common sense part, maybe—that was going to be alarmed if she just accepted everything at face value. For now, he needed her to simply accept, or they would not be able to move forward.

"Saban—"

"Margo, I didn't invite anyone to this party. I'm just trying to keep it from going out of bounds, y'know? I have secrets; you have secrets. For all I know, you could be the Alpha T-Com. Or you could sprout wings and fly away. You're not gonna, are you?"

She relaxed a little and smiled. "No."

"Okay. So we're two unique people thrown together by suck-tastic events. Do we analyze this now or later over a cup of coffee?"

"Oooo, coffee…mocha latte.... " she closed her eyes for a moment, lost in that pleasant idea. "You're really okay with all this?"

Saban wasn't sure exactly what she meant by "all this," but he felt like she needed to know he didn't consider her to be a part of tonight's freak show. Frankly, they both had some explaining to do, but in Saban's mind, there was enough mutual goodwill that explanations could wait. "No. I am not okay with 'all this,'" he said, waving his hands to indicate their surroundings. "But I'm okay with you. Are you okay with me?"

"Yes. Yes, I am. For now."

He exhaled slowly. "Okay. So, what did you get off Rambeau?"

"Right," she said, instantly focused. Saban liked watching her switch gears like that. When she wanted to, she did it so easily. "Well, I couldn't get the headset because it was, like, wired into his uniform. I did sort of rip it, so he can't use it when he wakes up." She tossed the small earpiece and microphone toward him, the glint of two small trailing wires flashing briefly. "And I also got this!" She held up something silver, a little larger than her fist. "Duct tape! How did you know?"

"C'mon. I'm a guy. *Duct tape*," he intoned, as if speaking some great universal truth. "Anything else?"

"Yeah. A flashlight. Everything else was too secure or in places I just didn't want to explore. I say we tie up Ford, duct tape his mouth and get moving. I already taped Rambeau."

They located Ford's flashlight and made sure both agents were secured, then taped their feet to each other. Saban was just about to apply the tape to Ford's mouth when he whispered, "Hey. Kid."

Saban did a mental double-take. He was sure he had told Ford to be quiet and wished he had been faster with the duct tape. He pointed at Margo to stay where she was and whispered, "Yeah?"

"How did you do it?"

"Which part? It's been a busy day." *I don't have time for this!*

"C'mon, don't mess with me, I'm a combat vet. Who trained you?"

"Excuse me, aren't you the guy who was going to wipe me out five minutes ago? Why should I tell you anything?" *The nerve of some people.*

"Ah, I wouldn't have killed you, kid. I won't kill an unarmed person." Ford was speaking the truth. "Some of my guys have personal firearms, but this was a non-lethal mission. I was going to 'wipe' you. Mercy bullet with a short-term amnesia additive. Like a high-speed roofie."

Saban picked up the rifle next to Ford and quickly examined the ammunition. Sure enough, the banana clip was filled with ampules similar to the one that had knocked out Mikey. *Two covert ops teams with mercy bullets? What kind of game is being played here?* "Oh." Saban responded without visible surprise. "Why was I worried?"

Ford ignored the comment. "I'm pretty good at close-quarter combat, but I've never seen a style like yours. I know the game; whoever you work for can't leave us alive. So before you do it, I have a last request: where did you learn to fight like that?"

And then Saban realized what was happening. There were several odd corollaries, mostly benign, to Saban's spin. One was the ability to completely read the emotional state of almost anybody. It was part of how Saban knew the best thing to say when persuading.

But Ford was experiencing another side effect of the spin, one that Saban found unnerving. While Saban was connecting with the target, the target would connect honestly with Saban. As such, they might ask and reveal things on any number of unrelated topics, things they might never discuss under ordinary circumstances. Saban made a mental note to query John for ideas on how to stop that. The experience always made him feel like he was snooping through someone's underwear drawer.

Saban tried to get a better read on Ford. All he came up with was genuine curiosity and a great weariness. The thought of death had no emotional resonance to Ford that Saban could discern.

The whole conversation made him feel sorry for Ford.

"First off," said Saban, "I don't work for anybody. Second, no one's gonna kill you. Third, you're not just pretty good. You're outstanding. You almost had me twice." Saban thought he saw a small swell of pride go through the downed agent. "Listen, I have an associate who's the best fighter I know. All I can tell you is he takes in very, very few students, and I was in the right place at the right time. Honestly," Saban said, leaning down, "the fight could easily have gone your way."

"I don't think so, but thanks anyway," Ford replied. "Keep your head down, kid." Ford turned away, ending the conversation, and Saban was relieved. This had gone on far too long, and he would rather not be nearby when Rambeau came to his senses, bound or not. He turned and saw Margo staring at him. It was obvious she heard every word.

"Now what?" he said.

"Nothing, nothing," she replied with a bemused expression. "I was just waiting for one of you to say, 'You complete me.' When's the wedding?"

Saban hadn't realized how honest he had been with Ford. This was the last and only dangerous aspect of using his spin: the connection of honesty seemed to work both ways. The more he got out of his target, the more compelled he was to be truthful himself. That could be a hefty liability in his line of work. If he ever mojo-ed the truth out of someone, they might just as easily get the truth out of him.

He realized Margo was still waiting for an explanation. "I…he was…it wasn't a friend thing. It's a respect thing. We were showing respect to each other as, uhm, warriors."

Margo appeared lost. "He tried to kill us, Conan. Plus, you already beat him."

"No, there wasn't…look," he said. "There's a difference between beating someone and shaming someone. There's no shame in losing. Why make it humiliating? Keep it professional. Besides," he concluded, "it's bad karma."

"I don't believe in karma, but I think I understand. I don't agree, but I understand."

"Good. Can we go now?" He pointed to Mayberry Manor. They made sure Mikey's breathing was still steady before departing the area.

"So tell me," she whispered as they crawled further away, "how did you really learn to fight? That was tight."

"Like I said," he replied as they made their way steadily through the dank underbrush. "I know this guy named John Smith. No relation to me. He hired me to work for him, then with him, and I never even threw a punch before three years ago. But apparently, I was gifted, and he taught me."

"Just like that."

"Not 'just like that.' It wasn't a montage; it was hours and hours of hard work, every single day. Got my butt kicked by him or Spar, every day, trying to get better."

"Spar?"

Oops. "Uhm…a spar. A sparring partner. Eight hours a day for over a year, and I still feel like we only scratched the surface."

"But you just—"

"It's no big."

"But—"

"Mar!" He didn't like to dwell on it, but she didn't understand. "If I were a painter and my hand slips, what's the worst thing that could happen?"

"Uh…you ruin the painting?"

"Okay. Now if I'm aiming for a pressure point or applying leverage to a bone, and I'm off by an inch or two, what's the worst thing that can happen? To them? To me?"

"Oh."

"Yeah. It looks cool, until someone gets crippled. Or dead." Fighting was one of his least favorite things to do. He just happened to have natural ability. "Can we drop it?"

She dropped it and began to take the tactical scenario apart out loud. "So we have blue bad guys and cammo bad guys," she observed. "We have a blue team leader—the Alpha T-Com—who may or may not be here. What do you think Alpha T-Com means? And how does this Leroy Brown person fit into all this?"

"I think he was kidding about that part. It's from a song for really old people; they used to play it on 'ape-track' or something." He hated having to withhold information, but the less she knew, the easier it would be if he had to spin her. However gifted she was, she was still just a civilian. She didn't deserve to get sucked into this. If only he could give her some kind of task that kept her out of…*Bingo!*

"I do, however, have a crazy idea about resolving this." *Talk fast, maybe she'll buy it.* "If we can get that crystal ourselves, we can throw it at one team or the other, and their game is over. They'll all leave. I vote the blue team. They're not trying to kill anyone."

"No, just paralyze them! How do we know when Mikey will recover? Why would we give it to either group? Being less evil doesn't make the blue guys good!"

"Shhh!" Saban gently reminded. "We don't know they're evil at all."

"Whatever. It's still the stupidest idea ever, and probably the best way to get us killed."

They crouched next to the bushes at the edge of the field, looked for movement, then darted across the road to get to the Great Wall. They could barely see the two members of Ford's team, partially hidden but guarding the campus entrance, so they started working their way back to the president's house. This time, they stayed close to the wall, relatively hidden from view. Between a tall thicket and the wall, they found a narrow path they could simply walk, albeit carefully.

Carefully, Saban pulled out his cell phone and began to check the company intranet to see if John had left any information for him. It was a slow load, but they were moving slowly anyway, and he was running out of patience for surprises.

"All this is moot," Margo continued unaware, "unless you happen to know where this crystal thingamabob is."

Saban said nothing. *Wait for it. She's as smart as I am. She'll figure it out.*

"Why would you even suggest…." She stopped in her tracks. "You know where it is! You *do* know where it is, don't you!" It wasn't a question.

"No, no. I don't *exactly* know where it is," he responded to her obvious disappointment, "but I do have a pretty good idea." They started walking again. "I've spent an awful lot of time in the library, doing research for my company. Did I mention I have a job off campus?"

"Yeah." He heard a bit of steel in her voice. "Tell me you're not involved in this."

"I'm trying as hard as I can to stay out of this, frankly." *Which is true.* "I work for Millennial Security. We do, uhm, historical excavations, and we were thinking of doing a project here, so I was sent to do the research. Like, uhm, like a work-scholarship. Sort of. Anyway, I went back into the early records of the school, and from what I could tell, there used to be some tunnels between the buildings."

"Is that why you used to walk around campus in weird patterns?"

"You noticed me? I was trying to figure out where they started and ended. I didn't think anyone ever noticed me." He glanced at his cell. There was some information for him, after all.

"I notice a lot of things, but how could I not notice you constantly shuffling around like a zombie spazz?"

She had such a lovely way with words. *I like it.*

Every so often as they were walking between the wall and the shrubs, Saban would stop and peer through the brushes, scanning for any activity on the field, but there was none.

Excellent. As far as Saban knew, the tunnels came out under the library and under the president's house. If he could keep her close, they would walk on past, and Alpha would not see them even if they were stationed at that entrance.

All we have to do is get safely past the president's house—then I can keep her busy pretending to look for an entrance over by the cemetery. That would keep them out of the way until everyone was gone. "Most of the tunnels collapsed, but I think there's still one, uhm, on the other side of the campus, near the cemetery. If we make it over there, I bet we can find it."

"It's still a dumb idea. We need to get off campus anyway we can and call the police," said Margo quietly. "I think there's a low spot in the Wall by the cemetery. We might be able to get both of us over. That's where we need to go."

"Good thinking. Let's just make sure to keep the noise down." Saban stopped. "You know, considering we have at least a dozen people with guns running around, this place sure seems deserted." They had almost reached the Manor.

"Yeah, what's up with that?" Margo asked. "What were they going to do, shoot everyone coming back to campus or wandering around?"

"Nah, I'm guessing the guns were mostly for show, psychopaths notwithstanding. See, the blue team dropped in from the sky, but when they leave, they're going to have to walk out, and there are only three places they can do that." Saban stopped again. They were directly across from the Manor.

"So the cammo guys are stationed at the exits?"

"I think so. They were going to drop the blue guys as they left. Now hush, they might be close by." Saban scanned the field once again, then glanced at the Manor, but saw no one.

Well, nothing to do but stay out of the way, keep Margo out of trouble and let Alpha handle things. A slight vibration in his pocket told Saban that the web page and attached files had finished loading to his hand-held. He pulled out his cell and scrolled through John's notes, which mentioned, among other things, Alpha's arrival this evening. *Sure would have been nice to have known that an hour ago.*

"I think everyone is gone," said Margo. "Oh! Talk about stupid!" She hit herself in the forehead. "Why find a phone off campus when I know there's one in the front foyer of the Manor?" She turned her head, grinned at Saban. "Race you!" she said before exiting the path that ran between the shrubbery and the wall.

"No! Mar, wait!" But Margo was too fast and Saban had been too distracted.

"I hate waiting," was all he heard. He dove through to follow her.

The yard surrounding the manor was well manicured, wet and sparkling in the light rain and moonlight. Margo moved across the lawn with speed and purpose. Even as he followed her, he glanced toward the storage shed attached to the side of the Manor. When they walked past it earlier, the doors were chained and padlocked. The doors were still closed, but the chain and padlock were gone.

Crap! In all likelihood, there's one or more agents in the immediate—

“This will only sting for a second,” a voice said from above him just as he caught up to Margo near the front porch. Saban saw a red dot of light materialize on Margo’s shoulder.

Crap, crap, crap! He looked up to see an Alpha with an A33 patch and his rifle aimed directly at Margo, who reacted before Saban could do anything. *Wow, she’s quick!*

Margo shoved Saban off to the left as she dove to the right.

This Alpha must be incredibly green. You never talk before you shoot. Saban landed a dozen feet away as A33 fired two shots that missed, right down the middle.

The agent was tracking Margo in his sights when Saban heard her cry out, “Stand…stand down! Stand down! I’m the Alpha T-Com!” She glanced over at Saban through her matted and tangled hair, then kept her eyes on A33.

“What are you doing?” Saban demanded of Margo.

A33’s face could not be seen through the gauze-like cloth wrapped around his helmet, but his stance indicated he was at least momentarily unsure. “Clarify and verify, please. This should be highly interesting.” He lowered his sights slightly.

She threw her hand up, palm out. “Be quiet, both of you! Someone needs to take charge. This is all completely out of hand. I never foresaw this getting so nuts, but it’s obvious I need to step in.” She stood up straight and brought her shoulders back, surrounded by an air of complete control. “Stand down, A33. Now!”

Saban couldn’t help but stare, like watching a crash-test dummy in slow motion.

“I require the pass code, Miss Alpha T-Com,” said A33 coldly.

Margo maintained her stance. “You’re going to be in a world of trouble if you don’t drop that weapon. I’m not bluffing.”

“And the probability of me getting bluffed is approximately zero percent.” A33 shifted his weight and pointed the weapon in her direction. The red dot of a laser sight appeared directly in the middle of her chest. “Pass code,” he repeated more forcefully, “or the defecation is going to hit the oscillating device.”

“I don’t even know what you just said, and I don’t care. Stand down!” She put her hands on her hips, but began biting her lip ever so gently.

A second red dot joined the first on the front of Margo's mud-soaked tee shirt. "He meant the poop is about to hit the fan," said a different voice, light-hearted but masculine. A similarly dressed agent, A19, walked over and stood next to A33. "Don't worry; you'll be fine in a few hours. I bet you're a knock-out when you're not such a mess, so this is like sweets for the sweet."

"Knock-outs for the knock-out?" Margo mouthed silently. "You…you're *not* hitting on me, are you?" She sounded indignant.

"Will be. This will only hurt for a second," A19 said. "Maybe a few seconds."

Saban saw Margo tense up. She was going to do something foolish, he just knew it. And someone was going to get seriously hurt, because neither side knew what they were dealing with.

He couldn't let it continue. *Damn it.*

"Hey, A33. Subnet, right?" Saban stood up as he spoke. "Stand down." For a moment, it seemed A33 had forgotten about him. A19 seemed to register Saban for the first time.

"Oh, not another one," said an exasperated A19. Then he stepped backward quickly. "Whoa, I didn't see—"

Margo interrupted. "Saban, don't. I tried. It's not going to work."

"That's because you're not the Alpha team commander," he replied to Margo as he stepped in front of her, the red dots passing from her chest to his. "I am." He addressed the two agents. "Pass code Alpha Delta Omega Omega Eight. You heard the girl. Stand down, 'Net. Stand down, Franklin."

Subnet hesitated before he stiffened to attention, saluting Saban. "Sorry, Mr. Smith, it's an honor to finally meet you and—"

"Yes, please get me shot!" Saban said. "Don't salute me while we're in the field." *What is it with newbies?*

Subnet brought his hand down quickly.

"Hey, 'Net," Franklin commented, "maybe if you pry your lips off his butt you'll get an autograph."

"At ease, both of you. Franklin, is Fax on this mission, too?"

"She's already down there. Boy, won't she be surprised," said Franklin, in a tone that warned of impending trouble—as if Saban did not already know.

Play it cool. "Excellent. 'Net, resume your post. Franklin, you're with me." Saban turned to Margo, but stopped before saying anything. One glance and he knew this wouldn't be pretty.

"You told Ford you didn't work for anyone," she hissed.

"I don't. I'm…well, I'm their boss. I don't work for them. They work for me." What else could he say? It was the truth. "At least you're not getting shot," he said, a flippancy he regretted it as soon as he said it. She was fuming.

There was just no pleasing some people. For a moment, Saban wondered if he should have let Franklin peg her anyway.

CHAPTER 5: The Ancient and the Agitator

Ford did not believe in luck, or much else for that matter, but he was hard pressed to explain how his "science guys" had stumbled upon him and Rambeau. A quick trip by Ford to the near entrance revealed that the two members guarding it had been knocked out by mercy bullets, and an attempt to raise the rest of the team by radio implied a similar fate for the other members of his team.

Ford made his way through the hedgerow as quickly as he could, but by that time, Rambeau had taken the science guys and was running off toward the library, most likely in an attempt to find those two kids.

Ford watched them disappear into the night and did not call them back. *That lunatic isn't trying to salvage the mission; he just wants to give worse than he got.* Judging from Rambeau's face, he might have to give more than he was capable. *Well, let him figure it out for himself.* Ford stood motionless in the raining dark and evaluated his choices, devoid of emotion or agenda. It wasn't the nicest way to make decisions, but Devon Ford had never been considered a nice man. Even when he was young, people had whispered that he was eerily dead around the eyes.

The down side of Ford's work was that any government that hired his team wouldn't cry if his team went down in flames. Also, there was no calling for backup. Whatever happened, happened, good or bad, and that required being able to look at all the angles, coldly, logically. Fortunately for him, it was one of the things he did best.

Fact: he had ten members on his own team, and two of the team had just gotten their butts kicked by a civilian. Not their best day. Strangely, this did not concern him as it ought, though he knew it should. Perhaps that fact merited an analysis all its own, when the time was right.

Fact: before his radio was destroyed, there were reports of another team of agents or commandos or who-knows-what running around out there. They called themselves Alpha, but they were probably just a small part of a larger group. If this was the same group whose intelligence they intercepted, then Alpha was most likely a part of the Ancient.

He pondered this for a moment as he decided against lighting a cigarette, despite wanting one more than he had in quite some time. *The Ancient.* The name was pretentious, almost comical. Were they "ancient" the day after they formed? But their reputation was not funny at all—only a handful of recorded incidents where their activities were uncovered. But nobody knew when they came into existence, their funding, their goals—nothing.

Come to think of it, it was disturbing how very little was known about the Ancient. None of their agents had ever been captured or even identified. No direct intelligence had ever been gathered on them, though some recent indirect findings put their inception at fifty to sixty years, or so he had heard. Not exactly ancient. Regardless, the frightening implication was not lost on him: the reality of a well-funded and well-trained covert operation escaping the notice of every major intelligence outfit for…oh, half a century or so…was mind-boggling. The global intelligentsia had been ablaze with gossip and speculation for the past several years.

The Ancient made the powers-that-be uneasy. Ford reminded himself that a life of spying brings a feeling of invisibility, untouchability. All the world's a stage and all the people merely players. *Wasn't that Shakespeare? Or Rush, maybe.* And one day, you find the camera eye in your own room, and you wonder for whom you've been performing. The superiority and control are gone, and it's replaced by something much more like panic.

Not that it affected Ford. All that emotion was for others. He returned to making his checklist.

Fact: he was not given armament or weaponry to combat another black-ops team. They were primed for non-lethal control only, which was good because Rambeau was not the sole psychopath on the team. As he had instructed Rambeau, no sense losing money over an unsatisfactory body count. One could, in fact, pay him enough to take on these other mercs, but not for the amount he was promised and not under these conditions.

Fact: their target, a crystal, was important enough to warrant two separate teams of highly trained specialists. Given its obvious value, the likelihood of it being destroyed was marginal, and anything not destroyed could potentially be stolen back at some point in the future.

All facts pointed to his immediate retreat, but before leaving, there was one other thing to consider: if Ancient operatives were in the immediate vicinity, he had a unique opportunity to kill or capture what the rest of spookdom considered to be phantoms. It would look impressive on a resume when trying to land his next gig. What about this gig? The bottom line was the risk had to guarantee the return of the one thing that, to Ford, made it all worthwhile. Money.

Would his current employer pay for all that extra effort? Probably not, and there were no guarantees of a tomorrow.

If he stayed, he risked capture or death. If he left, he could claim bad intelligence, go back and ask for more money, and resume the mission at a time of his choosing, when odds were more in his favor. Let the others fight for pride against poor circumstances. Perhaps a turn of Darwinian natural selection would help trim the more cumbersome members of his team. He could re-staff without them, and they would be better for it.

Ford slung his rifle over his shoulder and headed toward one of the unguarded exits, walking past his unconscious former-employees without even a sideways glance. He kept his gaze forward as he made his way off the campus and down the main road.

In retrospect, he probably should have looked back a least once. He might have avoided the rough hands that placed a black sack over his head without warning and pulled him into a slow moving van.

* * *

John Smith was upset. He paced back and forth in his office, an office that was spacious by most standards. Today it felt unusually confining. For so long he had been a man of action, then a man of great preparation, but he supposed he would never get used to sitting and waiting while others did the hard work. He sat down behind the large mahogany desk, then stood up again immediately, wondering if there was something he should do. Moments of indecision in his life were rare, and since this fact was not lost on him, he was even more upset.

"John Smith" was not the name he was born with. That man had been gone for many years. He was not the sort of person to reflect on the past, but this luxury he allowed himself once a year, and always on this day—for it was many years ago on this date that he was born.

He walked over to the large plate glass window that comprised an entire wall of this, his lower office, and flipped a switch that caused the blinds to part. For a moment, he caught his own reflection: tall, mustachioed, still looking dapper in the blue pinstripe suit he had been wearing since six a.m. His white hair drew a solid contrast to his dark brown skin. Try as he might, he had never gotten the knack of keeping himself completely out of the sun. Bekka used to warn him that being African was no defense against skin cancer. And he would reply, with a smile, that he was not African, he was British, and "God Save the Queen!"

The phrase always made him think of his wife. He hadn't said it aloud since she died.

I don't have time to go there. The mission was the priority now, though his life had always been riddled with some sort of mission. He looked past his reflection and himself—befitting a man with such a tremendous sense of obligation—and gazed at the mammoth facility past the window.

The lower section of John's office was in the uppermost corner of a cavernous underground room, ninety feet high and roughly the size of four football fields. Machinery and racks of supplies in an open-sided warehouse obscured his line of sight for much of it, of course, but he could get an instant status on the majority of the operation by simply looking in any particular direction. There was quite a bit more being used as living space, and even more that could be used but was as yet unoccupied. *All things in time*, he thought. Some things required patience, and when it came to planning, John could be very patient indeed. Forty years of patience, if need be.

In the middle of the massive room was the operations center; round and roughly one hundred feet in diameter, it rose up from the center of the room five stories high. Each floor was surrounded by a five foot Plexiglas wall, high enough to feel completely safe from falling, but with three or four feet of open air between it and the next floor to allow for the circulation of air. Every few steps, the barrier extended six feet high, then five feet high, then six feet again, like minarets atop a castle.

As usual, his eyes were drawn to the near upper right hand corner of the gargantuan room. Above everything was another protrusion of steel and Plexiglas, an exact duplicate of his own office, and on many days it housed the only person equal in rank to himself. But Saban had not occupied that office for a long while.

Feh. Such thinking was quite unbecoming, and dishonored his upbringing. *What has gotten into me? Besides, I'm not really alone.* He could see the evening crew still getting briefed by first shift.

He liked for there to be about an hour overlap in shift replacement. That way, the people who worked for him could easily build relationships with one another, and in a difficult job, the relationships were what kept people going. They might not understand the mission, they might forget the vision-casting of the person in charge, but they would hang on for the sake of the chap next to them.

And he had his own people to think about. He wasn't alone. So why was he (*dash all the "stiff upper lip" rubbish and admit it*) lonely?

He had not always been this way. A long time ago, when he had a different name, he had been an excellent spy, one of the best spies in the world—a club far harder to quit than join.

And to the people in this "club," the best of the best, he had been fairly well known and admired. They were they only people by whom he wished to be known and admired. But those people were dead and gone. And as of today, he was one large step closer to discovering the identity of whoever had betrayed them.

By an explosion we were created, and by an explosion we were almost destroyed. If only Bekka had…no. His wife was dead, and dwelling on it would not—

"Mr. Smith?" A small light on the top of his desk intercom flashed brightly red.

John returned abruptly to the present, drew a deep breath and let it out. He was still standing in front of his Plexiglas wall. From the vast open space between them, John located a young communications specialist staring up at his perch from her desk.

Back to business. He punched a few buttons on the speakerphone mounted on the wall near him. “Smith here,” he said. “Give me a sit-rep.”

“There’s been a problem,” she said. “I’m not sure to what extent. Bravo team is en route but has not yet arrived. I was getting a report from Alpha team, and then it cut out suddenly.”

“And you didn’t call me sooner? You must get me some information. Do they need more backup? Is it over? I’m not pleased with being in the dark.” His tone was conversational, and his British accent always sounded polite to the American staff, but there was no denying the crisp urgency.

“I’m sorry, Mr. Smith. I’ll give you an update as soon as I have one.”

“Very good. Please keep me posted every ten minutes regardless.”

“Yes, sir,” came the reply.

The U-crystals had surfaced, and as of this night, the stakes were much higher than they had been for the past few years. *If all of the crystals come together in the right place*—he shuddered to think. *Post-modern society doesn’t care much for the word “evil,” but how else could this be described? There were evil people, evil empires and then there was just…evil.*

The rest of the world pursued these trinkets without even knowing why. But the rest of the world did not have access to the lost pages of the Kronikon Vulternense, so how could they know? And who would believe? For this very reason they worked from the shadows.

More than two hours had passed since he gave the order to send out the newly-assembled Alpha team. Even accounting for ninety minutes of travel, there should be some news. In his estimation, that meant things were not going well, and if his team was not careful, the Ancient would be immediately compromised.

And that would have all sorts of unpleasant ramifications.

CHAPTER 6: Alpha in Trouble

Margo was cold, wet and angry. The gravel crunched under her feet as she and Saban followed the agent Saban had called Franklin into the storage shed. The air was musty and smelled vaguely of sulfur, but at least they were out of the rain.

For twelve feet on either side of the narrow room, she noticed neatly arranged rows of tools and gardening materials, but at the other end of the shed was another door, an open door. They walked through that doorway and down a short set of slightly moldy wooden stairs, which brought them to a basement with recessed alcoves to the left and the right. Saban said something about securing the shed behind them and vanished for a moment, giving her a moment to look around.

One weak and dangling bulb lit the room. The alcoves had been hewn right out of the ground, and more gravel made up the pathway they walked on. Margo pulled out the flashlight she had lifted from Ford and examined her surroundings. She counted several water heaters and saw a variety of pipes and electrical wires. *We must be directly underneath the Manor.*

One of the larger, door-sized niches housed an expensive looking collection of wines, champagnes and other assorted alcoholic sundries. She wasn't a drinker, so she didn't know if she should be impressed. She did notice, however, a broad metal base underneath the rack that seemed out of place in the dirt and the gravel. Franklin reached into the wine rack and pulled something forward. The entire structure began to pivot, revealing a passageway behind, just as Saban re-appeared.

The three of them slid past the sideways racks and through the opening. After a sharp turn, they began a sloping descent so steep she couldn't tell how far underground they were. Someone had put much more effort into this portion than the prior section. The support beams placed every few feet made her feel safe that this section was in no danger of collapse. If she were the least bit claustrophobic, it might have been unnerving, but as it was, the idea of being closed in was comforting.

She shivered as she walked and brushed her hands quickly across her forearms for some friction heat. The prior rush of adrenaline was still keeping her warm, but the air took a definitive chill.

Despite the poor lighting, Franklin did not slow his pace, nor did Saban. How had Saban pulled rank on the two goons up on the surface? At first, she was mad because of all the implications about his deceptiveness. Then she wondered if he had gotten the pass code from Rambeau or Ford while she wasn't listening.

But now that they were following this Alpha team down and away from the sub-cellar of the president's house, she wasn't sure what to think. And that made her angry again. She was a bottom line kind of girl, and the bottom line was nowhere in sight.

It occurred to her that her own reactions were as unusual as the events themselves. She felt she should be crying, screaming, hysterical—she tended to be very demonstrative with her feelings. *Aren't I? There's that stupid emotional fog again.* And yet, here she was, just moving forward. Even as she focused inward, trying to understand her own emotions, her mind sifted through data, trying to bring order out of chaos.

"I need an earpiece," Saban stated. "You know you've got multiple hostiles up there. What's our official head count?"

"We know, we're not engaging. Two Standards, four Talents," Franklin responded as he handed Saban something small. "Here."

"What's a 'headcount?'" Margo whispered.

"It's how many people there are," Saban answered, as he inserted a tiny device into one of his ears. Then to the agent, he asked, "Do you think that's enough?"

"Doesn't matter what I think. Sir. It's your operation now." Franklin's muffled voice was like wind chimes in an ice storm—melodic, but cold.

Margo was dying for more information. "So these people..." she began. "You work with them?" After another turn, the passageway leveled out with support beams about every few yards.

Several thick strands of electrical wire ran the length of the passage. They looked more modern than the thin wire tacked to each post, running from bulb to bulb.

"Sort of," Saban responded. "I've never met some of them. They're…uhm…contract help."

"They're mercenaries!" Her voice got a little louder. "They're crummy mercenaries, like the ones we fought!"

"Hey, I'm right here," said Franklin.

"Stay out of this." She continued on without missing a beat. "I can't believe you have mercenaries who work for you." She tried to be quiet and still project her voice, but it only made her sound like she was hissing at Saban.

"Well first, by definition, they have to work for someone, if they're, you know, mercenaries. Second, at what they're being paid, I'm pretty sure 'crummy' is the last thing they are." Saban counted on his fingers as they walked. "And third, they're not really mercenaries, anyway. They're more like employees. Employees with guns." He sounded almost chipper about it, which made Margo even more irate.

"Oh, and that's okay, because people don't kill people; guns kill people." Though they continued to walk as they argued, their pace had slowed.

"Actually, guns don't kill people," Saban observed. "Bullets kill people. Guns just make them go reeeeeally fast. Just think of my people as extremely proactive security guards. Normally."

"Right. And a teenage boy who runs his own security detachment is the most normal thing in the world."

"Well, who made you the 'normal' police? Why do you get to define that? John Quincy Adams was an ambassador to Russia when he was fourteen. Fourteen! Now we live in a society that needs warning labels on their coffee cups. What's wrong with that picture? Why do we sell ourselves so short?"

"Why can't you just address how abnormal all this is and let me know what's going on?" Margo was a little overheated, but Saban appeared as unruffled as ever. "You can't tell me this is normal!"

"Well what about you?" he challenged. "How normal are you, jumpin' Jackie Flash?" Saban adopted a mock French inflection.

"'Your mother waz a kangaroo and your fath-air smelt of elderberries.'"

He was always quoting from movies she had never seen, but he had a point. "You're not French," was all she managed to say.

Down the corridor, there was definitely a door—she could see it now—with two more Alphas nearby. One was her size, but the other was huge, half-again as wide as the door.

"Of course ahm Franch!" he replied with zeal. "Why do you tink ah have zis out-rageous accent, you silly girl!"

Franklin snickered behind his mask.

"Hey!" she said to Franklin. "Why don't you stand over there and have a big glass of shut-up!" She knew what Saban was doing—trying to make with the funny and distract her from what was making her angry. Well, she wasn't going to let him. "You haven't told me anything about anything, and I'm just supposed to go along for the ride? What are you doing here? What am I doing here? What are they doing here?"

"The philosophy midterm is over, Mar. I'm not going to talk if you're getting all existential."

That does it. She stopped walking. "I want some answers, and I want them now!" They were almost to the door and two blue teamers that were huddled next to it, but she didn't care.

Saban and Franklin both stopped and looked at her. Franklin's head was cocked in such a fashion that he just as easily might have been watching a third arm grow out of her forehead. He looked at Saban. "Boss?"

For once, Saban appeared worried. "Go ahead," Saban told him. "We'll be there in just a sec." Franklin shrugged and began to walk the last fifty feet to the other Alphas. Saban watched him go, then turned to face her.

His easy-going manner was gone. He looked…angry? Scared? She could not tell.

"Listen," he said, leaning close to her face, "what *they* are here to do is retrieve something valuable that needs to be kept safe. These are the good guys. So am I. What *I* am trying to do is keep you alive. What *you* are trying to do is get yourself killed, and maybe me, too. Is that enough information for you?"

"Killed? You just said you were the good guys!"

"Yes, but there are good guys who want it and bad guys who want it! Aren't you paying attention?" He tapped his head for emphasis. "Now, this is how we're gonna play it. In ten seconds we're going to saunter over to these nice commandos like I own the place, and I'm going to run this crazy show to the best of my ability. *You* are going to put a sock in it and make nice, or so help me, I'll take you out, and I don't mean on a date." His face softened a bit. "If I've figured this out right, then we're close to over and we can all go home. But you must *chill*." He stressed the last word. "You need to start listening, and you need to trust me. Stay here for a minute and let me get an updated sit-rep."

"A what?"

"A situational report. Now be quiet. Please!" He walked over to the door and began talking with the immense Alphan, leaving her by herself for the first time all evening.

What has he gotten me into? What have I gotten me into? She really did want to trust him. She considered his words as he finished getting whatever information he wanted, and as he came back to her, she focused on one thing he had said. "You said you were figuring it out," she stated before he could say anything. "So, you're really not their team leader?"

He sighed. "No, I really am. It's a long story." He smiled, took her hand and pulled her behind him. "And complicated. Besides, if I told you more, what would be the fun in that?"

"Saban!" He had a lot of nerve, but she let herself be pulled behind him. "Okay. I'm with you. For now."

They finished the short distance to the door where the Alphas were congregated. The tunnel ended abruptly at a stark steel wall, embedded with a door that could have been misplaced from a bank vault. Standing a few feet away was Franklin, apparently in the middle of being chastised by the short and petite Alpha whose shoulder patch read "A47," and whose voice was distinctly feminine.

"…can't believe you and Craig would be so stupid. I've told you a hundred times, shoot first, smart off later! How are you ever going to make Bravo?" She popped the front of Franklin's helmet with a gloved hand.

He said nothing and turned away.

"I…it's alright," said A47, her tone oddly conciliatory. "I'm glad you're not hurt." From behind their helmets, a sound, like two tape recorders stuck on fast forward, filled the air for a few seconds. *Weird.*

"Okay," said Franklin meekly, as if finishing some unheard conversation. He turned his attention toward the metal door that took up almost the entire wall, and Margo turned to face it as well.

Halfway up the door was a metal handle, and above the handle, there was a combination lock that must have been infinitely fascinating, as far as Margo could tell. Saban and all three Alphas were staring at it like it was the well of eternity.

Margo tried to get a closer look. "Can't you just blow it up or something?" she suggested, trying to be helpful.

"I wish," said the largest Alpha. "I got a pocketful of cordite, and I'm—"

"Let's just work the problem," Saban said, as he glared at Margo and put his finger to his lips.

Margo mouthed the word "sorry" to him while A47 made some adjustments to the lock.

"Well, well, look what the cat coughed up," said A47 without turning around, apparently noticing Saban for the first time.

"Good to see you too, Fax." The expression on Saban's face was anything but happy.

"You must be the Alpha T-com. Who's the civilian?" Fax finished her adjustments, but never turned around as she let the largest Alpha continue.

Boy, if these are his employees, I'd hate to see his enemies.

"She's with me, Fax. Not to worry. She's on our side; she's not hostile."

"Don't be so sure," Margo and Franklin grumbled at the same time. They looked at each other. Behind his wrappings and goggles, she was sure he was smiling. He extended a hand toward her. "Call me Franklin. Sorry about the 'knock-out' thing up there."

She shook his hand. Such an ordinary gesture, but it did put her more at ease.

"People," said Saban, "let's secure the chit-chat. How's the door coming, Demo?"

"Steady," said the mammoth agent. He was dressed similarly to the others, but around his waist rested a belt holding several odd-looking gadgets. One of them, in a hip holster, was a device very much like a cell phone, with a small screen and some arrows pointing in each direction. All four arrows were blinking. "Steady…," he repeated. The handle gave a loud click.

"We're in," said Fax.

Margo's shock and irritation were momentarily overcome by fascination at the opening door. A slight rush of stale air brushed her face, but when the door had swung completely open, she could see nothing inside. It was completely dark.

"I have a flashlight," Margo said helpfully, but no one seemed to be listening.

"They all have one. Standard issue," Saban whispered to her. "Take your time," he said to the Alphas. "I'll stay back with the civilian."

The who? Oh. Me. "I'm not staying back anywhere."

"Mar, don't start. There could be danger, the kind I might not see until—"

"I'm going in, because I'm not going back, and you know you can't make me." That sounded more immature out loud than it had in her head.

"Okay, whatever," Saban sighed his surrender. "Just stay close to me."

The three Alphas entered quickly and without any noise whatsoever. A minute passed by, then two. There was another, quieter click, and gradually, light began to fill the room.

Fax was standing near the door and addressed Margo. "Please try not to…touch anything. Or drip on anything. Or do anything, really." She seemed irritated by Margo's mere presence.

Saban either didn't notice Fax's annoyance or didn't care; he took Margo's hand and together they stepped over the threshold of the vault. As they walked into the room, Margo briefly felt the sensation of being covered, as though a gossamer fabric had gently fallen on top of her. She waved her hand in front of her face, trying to brush away what felt like a spider's web. Then it was gone.

The Alphas spread out quickly and began searching the room, leaving Margo to her own observations. The room was much larger than she would have imagined—square, maybe twice as large as an average living room, with a high ceiling. The walls were metallic and the floor was comprised of what appeared to be slightly dusty steel plates, laid out on the floor into tight-fitting grooves, like ceramic tiles. On each side of the room was a large shelf housing row after row of jars. She could see green beans, corn, beets. There were bags, too, and some boxes, which she presumed had other foodstuffs. A rumbling in her stomach made her suddenly aware that it had been hours since she had last eaten.

Next to each set of shelves was a set of bunk beds. The bottom bunk on one side was smartly made; the bottom bunk on the other was messy, as though it had just been used. A wool blanket and old-time comforter were at the foot of each, sitting atop twin chests. The two bed sets were well preserved, but clearly many years old. Next to each set of beds was a small writing desk of equal vintage, and between each desk and bed was a simple full length mirror.

On each writing desk were papers and books with book marks and some old drafting tools. The desk nearest the neater bed had all its accessories neatly intricately arranged. The desk closest to the messy bed had adopted a piling system instead of a filing system. Only a small space was cleared for work, and the rest was a disaster waiting for a match.

Directly in front of Margo was another doorway, like the one she had just come through. On either side of the door were bookshelves, extending almost to the wall in either direction. Each shelf was filled to the brim with books, papers, and odd looking bric-a-brac.

But the oddest thing about that doorway was the two large poles, ten feet high and gleaming jet black, on either side of the far door. They couldn't be support beams because they didn't reach to the roof. Their only purpose seemed to be marking the doorway.

Intuitively, she glanced over her shoulder and, sure enough, there were two large poles behind her, each about a foot wide. Everyone had walked between them to enter the room. She reached out tentatively and touched one. The slender obelisk was warm to her fingertips and felt like Teflon, and she could hear the hum of electricity when she pressed her ear to it.

Behind her were also shelves, similarly populated and extending to each wall, except for two small closets, in opposite corners. She began looking at some of the books, scanning the titles, and noted them all to be at least fifty years old. She pulled a few out, one at a time, and was surprised to see that some were first editions and relatively untouched. More surprising, others had been radically altered, the interior of their pages cut away, hollowed out as it were. Each of those books contained a chamber large enough to securely hold an object roughly the size of a woman's fist.

She continued to scan the shelves, searching for something without really knowing what for or why. She would know it when she saw it. *Ah-ha!*

A notebook caught her eye, wedged between two oversized tomes. She pulled it out and began leafing through it. There were several maps, but she could not tell if they were from the same state, or even the same country, because whatever handwritten notes she saw were not written in English. One particular page showed a large circle with a five-pointed star—a pentagram—inside it. She turned the page.

More sketches—pictures of odd-looking crystals, perhaps twice as long as they were wide. The pages following showed the crystals being placed at the points of the star in the circle. She felt a shiver and quickly put the pad back where she found it.

Another pad near it had some words on the cover from a different language. She couldn't make out some of the characters. It spelled…*Vultanase? Vulcanese? Or something very similar, kind of Spanish-y.* She knew some Spanish, but this wasn't quite the same. Inside the tome, page after page was filled with the same language, as well as some sketches of mountains, tunnels and doors. She was able to pick some words here and there: "opening," "danger," "death." Not a bedtime story, unless you wanted the kids sleeping under their beds.

And whatever story was in this book, it came complete with a boogeyman—an occasional drawing of a gentleman with long, long limbs, bony hands, and a nasty set of canines. Underneath one of the pictures was a three-word phrase in that same obscure tongue. The first word looked like "Nos," Margo knew that should mean "to us." Then the word "fera," then "tu," which Margo thought meant "you" or maybe "from you." *To us "fera" from you. What in the world was a "fera?" A gift, maybe? A punishment?* She closed the book and put it back where she'd found it.

Some evil things had been dealt with in this room. She was sure of it. Her first instinct was to ignore them and leave. Still, she was curious. Were the former occupants defending against some raw malevolence—or propagators of it? A discussion had ensued while she was distracted.

"…and since we're so close, I just can't get a more specific reading," Fax said. "It must be in here. We unlocked the opposite door, and there's nothing past it but another tunnel. Any one of these books could have a false cover with an empty space inside large enough to hold it. And to make matters worse, some tiles appear to be welded together near the pantries. We think they might lead to a sub-basement."

"Yeah, that would make sense," Margo heard Saban say, "since extra storage space was referenced in my research, but I could never decipher where it was."

"Who cares?" Franklin came running up from across the room. "We have our hands full just searching this room. I know I'm not the resident worrywart," Margo was sure she saw him glance at Fax, "but there is no way we can get it all done in time. Check your watches."

Demo and Fax did so. "Franklin is right, amazingly," said Fax. "The next shift of campus security is going to show up soon. And what about all those camouflaged agents running around?"

"One crisis at a time. Our immediate objective is retrieval." Saban sighed. "There are only two of those cammo guys roving, the rest are stationed at the exits. Franklin, run up through the far entrance and call Anni. Have her and Spar keep an eye out for that other team and meet us down here as soon as Bravo team arrives. Then we'll just split up and search through these books."

Franklin ran to the far door and pulled down the massive lever, opening it, then bolted through as Fax began examining the various books that stocked the shelves.

"Did you notice that many of these volumes have the exact same titles?" said Fax. "That could be a problem." At first, she was rifling through the shelves with superhuman quickness, but gradually she slowed to normal. *I wonder if she can run fast, too. Is she like me? Are they all like me?* Her heart leapt with the thought, but it was not the time to explore such things. *What have I stumbled onto? And why does all this seem...familiar?*

"Then we'll search every book in the place," Saban stated. "With any luck we'll be done in…" he was looking over the stacks and stacks and furrowing his brow in concentration. His expression soured. "…three hours. Oh, man. No, wait! I think I know a way to cut that in half! See, we can—"

"What are you looking for?" Margo interrupted. "I mean, how big is it?"

Everyone froze and looked to Saban for direction, but he too appeared frozen and said nothing. Fax broke the silence. "We're not at liberty to say. If you would step outside with—"

"Oh, give me a break! It's some kind of crystal, right?" No one spoke. "Right?" Margo turned to Saban and repeated softly, "Right?" *Okay Saban, make a decision; don't leave me hanging, don't put me with these people and then make me feel alone, like some kind of...*

"Right," he replied firmly, as if he had made some mental adjustment. "Listen up, guys. If you hadn't figured it out, this civilian is one of us. For now," he emphasized. Saban walked over to Margo, and as he passed by Demo, he removed the big man's cell phone-shaped device from its holster and turned it over. A moment later, he popped out a walnut-sized piece of glass and showed it to her. "It's exactly this size. Ford's team has one. We have the other."

He held the crystal up for her to see. It matched the drawing she had seen in the notepad—kind of pretty, but it could just as easily been hanging from a chandelier.

"And there is just the one?" Margo asked. "We're not looking for two?"

"Ford thought there were three; actually, there are five total, but only one down here. What are you on to?"

"Yes, do tell," came Fax's voice from across the room.

Margo ignored her. "Then it's not in any of the books." And she had a very good idea where it was. *Why do I know this?* She got down on her hands and knees. From one door to the other was a straight line of platelets. She started on the floor platelet in the exact middle of the doorway and gave the panel a rap with her knuckles. It was solid. She went to the next one, then the next.

"Hey," said Franklin, as he re-entered the room, shutting the massive door behind him. "New problem. Anni's not up there and I…what is she doing?"

"What do you mean, Anni isn't there?" said Saban.

"She's not there. I couldn't raise Subnet or Spar, either."

Margo continued to sound out the floor as Saban pondered this for a moment. "Spar probably took them to deal with the new security shift," he said, "and as deep as we are, the radios are out of range, so she couldn't have told us. They'll be okay, they're professionals. And we're safe as long as we're down here. There's no way Ford's team will find either entrance."

Margo concentrated on the floor platelets. Ten seconds later, one of the plates gave a hollow response. She looked up. It was in the exact center of the room.

Franklin came closer and took to one knee, a pen knife in his hand, and began to pry up the steel tile. It was wedged, but gradually it loosened.

"Got it!" Franklin yelled triumphantly. He held the prism up so the others could get a better look. Margo saw relief wash over Saban's face. Whatever was going on, the whole thing had just taken a turn for the better. Maybe now, without the pressure of "the mission," she could get an explanation as to how all these puzzle pieces fit together.

"Well. Welcome aboard." Saban smiled broadly. Margo felt a little flush of excitement.

"Yeah, good job," echoed Franklin, who walked over and stood next to Saban. He still had the prism in one hand, but pulled off his headgear with the other. A shock of strawberry-blond curls cascaded over his shoulders, framing a happy blue-eyed face of no more than twenty-two years. "How did you know?"

"Yes, I'm also curious." Fax had also taken off her headgear. She had the same hair as Franklin, though shorter, and her features were a more delicate version of his.

Twins? Both were beautiful, though Fax gave the impression she had just swallowed something that disagreed with her. *Probably her pride*, Margo thought with a mental smirk. *Or maybe some crow.*

"So how did you know?" Saban repeated Franklin's question.

Well, how exactly did I know? Margo wasn't sure she could answer.

* * *

Wow. So that was Saban Smith. How was it that some members of Alpha seemed to despise him, Craig wondered, but everyone else in the Ancient wants to *be* him? Or at least work with him? *He did seem shorter than I would have guessed.* Craig peered though his night-vision binoculars, checking the positions of his teammates, as well as the positions of the rogue team Saban had encountered. He could see the two men by the far entrance, where Saban and the girl had come from. Two more at the next entrance.

He shifted his view to Anni's position atop one of the dorms, and saw her scanning the field as well. *And why doesn't anyone think Subnet is a cool name? I think it's a cool name.*

"You can call me…Subnet," he whispered aloud. *Yeah, it's a cool name. Cooler than Fax. Cooler than Spar. What kind of name is Spar, anyway?* He adjusted his view to Spar's position, but she wasn't there. Again. He radioed Saban to let him know, but there was no response from Saban. No cause for alarm, they had anticipated a radio blackout due to the location of the crystal. He continued his rotation back to the first pair of enemy agents.

"Ow." Craig heard a girl's voice through his earpiece.

He kept his eyes on the men while he toggled his headset. "Was that you, Spar? Anni?"

As Craig watched from afar, one of the men collapsed to the ground. The other looked around quickly, then also fell to the ground. Craig shifted quickly to find the second enemy team, but they were no longer there. There did appear to be two human-sized lumps where they had been standing, however.

Was Anni engaging? He glanced at her position and saw slumped shoulders barely visible over the top of the dorm. *She's down, hopefully not permanently.* But who, then?

A flash of movement caught his eye. One of the rogues—a bearded fellow—and two more were headed toward the library, where Spar had been posted. Did they take Spar down? They didn't seem concerned about being detected. But they couldn't have taken out Anni. The angle was all wrong. *And what about their own members? Saban would need—*

Craig felt a burst of pain on the side of his hand. He lowered his binoculars and saw the tiny shards of embedded glass just as his vision began to blur. *Someone is taking out both teams? I have to warn Saban.*

Craig fell onto his knees, toppling forward a moment later. His head hit the ground in front of him with a graceless thump. *I have to...whoever...whoever did this...is a magnificent shot. Whoever...aw, no!*

He was briefly aware that his behind was sticking straight up in the air, and as dismaying as it was that he could not warn his friends, it hurt him more to know that, if and when he was discovered, he would most likely still be in this very undignified position.

* * *

Margo took a deep breath.

"Well, first of all," she began, counting on her fingers the same way Saban had earlier, "the whole room is an exercise in symmetrical architecture, and the former tenants seemed so dissimilar. I figured the people who stayed here would have to agree on a common location for non-divisible items, so they must have had a central place where they kept important things. Ergo, the exact center of the room."

Saban stared at her.

"Don't look so shocked," she said, slightly offended. "Just because I don't display my vocabulary with every sentence, like *some* people, doesn't mean I don't have a brain."

A tiny snort came from Fax. "She's right. It wasn't too hard. I could have figured it out," she said, disdain evident on her face.

"But you didn't," said Franklin.

"Will you grow up?" Saban barked. Franklin became serious, and Margo sobered on the outside as well. Inside, she was starting to enjoy this. *There's a fellowship here, like in sports.* She was beginning to wonder who these people really were and what sort of strengths they had, from a tactical sense, but she also had a desire to know them on a personal level. *Except for Fax.*

Saban pulled a little closer. "You just…figured all that out? How did you know there might be a fake floor like the fake books?"

"Well, that part I just knew. I don't know how."

"No, really. Tell me," he said expectantly, "how did you know? You want me to believe…I mean, I'm not saying you're lying or anything, but…but…is that it, you really just knew?" He was searching her, evaluating her, but not about her intuition. The real question was about her integrity, so she answered that question.

"Saban, I have no idea what kind of life you have, but for me, all I have is honesty. I hate that I have to hide who I am sometimes, but I've never tried to be dishonest."

The others had drawn in close around Margo, forming a semi-circle. She felt slightly crowded.

"So, about the plates and the false floor," she continued, "I just…knew it, in my spirit, I guess. There was no doubt. I honestly don't know why." She looked down at their muddy shoes. Both she and Saban had the right to question the other, so he either believed her or he didn't. *The truth stands on its own, always. Doesn't it?*

Fax let out an exasperated utterance. Franklin shushed her. The rest were quiet.

Strangely, she did not find troubling the issue of Saban not completely trusting her. In fact, it made her trust him more. *If he were trying to be deceptive*, she reasoned, *he would be more concerned with me believing him rather than him believing me.* And in her mind, that made sense, though she doubted a man would understand.

Saban struggled to respond. "That's…well, that's good enough for me." He grinned at her, and everything was good between them. She was relieved. The others made no comments, but it appeared that if Saban had no problem with it, they didn't either. Or at least they weren't going to say anything in front of him.

She glanced over Saban's shoulder at the other three. Fax had already put her headgear back on, while Franklin and Demo were bickering about his—Franklin was complaining it gave him helmet-hair. Despite Saban's claim, they were obviously a team and not just employees. They seemed to be on the trail of something important—she had no idea how high the stakes might be—but she could see how doing this sort of thing could be exciting!

Margo took a step toward the side wall where she had seen a long mirror earlier. She felt like she ought to…ought to…. Her hand flew to her mouth, muffling a scream.

"What? What?" Saban rushed to her side.

She raised one arm and pointed one arm to the wall. "Look," she croaked in horror. He looked. In the mirror, she saw their reflection: two of the filthiest bedraggled youths in the world. He started to laugh.

"It's not funny! I can't even tell it's me! I look like…like the thing from the Black Lagoon! No, I look like its ugly sister! I have mud for hair! Saban!"

Saban was still laughing. "I don't look much better. And look at it this way—you'll always remember our first date."

It is kind of funny. And that was the last pleasant thought she had before things turned very, very bad.

"I can't believe you," she heard Fax say in an accusing voice. Margo whirled to confront her, but Fax was addressing Saban, not her.

"I'm sorry?" Saban's face was absolutely emotionless.

"You…you…." Fax was apparently trying to keep a handle on her emotions. "We've put thousands of hours into this operation, and at the last moment, some strange girl—"

"Hey," said Margo. "I'm not the one in a smurf suit holding a gun."

Fax ignored her. "—who shouldn't even be here, gives you one smile and has your complete trust? What is wrong with you? You never trusted me that—"

"Hey! You can stow it, Fax." Saban's jaw was set. "This is not the time or place."

"There is no time or place as far as you're concerned."

Franklin ran his hands through his hair. Demo shifted nervously from foot to ponderous foot, but said nothing.

"No, there is, but it's not right now!" Saban raised his voice. "We have bigger things to worry about. We still can't raise Spar on the radio, and her team was supposed to be…." Saban and Fax began arguing in earnest, but Margo tuned them out. Something was wrong.

She was the only person facing the unopened door to the vault, and thus the only one who saw its handle moving slowly down. Before she could say anything, the door flew open and boomed into the wall outside it. A muddy, bloody figure stood in the doorway. "Yew don' have to go so soon," said a familiar voice. "Yew can stay raht here foreveh."

"Rambo!" Saban turned around, ready for round two, fists balled up. The other team members started to fan out.

"Ah! Ah! Ah! Stay still, won't you, child?" His rifle, presumably armed with mercy bullets like the ones Alpha used, was in one hand. In the other hand, however, was a pistol, maybe a .45, and he waved it at Saban as he talked. "An dat's Ram-beau! Ram-beau! Don't ya'll know how to speak no English?" Rambeau leered at them with a bloody grin. His nose was pushed a little to the left and the cammo makeup had been rubbed off one side of his face to reveal a puffy purple shadow underneath. "Ah don't know how you did what you did back der, boy, but dis time I brought a few more of mah friends."

Two camouflaged mercenaries appeared in the opposite doorway, the one they had all come through earlier. Both mercs had their rifles at the ready. Alpha team was surrounded. "Give it up," said one man who had a small device about the size of an oversized cell phone in his off-weapon hand. *Could that be the science-guy-thingy Ford had mentioned?*

"Okay, everybody just calm—" Saban began.

"Hey!" shouted Franklin, cutting him off. "You can't just give them—"

"Shut up! They got us." Saban raised his hands, but his eyes were locked on the device in the merc's hand. "You got us."

"Yew's raht I got you," Rambeau responded to Saban. "Stinkin' mercy bullets. I hate this mission!" He spat on the ground, and a faint scent of tobacco wafted into the air. "I may leave most of you alive, but boy, when you go down, yew gonna stay down. You best say yur prayers." Rambeau leveled his .45 at Saban.

"Then I guess there is only one thing I can say." Saban shifted a little on the balls of his feet. "Lima-19-53."

Demo crouched and took a shot at the two mercs, while Franklin whipped around and aimed dead at Rambeau. Fax dropped and rolled to the floor, so Rambeau would have to enter the room if he wanted to take a shot. Saban grabbed Margo and rolled in the opposite direction. The sudden flurry of activity took the camouflaged men off guard.

Saban landed on top of her, smacking her head onto the floor, his weight pressing her face against the cold metallic tiles. Margo heard several shots, but they were hard to distinguish since her head was ringing from the impact of the floor. Some sounded like gunfire, while others sounded of bigger caliber and more hollow.

Then the pressure of Saban's body was gone. She heard Rambeau curse and Saban's shout of "Stay here!" followed by the sound of running footsteps. She picked herself up and looked around the room. Saban, Fax and Rambeau were nowhere to be seen.

Demo was still standing, though he was bleeding from his leg and arm. "Scratches," she heard him say under his breath, though he was holding himself in such a way that indicated they may have been more serious. The two camouflaged mercs were in a pile at the doorway, and Franklin was lying face down on the floor. Margo watched a thin trail of blood trickle down from the side of Franklin's forehead. "Asleep, not dead," Demo commented on Franklin's condition, "No headgear. Fool. I t-t-told—"

Demo put his hand up to his mouth and was abruptly quiet. He lurched over to the unconscious men, and thrusting his hand between the two bodies, pulled out the cell-phone looking object. He turned it over, slid up a small panel and popped it against his other hand. Out came a crystal, which he pocketed silently. He turned to Margo and dropped to his knees, falling backward to rest against the wall. "You okay?" he slurred.

Oddly, she was okay, albeit stunned. *But what about…oh my!* "Where are the others?" she demanded.

"Gone," he said, pointing down the newly-accessible tunnel. "Th-that way."

She ran past Demo and dashed through the doorway, brushing cobwebs off her face.

"Don't! Come back!" Demo's warning was barely heard, because Margo was down the hallway, sprinting toward a spiral staircase of wrought iron. At the bottom of the staircase was a bluc helmet with the one of the eye-pieces cracked. *It had to be Fax's, but where was she?*

Up the spiral staircase she raced, through an opened trap door. Nothing visible to the left or right, but a light shone dimly just a short distance away. She ran toward it and found the light coming from above a long flight of stairs. She took the steps three at a time, and the closer she got to the top, the more she could hear noises from above that sounded like fighting.

Her nose recognized the musty and familiar air, but she could not place it, and there was no time to think about it. She dashed up the last few steps, tripping on an Alpha rifle as she came to ground level. It had been resting on the top step, blood on its grip. She forced herself to slow down and scan her surroundings as she stepped carefully over the rifle.

She was in a large, shadowy building with a vaulted ceiling. Even in the semi-dark, she could tell there were shelves with books everywhere—the library!

The tunnel must run from here to the Manor, she thought, *with the underground room somewhere in between, just as Saban had said.* That's why those cammo agents couldn't get a fix on the location: they were thinking horizontal, but they should have been thinking vertical. *So much like life.*

As she fit those pieces together in her head, her eyes came to rest on a strange tableau. Rambeau and Saban were half a room away and a good distance apart. Saban was trying to advance, but Rambeau kept firing to keep him at bay. It was not going well for Rambeau, because each time he fired, Saban shifted out of the way and got a little closer. Judging from the flecks of spittle flying from Rambeau's mouth, his inability to hit his target was driving him further over the edge, if that were possible.

"Stand still, yew damned ghost!" Rambeau was retreating, but not quite as fast as Saban was advancing.

"Do you even think before you talk? Sure, let's all stand still! That'll help," Saban replied. "Can we get this over with? I really have to go to the bathroom."

Margo was out of his field of vision, but not Rambeau's, who threw his rifle to one side.

"I don't know what you are, but ah do know one thing dat will slow you down." He glanced over at Margo and pulled out a throwing knife with a nasty serrated edge. Saban stopped and watched the knife dance in Rambeau's hand between his palm and his fingers as though it were alive. Still gripping his .45 with one hand, the knife tip came to rest between the thumb and fingers of the other. "Say goodnight, mon cherie. Ah hope yur funeral is a lovely affair." With a flick of his wrist, the knife sailed through the air, straight toward her throat.

She couldn't budge. She could not even think. If she had tried, she might have moved out of the way, but she was frozen, unable to process the deadly reality hurtling toward her. Saban's shout of "No!" reached her ears as she registered movement from her right, closing fast. Suddenly, there was a body in front of her and a blur of hair in her face.

Fax tackled Margo to the ground.

They both tumbled backwards and came to rest in front of the periodicals desk. Margo untangled herself from Fax, who was half-sitting, half-lying against a large counter. Margo scrambled to her feet, trying to come up with something to say that might be both clever and grateful. The comment died on her lips as she turned to face Fax.

Fax was like a broken marionette with its strings cut. Her right hand was covered in blood. Her left arm had an unnatural angle from elbow to shoulder: it was broken. And coming out of her left shoulder was Rambeau's throwing dagger, sunk up to the hilt. Barely conscious, her head lolled over to observe the knife jutting out of her body. Then she swung her head back and cast a glassy gaze at Margo. "Stupid girrrl," she said thickly, and passed out.

Margo's mouth was agape in horror. A sick feeling rose in the back of her throat, interrupted by a noisy crash that reminded her Saban and Rambeau were still locked in combat. She turned around to see what had happened.

Rambeau was unconscious. Saban appeared to be unhurt, though one side of his face was red. Standing over Rambeau, his attention was fixated from across the room on Fax's limp body. His face was a mix of shock and revulsion that faded to a dismal resolve.

Margo watched him take the clip from Rambeau's abandoned rifle and remove something from it, then approach her.

"Are you hurt?" He would not look at her directly.

"I'm fine. But…her arm! I think she was shot through her hand. And that knife! Is she going to be okay?" Margo blinked through tears. *Tears?* They streamed down her cheeks.

"If we get her some medical attention. I think so. But you…you are done." He took each of her hands in his.

"What do you mean? I'm stronger than you, I can carry her! We need to get her to a hospital." She felt Saban push something cold into each of her hands, then squeeze. She opened her hands. A small piece of cork rested on each of her palms, and tiny shards of something that looked like glass. Small blurry beads of liquid were already disappearing into her skin. No, they weren't blurry. Her vision…something was wrong with her vision. Her knees felt weak. She reached out to grab Saban's shoulder and missed. "What did you do to me?"

"What I should have done hours ago. I told you to stay back. You just don't listen." His voice was laced with a profound sadness. "I should never have let you come so far."

Her body was becoming very heavy. She listed to one side, but his surprisingly strong hands guided her fall so she merely eased down next to Fax's unconscious body. They were like two grotesquely shaped bookends. She had an irrational notion that someone should stack some oversized hardbacks between the two of them.

Her senses dimming, she saw Saban gazing at Fax, then her, then Fax. He took a first aid kit from Fax's belt and began to bandage her bleeding hand. And he was saying something.

"Stupid. Stupid."

Well, that's what I am: stupid. I should have stayed back and not become a target, but I didn't listen. She didn't blame Saban for calling her stupid.

As the last fleeting vestiges of awareness left her, she was groggily astonished to note that though Saban was tending to Fax, he was watching Margo, and heard him say even more softly than before, "I'm so stupid. I almost got you both killed." A tear rolled down his cheek, cleaning a small path on his otherwise grimy face. Then she saw nothing.

* * *

Margo dreamt. She briefly felt the sensation of being weightlessness (or was someone carrying her?) before falling to the ground, unhurt. Night had fallen and people were running after her (running around her?), chasing her through a huge meadow. She stumbled across a creek and tried running upstream to throw them off her trail, but they continued to pursue her.

In the distance she spied a waterfall. With a burst of speed, she attempted to dash through it (or was someone washing her?) It seemed like forever before she came out the other side. Then she was in a cave, and saw a group of people encircling something on the ground.

As she approached, she was dry again. The small crowd was not talking, so she walked up and gently pushed her way through them. They were staring at a body lying on its side, a knife sticking rudely out of it. She could not tell if the person were dead or alive, so she knelt down and rolled the body over. She knew what she would see: Fax.

But she was not prepared for what she heard them say: “It should have been you.” They were right. It should have been her. But it wasn’t. For a moment, she truly wished it had been.

She began to consider a way to take Fax’s place, but in the distance, something called her attention. There was a river…and a village…and a thin, bony man who stood atop a hill, watching her. Smiling.

Oddly, this part of the dream felt more real than any other.

PART TWO:

The Next Morning, and the Weeks Between, When the Pieces were Played

CHAPTER 7: Saban Gives an Explanation

Margo woke up. The sunlight hurt her eyes, so she closed them, still disoriented. She decided she would explore her surroundings one inch at time. Her left hand moved slightly, then her right. A soft fabric was under each of them. Cloth is good. Better than mud, dirt or wet grass. She moved her hands out, and they dropped off the edges of whatever surface she was on. She actually felt like she was on…a bed. She opened her eyes. Above her was a ceiling with an autographed *Plumb* poster tacked to it. It was her ceiling. Her bed. She was in her dorm room.

Her sheets! They had to be a complete mess, what with all the filth on her…clothes….

She looked at her jeans. They were clean. Some dirt on one knee, some mud spattered near her ankles, but otherwise, pretty clean. She touched her hair.

No muck. No twigs. What was going on now? Nothing in the room indicated she had ever been mud-wrestling with secret agents, except for the young man asleep in a chair a few feet away. This young man was also wearing his same outfit from yesterday, now clean. This was the young man who was about to get the butt-whipping of his life if he did not give her some straight answers.

"Saban!" she yelled

Saban awoke with a jolt and fell face first on the floor, then popped up and stumbled in a circle, apparently trying to determine what woke him. Margo hopped out of bed and intercepted him just as he was about to speak, slamming him into the wall by his shoulders.

"Ouch! Y'know, Margo, there are many decaffeinated brands that are just as tasty."

She slammed him again, shaking him like she was trying to reboot an etch-a-sketch. "What happened? Why are my clothes like this? What did you do to me?" She wasn't sure if she was over-reacting, but she just couldn't muster the will to bring herself under restraint. She needed to find some measure of control over events more than emotions, and right now, information fit the bill.

"Ow! Ow! Are you mental? I didn't do anything! What the heck did they put in your drink, adrenalizine? C'mon, Bionic Woman, let me go!" He struggled weakly, but could not—*or chose not to*, she thought—get loose.

She let him down, but stayed in front of him. Something was wrong, and wrong in an even more weird way than last night. "Where's Fax? Where's Rambeau?"

"Fax? I don't have a fax. Was I supposed to pick one up? And Rambo is gone. I don't think he went to school here, anyway. I tell you what, you got some 'splaining to do, Rucy, 'cause you're acting like you're…you're…on drugs, or something!"

"Why are we having two different conversations?" It was all she could do not to scream in frustration. She gritted her teeth. "Will. You. Tell. Mewhathappenedlastnight?"

"I will. Just sit down, or at least back the heck off!"

Why is he angry with me? She hadn't intended to get Fax hurt, but sensed this was not about Fax. "Backing off," she said, retreating to the middle of the room and sitting down on the end of her bed. She saw her shoes on the floor; they were muddy, but not caked like last night.

Saban sat down, too. His pants, his flannel shirt—they were all clean. His tee-shirt had a stain that looked like cola, but otherwise, nothing of what she remembered from last night.

My backpack! We threw it…whoops. It was sitting in the corner.

She heard him take a deep breath. "Do you remember what happened when we got to Armando's party?" He appeared hopeful, as though trying to explain something complex to a small child.

"No, of course not, because we never made it there. Your Alpha teamers or blue-teamers or whatever landed on our heads, and we were on the run the rest of the evening."

"No. We met after class and wandered over to Armando's. Two seconds after we got there, you had a soda in your hand, but I think someone must have slipped a roofie or something in your drink, because you staggered out of there about five minutes later, and you were completely whacked out. Do you remember any of this?"

Margo shook her head no. She did not believe him, but wanted to hear the rest of it before busting his bubble or possibly his jaw.

"There were some paint-ballers on campus. Two teams. One was dressed in sky-blue jumpsuits, the other in camouflage overalls. The blue team's base was outside Quinlan Hall. I was walking you home when we went past a bunch of them. The camouflage guys decided to harass us. I tried to stick up for you and got a black eye. The guy who clocked me was calling himself Rambo. Does any of this ring a bell?"

She hadn't noticed because he had been sitting out of direct sunlight, but he did have a shiner on his right eye. *Didn't Rambeau do that?* She didn't remember actually seeing it happen, but she couldn't have imagined the whole thing. "You fought someone," she persisted. "You totally put the moves on him. You had mercenaries working for you. You were looking for crystals."

Saban laughed. "Oh, Mar, that stuff really messed with your head. Yeah, I got into a fight with one of those camouflage guys, but I lost. The blue guys came to the rescue when the Rambo guy was beating me up, and they escorted us the rest of the way here. And guys from both of those teams kept asking where they could find a Krystals restaurant. To buy some *burgers*. They don't have White Castles down here."

"You have got to be kidding me," said Margo. But the groggy feeling in her head didn't soothe the gnawing apprehension that was building like a dammed river.

"They had the munchies. I think they were all doing drugs, personally," Saban continued. "They busted into the library and paintballed the Manor, and…it was just a really out-of-hand evening. After we got back here, you were mumbling and shouting and stuff, but you weren't falling asleep, and I felt like I needed to stay close by, so I slept in your chair in case you did anything strange. You know, like acquire mutant strength and smack me around. I can't believe how strong you are!"

Margo felt a surge of panic. Could it be true? Her metabolism *was* different from other people's. Could a drug affect her in such a way? *I actually am a little woozy.* If she hadn't dreamed the whole thing up, why would Saban go to such elaborate lengths to cover last night's events? How could he even accomplish it? And which was more probable, that she had some sort of drug-induced hallucination, or that a lovable nerd she had known for two months was actually some sort of secret agent man? Or boy. Or whatever.

She may have just blown her own secret by rag-dolling him a few minutes ago. She needed to talk fast. "My head is spinning. I could use some fresh air." *Lord, it was true.* She started to stand up, but got dizzy and fell toward Saban, who caught her. They almost both went down, as he seemed to struggle under their combined weight. *How could I have thought last night was real? But it seemed so real.* She leaned on him and walked toward her window.

As she opened it, she could see the library off in the distance. Police tape had been wrapped around the entrance, cordoning it off, and if she squinted, she could make out blotches of white and blue paint on the side of the building. "I think you're right. Whatever I drank is still in me. I think I need to lie down."

It was a dream? She couldn't believe how close she had come to ruining the normalcy she craved. She would have to be more careful. *And Saban took care of me. He watched out for me. And here I am, treating him like a criminal.*

Gratefully, Margo took his hand in hers. "Thank-you, Saban. I'm sorry I was so rough on you. I was just…hyped up. You're a good friend." She leaned forward to give him a kiss on the lips, but his countenance darkened. He turned his head and took the kiss on his cheek instead. He closed his eyes, appearing downcast.

"Uhm…you're probably still not yourself, so let's hold off on that." He paused. "One more thing."

He took a deep breath, let it out and began to speak. "So we are still just friends. Just friends. Last night was a dream. Just a dream."

In that first instant, one thought flashed through Margo's brain: *he's trying to put his mojo on me! But wasn't that a dream?* Then she listened to what he was saying, how he was saying it.

"Each element is easily explained. It would be best if you forget that dream. It's not important. And—" He struggled to continue. "And...and...you are not attracted to me. We are only friends. You could never see me as anything more."

His cadence was measured and controlled, but he had a hard time forcing the words out. "We are very different. It would be a good idea to forget the dream you had, and...and after finals, to forget we were friends. You have many friends more interesting than I am. It would be a good idea to forget. You should get some rest now." His voice took on its normal tone. "I mean, you should get some rest now."

"You know," she said, "I think I'm going to rest now and try to forget that dream. Each element was pretty easy to explain." She looked at him blankly. "You're a good friend, Saban." She gave his hand a polite shake. His eyes would not meet hers.

"Thanks," he mumbled. "I'll see you in class on Tuesday." He shuffled across the room and let himself out without another word or even a glance behind him.

Just as well. She wasn't sure she could've hidden much longer how furious she was! Why had he tried to use his stupid mojo on her? And it didn't even work. Did it? Could she trust any part of what she thought she remembered without physical evidence? She had no idea what to believe. *God, give me a sign!*

Margo flopped down on her bed. She tried to process all that had happened but was distracted by something in her ear that must have just jarred loose. She dug her pinkie into her ear and came out with a brown substance under her nail. Tentatively, she gave it a sniff.

Her eyes narrowed. It was tobacco.

Eww!

CHAPTER 8: Rest and Recovery

"...Lo! Hello! I need to throw up, and I canna...I canna move m'arms!" Fax, barely awake, was aware of two things: her stomach was doing back flips, and her arms were...stuck. Or something. Bad combination. She tried to look around but her eyes weren't cooperating either, and the room was dark, too dark. Or were her eyes still shut? She couldn't decide. "I'm serious!"

She heard a door open and then the scrape of metal on metal and the rustle of fabric. *Curtains?* A girl's voice was saying, "Get a bucket! Get a bucket!" *Is that Spar?* Fax tried to lean onto her side in case her regurgitive system moved faster than her teammate, but the pain that shot up both her arms halted her efforts and caused her to cry out in agony.

She passed out.

* * *

Fax smelled the antiseptic before opening her eyes. She had been awake three or four times, but this was the first time she had not been in extreme discomfort; the nausea and pain had subsided and been replaced by a dreamy lassitude. Her arms still did not obey her, which was mildly troubling, somehow, but everything would be okay if only someone would scratch her nose. Where was she? Had she been in a training accident? She needed to figure out how to free herself—as soon as she got someone to scratch her nose.

"Hey!" Her voice sounded far away. "Hey! M'nose itches...." She closed her eyes. "...itches...." A shadow passed over her face; she was able to blink her eyes open for a moment. Strange, there was a boy standing over her who looked just like Saban. But it couldn't be him. He had left months ago, that miscreant, on his little "secret mission." When was the last time they had talked, really talked?

Well, whoever it was, they were scratching her nose. *Aaahhh...* She went back to sleep content.

* * *

Fax finally awoke with a desire to stay awake, and she could somewhat move her arms again. Though groggy, she began to get a sense of her surroundings. She was in a reclining bed, surrounded by various medical apparatuses. One of her arms was in a cast and suspended in a sling, the other was bandaged from wrist to fingertips, with tubes coming from the crook of her elbow. She lifted one leg up, and then the other. No pain, that was good.

She turned her attention further outward. The room itself was mostly white with a large window, various floral arrangements, and a chair that contained what appeared to be a small sleeping girl.

Ach, I'm thirsty. Despite her newfound mobility, the glass of water she spied was too far away to reach. Maybe the little girl could....

Fax looked again at the chair, but it was empty. Did she imagine the girl?

"Let me help you with that." A straw appeared in front of her lips. Fax drank long before seeing who was holding the water. The girl was little, but she was no little girl.

"Spar!" Fax struggled to think of the last time she had seen Spar. At the college—she remembered! "How is Franklin?" She rolled her 'r's when she spoke. "And—"

"Shh! Time-out, Jesse. You—"

"And Demo! And m'arms! I canna—"

"Jesse, hush! Can you belt up for a minute? Your brogue is showing."

She wisely hushed. Normally Fax spoke perfect English, but she had slipped into her old accent without thinking. For Spar to notice, it must have been heavy, because Spar didn't exactly speak perfect "American," either.

Spar always reminded Fax of a life-sized oriental doll, except with muscular steel struts for arms and a mule-strong kick. And Fax was perpetually fascinated by the delicate British accent that came from a face that looked anything but Anglo-Saxon. Making matters even more surreal, Spar was always using slang that no one but John understood.

But Fax knew what "belt up" meant: be quiet.

"You were hurt. We're in a hospital," Spar said. "A pub-lic hos-pi-tal."

"Yes, I unnerstand." *I'm unsteady, not unconscious.*

Spar continued. "We're alone right now, but someone may come in at any moment. Do you un-der-stand?"

Got it. Civilian names only. Be ready to switch to a cover story at a moment's notice. *And pretend this is normal, hah-hah. Got it.* "I understand," she repeated, forcing herself to annunciate as she had been taught. Her head was already clearing. "Good to see you, Asabi. How's my brother?"

"James is fine. A scratch and a bruise on his head, so nothing he uses, anyway," Spar said with a laugh.

"Who else got hurt?"

"Bernard was hit by mercy bullets, but no real bullets, so he was fine. Saban got himself a cracking shiner. And Margo—that other girl—thanks to you, walked away without so much as a nick. Now let me ask you a few questions. Where are you?"

"You said 'hospital,' so I'm thinking hospital."

"Smart-alec is what *I'm* thinking. Now what's your name?"

"Jessica O'Kane." She had gone by "Fax" for so long that her real name sounded strange.

"Correct. And what is today?"

"Hmmm." This was the only one Fax wasn't absolutely sure of. "We dropped in Thursday night, so I'm guessing Friday morning."

"Jesse," Spar asked carefully, "what *year* do you think this is?"

Fax answered without hesitation. "Hah-hah. I can't much move m'arms…" *Annunciate, woman!* "…but there's no atrophy in my legs. Nice try."

"Heh. Thought I'd have a bit of fun. Well, the joke is still on you. Today is Monday, not Friday. You've had a nice four-day kip, you have."

"Really?"

"Aye."

No sense getting worked up without the facts. "So," Fax struggled to take another sip of water without assistance, "what happened?"

"Short version or long version?"

"Accurate version."

"Ah, now there's the Fax I've heard about." Spar glanced quickly toward the door. It was closed. "Oops. Do you hate these codenames as much as I do?"

"I've had mine since I was a child. I probably hate them more than any of you."

"There you have it. Anyhoo, while all of you were wrestling with the door down under the library, someone knocked out me, and Anni, and Craig-call-me-Subnet. When we came to, all the action was over. Saban had tied up Rambeau and managed to get all of you up to the surface; the runt is a lot stronger than he looks. Then Bravo team arrived, and their Revver got me all feeling better—"

"Bravo has a Revver?"

"Sure. Nice girl, I forget her name. Better than espresso. She had me all perked up in no time, so Saban took one half of Bravo to do clean-up, while I went with the other half and arranged the window dressing for the cover story."

"Such as?"

"Saban decided there would be two rival teams of hooligans in a paint-ball war that got out of hand, so we added the paint splashes, some vandalism and a few other touches—you know the drill. Margo and Saban's cloths had to be laundered and re-soiled in a manner consistent with being caught in the rain, et cetera, et cetera. Standard stuff."

"I'm assuming her memories were altered—was she spun or drugged?"

"That's 'need-to-know,' Jesse, but I'm pretty sure she was spun. Brrr." Spar shuddered. "I hate the thought of someone mucking about my head."

"Just asking. I'm surprised there was anything for you to do. I would think Bravo or Charlie team would simply sweep in and take charge. They have more experience than Alpha."

"Everyone has more experience than Alpha; that's the way it works. We're the new kids, but to be candid, they didn't act like they knew much more. As soon as they arrived on the scene, the whispers began, wondering if that was really Saban Smith. Before we knew it, they were all like star-struck children, wanting to see what he would do and afraid to make a mistake in front of him."

"Ugh. That's so bizarre. I don't think anyone in Alpha even likes him. Why does everyone else worship him so?" Fax tried to put a finger part way down her throat, but the tubes attached to her hand wouldn't quite let her reach. "Makes me ill just thinking about it."

"Really? The bucket is still next to the bed." Spar cleared her throat. "Perhaps familiarity does breed contempt. It's not like he lets anyone close to him. Not anymore, anyway." She cast a sideways glance at Fax. "But didn't you used to be friends?"

"Saban doesn't have friends. The people who love him don't know him. The people who know him don't like him. And that's the way he wants it."

"Maybe that's part of his talent. I don't think he can turn it off."

"Well, that's his problem," said Fax. *And not mine, not anymore.* "So did 'mister perfect' find a high horse from which he could issue all of his very important orders?"

"You would think so, but it wasn't exactly that way. Mind if I get some of that water?"

"Help yourself. So how did it go down?"

"Honestly, 'twixt you and me? He surprised me." Spar poured herself some water. "Once he realized his own reputation was slowing things down, he began directing traffic and delegating responsibilities. He was very…I suppose 'gracious' is the best word that comes to mind. Like I said, I was surprised. Cheers." Spar lifted the cup and drank.

"And I don't suppose the high and mighty Saban came by to check on me, did he?" Part of her hoped he had, but most of her wished he had not, because then she wouldn't have to adjust her attitude toward him. *Once a creep, always a creep.*

"Actually," Spar said, pausing as if to consider how much she should reveal, "you might be surprised by that, too. Once he got little Miss Margo all situated, he almost never left your side. Did all his after-action reports sitting right there in that chair," she said, pointing to the chair she had been in. "He's been here sixteen hours a day for the past seventy-two hours."

Drat. "What about Rambeau?" Fax asked, changing the subject.

"Spun and left with the local police. Didn't you hear what I said about Saban?"

"And the rest of them?"

"You can read the report when you get out!" Spar folded her hands in her lap. Her casual tone became serious. "Jesse, I have to ask, what is it with you and him? I mean, I've heard rumors and mostly have no time for them, but now that we're on the same team—"

"I don't mean to be rude, but it really is none of your business."

The change in Spar was immediate; her visage went from somber to stern. Fax didn't make many mistakes, in her estimation, but it occurred to her that the count had just increased.

"I'd box your ears if you weren't off colour," Spar said, "and I would appreciate it if you never take that tone with me again. I'm galled that my brother has to depend on three people who have such an odd history—you, Saban and your brother. And didn't you and Franklin recently resume a speaking relationship?"

Fax nodded yes.

"I thought so. Listen, I need to know if you and *your* brother are capable of covering the rears of me and *my* brother. He's your squad leader for the foreseeable future—or are you planning to be distracted by this rubbish indefinitely? Bernard is tough, but he isn't invulnerable. So before I make a big stink up the chain of command, and since it's just us girls, so to speak, I would like to hear from you what happened, and how 'over' this really is."

"Short version or…." Fax watched one of Spar's eyebrows rise. "Accurate version. All right." Fax shook her head to clear the last of her fogginess. "You know, Saban only joined the Ancient about three and a half years ago. Most people think he's been around a lot longer."

"Closer to four. I was there."

"Right, I remember seeing you back then. You had long hair. Why did you—it doesn't matter. Anyway, Saban and James and I were the only ones who didn't wash out of that group, so the three of us became close, and Saban and I became…very close. Closer than I should have allowed myself."

"Don't you Americans have a phrase about not doing something where you eat?"

"There are many things one shouldn't do where one eats. At any rate, after the senior agents, the Primes, went deep cover, Saban became distant. He transferred to a different part of the Ancient, and a year later I found out he was my boss. And all that other stuff about him. That was the last James and I saw of him."

"Other stuff?"

Oh, you know. All the things that John told us about Saban. That he's much older than he looks. That he was an agent from some other agency, brought in to learn our operation from the bottom up. Brought in from day one to assume command. And all the things that Saban told me while we were together, about feeling confused and angry and…I thought he had opened up to me. But he was just selling his cover story to us, like any other agent would in the field."

"And…?"

"And embarrassingly, I suppose I let my feelings get the better of me. Thinking I had meant more to him than I actually did."

"And Agent Frank…excuse me, I mean James? What happened with the two of you?"

"Well…." This was the part that made her cringe. "James and I argued about Saban constantly. I couldn't let it go. I was convinced Saban would make things right and clear the air. James said that Saban did what James would have done, what guys do: they accomplish the mission and they move on. I don't know who James resented more for that, Saban or himself, but it became a sore spot between us. And I wouldn't…I didn't.... Saban may have destroyed our supposed friendship, but I'm the one who made the poor decisions that almost cost me my brother."

"You and James didn't talk for over a year."

"That was then. James and I are fine, and Saban is whoever or whatever he is now. Mission relevancy is nil. Uhm…there's no need to tell everyone all that, is there?"

Spar didn't say anything. She was obviously thinking hard. Her face was soft but sad when she finally addressed Fax. "No. I'll talk to Bernie, that's all. But…." Spar appeared to be still deep in thought. "You did something very good for me when you saved that girl's life. So I want to do something good for you and give you some advice: let it go."

"Let it go. Thanks, Miss Therapist. How could I have missed that? It's all better now."

Spar's eyes flashed dangerously. "I'll give you that one for free. But I'm serious. Let it go. Or at least, when the topic comes up again, approach it with an open mind." Spar stood up. "Get some rest."

"Is it safe for my brother to see me?"

"Hmm. Probably so. The worst of the infection seems to be out of your system. I'll send him up, but if you begin to relapse, send him out that very second."

"I will. What's next on the agenda?"

"Not sure. We may be sticking around. Millennial Security is about to get the contract at Dauphin Hill College. Seems that in addition to other problems, they recently had a paintball war on campus and no cameras to record the perpetrators."

"Do tell," Fax commented wryly.

Spar smiled and walked toward the door. "They needed it anyway, and as M-Sec, we'll do a better job for the money than anyone else. Don't let your brother stay too long. You know what you two are like when you get close together."

"I'm counting on it. This body needs to mend." Fax watched Spar close the door behind her.

That was a strange encounter. Fax would have bet money that Spar used to resent Saban as much as she did, though for vastly different reasons. Something had changed Spar's mind. The question was: had she misjudged Spar or Saban?

CHAPTER 9: Life Goes On

After the bustle of the past few days, Tuesday arrived for Saban with little fanfare. He gunned his vintage Volkswagon Bug (as much as anyone can gun a Bug) the last three miles to the building that had been his home of the past few months. Saban was well aware that he was cutting it close for his Tuesday class with Margo and Mikey. Skipping would not be the smartest thing he had ever done, but since he had spun Margo out of his life, it wouldn't make much difference to her.

And now that Jesse was on the mend, he could take time away from the hospital to do the legwork he had been putting off. So he was really too busy, he told himself, to go to class or go back to the hospital. As an added benefit, he could continue to avoid both Margo and Fax for another day or two. Being in charge had its benefits, and procrastinating on non-essentials was a perk of which he never tired.

Regardless, his mind whirred through myriad details—coordination efforts with Bravo team, after-action reviews, status checks on Fax, Demo, Margo…and how the bid for the Millennial Security contract was going with the college. *And was Ford ever located?* His mind ached from over-stimulation, distracting him for most of the familiar trip "home."

Home was a converted warehouse in a dilapidated section on the outskirts of the city. As usual, he activated the garage doors fifty feet from the entrance, but was surprised to see someone waiting for him—a tiny girl with delicate Asian features and short-cropped black hair. Spar should have been sound asleep, having just finished an overnight shift watching Fax. So she was either waiting up for him because there was a problem or…. Well, there was no other reason he could think of. They were co-workers, not friends.

Spar was also the only person on Alpha with whom he currently had any sort of relationship, though it was strictly professional and limited to training.

"Training" was the word Spar used whenever she wished to pummel Saban mercilessly. Spar had been John's first student in a fighting style so unique that few could master it. Saban was John's last student. On those occasions when John had been too busy to train, he would ask Spar to fill in, and she had happily beaten Saban several times a week for over a year. He could joke that their relationship was purely physical, but that would be asking for another beating.

Still, he had a lot of respect for Spar, and anyone who took Spar at her appearance risked a thrashing. She was a fighter without equal, and she could probably bench-press Demo if she felt the urge.

"What are you doing still awake, Asabi?" Saban stopped the engine and got out of his car.

"Oh, I hadn't planned to stay up, but we got a ring on the answerphone."

"Someone left a message?"

"Isn't that what I said?" His ignorance of British vernacular typically left her "brassed off," but she seemed pleased to see him, which was unusual—normally she was all business. He watched the garage doors close automatically before asking, "When you say 'we got a ring,' do you mean Alpha-Ancient or M-Sec?"

"Millennial Security. We have the job if we want it. Dauphin Hill's president called this morning and accepted our bid. Depending how fast we move, we start next week. Nothing is signed, of course; we could walk away…." She put her hands in her pockets and grimaced.

"But nobody expected the fledgling Alpha team would walk out with that crystal in just a few hours. I know. We spent a good deal of prep work setting up this gig, in case we needed to put heavy machinery on campus. Seems a shame to just walk away."

"Risk versus reward, mate. What benefit would there be from staying?"

"I dunno, it's…despite the target being acquired, this whole thing turned messy so fast. Ford. Fax. That civilian girl." *This has nothing to do with Margo. Nothing.* "Be nice to stick around and leave with something else accomplished."

"You're too hard on yourself," she said. "Ford will turn up. Fax is healing. Mar will be fine. We went down for one crystal and came up with two. It's all good." She drew herself up to her full height, a bit intimidating even though she was a head shorter than he. "I must confess, I haven't thought much of you for a long time. After all, I helped teach you, and then John puts you in a spot over me and everything. But I did read your after-action report. More importantly, I got to see you work up close and realize now that you have something I don't. Something I didn't notice before last week."

"Something good?"

"Quite. I make things break. But you…you have a way about you. Isn't that a song? You get people moving. You make things come together."

"Oh. It's nothing," Saban said, embarrassed, then embarrassed that he was embarrassed. *Why did John put me in charge of anything?*

"No, it's something. But you should know I…I complained to John before we left. I didn't think it was fair that you were placed in a tactical command. Actually, I'm still not completely sure. But I *might* have been wrong about you, and I told that to John this morning. I wanted you to know." She looked away. "Anyway, you need to talk to John yourself. Decide if we take the job. You lead; I'll follow."

Her lips formed a wicked smile. "This doesn't mean I'll be any nicer."

Saban caught a glimpse of what she was going to do next. His hand darted out to the side of her head to hit her first, but it was too late. She deflected his blow and landed one of her own on the bruised side of his face. "Ow!"

"Nice try, *Sidai*," she said. That meant "newcomer," he remembered, or sometimes "younger brother," a term she used with him when they trained. "How ever did that Cajun hit you? Sloppy, sloppy." She was grinning. "I know John taught you better."

"Sorry, *Sifu*," which meant "instructor," the appropriate response. "I was distracted. Hey, for the record, I'm glad you're on my team."

"I think…maybe I am, too."

"Good. Get some rest. I've gotta jet, or I'm going to be late." Saban was bolted toward the warehouse entrance to get his books, but stopped and turned around. "Spar. Asabi."

"What, then?" She eyed him curiously.

"We're…uhm, we're covert agents, right? We do what very few others could do, right?"

"Well, yes." Her nose wrinkled as she answered. "What are you—"

"It's just that sometimes I…why do I get the feeling sometimes that we're just playing at this? Like it's all some kind of game?"

"Because you're daft, that's why!" She took a jab at him that he easily evaded. "Get going."

"Right." He was only in the warehouse for a minute, but when he came out to ask her something else, Spar was gone. He re-entered and took care of a few things that could only be done at the warehouse then hopped into his car and sped off for school.

He would have just enough to time to call John before getting on campus, so he had better get his thoughts in order. Even if he and John were technically equals, protocol dictated that neither one waste the time of the other.

His car exited a short service road and pulled into traffic on the highway, with the comfortable putt-putt-putting of the engine already working its magic on his frayed nerves. He rolled down the window and let the fresh air rush through the interior, and when his head was clear, he called John.

"Hey, it's Eight. Patch me through to Six." He had no idea what "patch me through" had to do with cellular communications, but that was what John always said, and John had been like a father to Saban almost since the day they met. Good enough for Six was good enough for Eight.

"Hullo? Six here," came a voice from the other end of the phone.

"Yeah, it's Eight. I have ten minutes until I'm back in the field. Is this line secure yet?"

"In three…two…I think I heard…ah, there's the signal. Hullo, Saban. Seems as though you've made a favorable impression on Spar."

"I guess I have my moments. And Fax is healing fast. Have you talked with her?"

"Yes. Once, to let her know I care. You should try it," John replied in his gently British way. "She's quite fussed with you. Is there something I should know about?"

"No, I think she's more steamed about being taken down than actually getting hurt. There may be other outstanding issues, but I'm going to check in with her after class."

"And have a long-overdue conversation, I hope. Screw your courage to the sticking place, Master Eight, and you will prevail."

"I always wonder about the phrase. I mean, if it's a sticking place, why would you have to screw things to it? Shouldn't stuff just…you know, stick? Of course, if Shakespeare meant it like tuning a guitar or a lyre, I guess, then—"

"Was there anything else?"

Oops. "Were you able to do a background check on that girl?"

"Yes—the lovely and talented Ms. Margo Weissmann. How is she, by the way?"

"She's out of the picture, so she should be fine. I'll confirm that in the next few hours. But there's something about her; she's so strong and fast. And the fact that I had such a hard time spinning her…I don't know. She ignored everything but my most direct suggestions."

"Sounds as if she suffers from 'estrogen poisoning.' I'm not sure there is a treatment."

"That helps so much," Saban replied, not amused. "You know what I mean. I don't have problems spinning females anymore, like in the old days, but I really couldn't tell if it stuck all the way. I want to know why. I don't like being in the dark."

"Well said. But if that's the case, why have you avoided contact with her?"

Now, that's an excellent question, isn't it? Fortunately, he could easily avoid the real answer and still tell the truth. "I don't want her drawn into this any more than she already was, and I don't want to take any chances until I have more data, if it's available." No sense revealing a romance that never was and never could be. John would only think Saban was repeating past mistakes.

"Ah, very prudent, Master Eight." John didn't quite sound convinced. "However, I regret to say there is nothing unusual I can tell you about her."

"Nothing?"

"Nothing. No state police records, and her transcript indicated home-schooling, so there are no school records. I'll transfer what I can give you to our intranet page, under Alpha, access code four-six-four-nine. You can look it over if you wish. It's entirely possible she may have a natural resistance to your charms, and it is also possible you simply need more practice in this area."

"But…." Saban floundered, "How do you explain her—"

"There are diverse unusual people in the world, as you well know. We try to find them, employ them, but there are others undiscovered, and good for them. I will let you know if there is anything else I can tell you about her." His voice had a note of finality to it.

Was John not seeing what Saban thought obvious? Saban pressed on. "Sir, Margo herself is not the point. There's something not right. I think we were compromised. Those men knew where the entrances were; they took out our people. And someone took out *their* people. We're lucky no one died. And why were some of our adversaries carrying mercy guns like we do? I think we should just roll up this entire operation and go home. It's not safe."

"You think there is a mole, and I agree that may be the case. But if there is a mole, I'm not certain a 'safe' place exists. If you roll up now, you alert the mole that we know of his existence. As far as the entrances being compromised, it's more likely that Ford's men followed our people and discovered the entrances that very night."

"So how do you explain the fact that Spar's team was laid out all nice and neat? And except for Rambeau and friends, Ford's team was knocked out as well? What reason would a mole have for doing that?"

"Patience, Master Eight. There is most definitely an independent force at work here, but if there *is* a mole…." John seemed like he was thinking out loud, but Saban knew he was calling on decades of experience. "No, as much as it pains me, the best action is to stay the course, if only to reinforce any current spins you have out there. I believe that Millennial Security should take the job they have been offered, which will allow us to help the college's security situation and give us a reason to stay in the field without drawing attention to ourselves. Keep your eyes open, and wait for our possible mole to make a careless mistake. They always do."

"Well, that's why I love this job. Except for the whole 'constant danger' thing."

"There is another reason you need to stay," John said. "The class body is too small for you to vanish in the middle of a semester. If you leave now, there will be a sucking chest-wound where your cover story was. That will raise some questions with anyone who may be looking for answers, with Ms. Weissmann left in the crosshairs. Don't forget, Mr. Ford is still at large."

"I understand. If I go, it makes her look suspicious. I'm getting close to the college, so I need to cut this short, but I'm sorry I missed your birthday."

"Oh!" John sounded genuinely surprised. "Well, very good, then." He paused. "It was a day like any other, entirely unremarkable and unimportant in the grander scheme."

"It was important to *me*," Saban responded quietly. "Take care."

"You too, Master Eight. You too." The phone beeped off.

Saban eased his phone into its dashboard holster. Someday, they would talk about the wall John kept between himself and the living. Saban had been new to the Ancient when John's wife, Bekka, and the others died, but even Saban had noted his change. As close as he and John had become over the past two years, it was only so close and no closer. Saban had no idea how to bridge that gap, or if he should even try. He was much better at keeping people at a distance.

The irony did not escape Saban. Most people didn't notice Saban unless he wanted to be noticed, and when he did, their casual interest tended toward adulation—the same way Saban felt around John. Except John didn't have a talent that made it so. John was simply that cool.

Saban's Volkswagen turned into the main entrance of the college. He saw the shortcut Mikey had run through to surprise Fax and Franklin, the shrubs where he and Margo had interrogated agent Ford. Hard to believe this was the same road he and Margo had taken thirty minutes to…no.

There was no "he and Margo." He had responsibilities: to John, to the Ancient, to Alpha. There was Saban. There was a girl. And there was a class the girl attended where Saban needed to be in less than an hour. That was all.

CHAPTER 10: Back to Normal?

After the boredom of the past few days, Tuesday arrived for Margo with little fanfare. She lay in bed and considered the fact that she had spent the better part of the weekend in a daze, trying to sort through what was true and what was not. She was not one who dealt in shades of gray, so on Saturday she had naturally gone to temple, which helped. There was no question she could not answer in the context of God's timing and providence. And while this was certainly a truth, it was not the precise truth she sought. She needed very specific answers, but all she seemed to accomplish were questions upon questions.

Yesterday, for example. She had run into Mikey, who told her about getting knocked out by a stray paintball last Thursday night. Did he think that on his own, or had Saban gotten to him? She asked him if he had talked to Saban lately, and he appeared puzzled but responded that he had not.

Did he really not see Saban, or had Saban convinced him otherwise?

Saban said he could not completely dominate another person, but how could one believe anything he said? And anyway, did he really tell her that, or did she only think he said that? He was the last thing on her mind when she fell asleep, and the first thing running through it when she awoke. The whole thing was driving her crazy.

Thus, Margo began her familiar morning routine feeling out of sorts. She wasn't incapable of logical reasoning. Her GPA vouched for that. But questioning the natural order of things was unusually…unnatural, as though it were a muscle she hadn't used in a while.

That muscle was definitely getting more exercise. Lately, she had a frequent and burning desire to peek around corners or tread unknown staircases, and that wasn't like her. Was it?

She showered and changed into jeans and a tee-shirt, then on a whim, took out a legal pad to try and bring some order out of the chaos before class. After all, this would be the first time seeing him since Thursday. How would he act? Would he be there? Would she?

She wanted to make a list of known and unknown issues, but when it became apparent that the legal pad was not filling up on its own, she decided to take a stroll around campus to clear her head. Her room seemed very small, distractingly small.

Though early in the day, the sun shone brightly, and the air was cool. Everything seemed normal. She almost couldn't imagine anything outside that realm of the mundane. So why was it that with each passing day, the color of everything seemed a bit brighter, every sound a bit clearer? Even the air smelled wintry and fantastic.

As she walked, her ever-present flannel shirt made its way from her waist to her torso, blunting some of the chill. The fall season had not completely given way to the next, making the walk wonderfully brisk. She made a mental note to try and run a few miles later, after dark. More fun to run then; she didn't have to hold back as much. Safety issues were a factor; she wasn't that naïve. But she hadn't met anyone who could outrun her, and she pitied any would-be mugger who, by some means, caught her.

The thought of venting her frustration on some petty thug brought a silly smirk to her face, and smiling made her feel more normal. *But there's nothing normal about looking forward to beating up a mugger. What's wrong with me?* She was not one hundred percent herself; something was…different. Even for her.

Without meaning to, she had wandered over to Mayberry Manor. In front of the president's house was a cul-de-sac with a large dogwood at its center, surrounded by thick green grass that had not yet begun its annual withering. She took off her shoes and felt the soft blades; they were still cold and wet from the morning dew, and lovely against the soles of her feet.

From where she stood, she could see the corner of the outside shed and decided to check it, as she had done yesterday and the day before. A large padlock was still on the door, maybe even the same one from last week. There were no signs of a struggle, nothing to indicate anything had happened. It didn't matter; she knew what she knew. Didn't she? Saban was the one who didn't know what she knew. And she knew Saban didn't know that…that…. She pounded her fist on the masonry next to the door and felt it give slightly.

Rein in! Deep breath. *Let's not leave holes in buildings.*

Sorting through fact and fiction was a big problem, but very few problems were insurmountable for her. *"I can do all things..."* Margo reminded herself. She just had to find the right handle with which to bludgeon the issue. *Again with the violence.* She returned to the dogwood, sat down, leaned against the trunk and took out her pad. She still had a few minutes. Here and now was as good a place as any to work.

So where do I start? The problem she faced was more profound than Descartes ever wrestled with: *I can think, but how can I know what to believe?* Was it possible that Saban spun her partially, but not fully, or was she completely immune? She decided that as fantastic as the entire situation was, a partial spin was too hard to explain. It was all or nothing.

After framing these thoughts, she wrote her conclusion on the pad: "I am not crazy." Descartes she was not, but that was a better starting point than the alternative.

So why would he tell her it was all a dream and then try so hard to cover up all the evidence? She was sick of dreams, especially dreams of rivers and villages and—

She stood up, put her shoes on without bothering to brush off her feet, and headed toward class. Whatever happened (or didn't happen) with Saban, at least Mikey would be there.

Mikey had a fraternal affection for Margo that she found truly touching. He seemed to live from moment to moment, just enjoying life. She figured him to be a junior or senior, or else he was on the "five-year" plan.

Also, Mikey occasionally displayed a Gump-ian wisdom about life and relationships, but as far as sheer I.Q.—ot-nay oo-tay ight-bray. Not that it mattered to her; when it came to friends, it was the heart, not the brain, that could be a deal breaker. And Mikey's sporadically profound observations made their study sessions all the more interesting. She and Mikey were already study partners before Saban joined in, making it a trio of different perspectives. They had the viewpoints of Saban the "thinker," Margo the "do-er," and Mikey the…*liver? The experiencer?*

She couldn't think of a proper word. Well, it hardly mattered. She preferred action. She didn't have the time or desire to anguish over the particulars of self-expression.

She neared Quinlan Hall and stopped to wait for Saban and Mikey. Their habit was that each person would wait until the others arrived, and they would all go into class together. But maybe not today.

She opened the double doors to Quinlan Hall and went in by herself, a relative term, of course. There were lots of other people in the hallways, at least ten or fifteen—a crowd on this campus. The total enrollment was less than a thousand.

She had heard of colleges where there were tens of thousands of kids, but the thought of being around that many people struck her heart with an irrational dread. Coming from a small town, she had never been in a room with more than thirty people in her whole life. She had never even been to a mall, nor did she have any desire to go.

As she walked through the corridors of the aged building, she had an unusual idea about the mall—why not? The "why not" part wasn't unusual, she always had a hard time backing down from a challenge. No, the unusual part was, why had she never before considered going to a mall? It was not agoraphobia, or whatever phobia made you afraid of people. *Saban would know the word, darn him.* She loved people. In fact, after a few days by herself, being around others gave her incredible energy, like an adrenaline rush squared. So why the avoidance, and why had she never deemed it odd?

And why was she questioning things she had never questioned before?

She was aware that things were shaking loose in her, adding to the feeling she was not quite herself. Maybe she wasn't less than normal. Maybe she was becoming better than normal. Margo liked to think optimistically.

Or maybe her feelings weren't strange at all. After all, there were no shopping malls in…in…that's bizarre, she'd lived there her whole life and couldn't remember the name of…Salinamas. Of course, how could she forget? Salinamas. No malls there. So that might explain it.

Margo found herself sitting at her desk. Her brain had taken her there on autopilot while her mind was occupied. She patted herself on her head with a tinge of irrational pride.

"Were you a good girl, then?" Saban said from behind her.

He came! Here we go.

She whirled around in her seat. Saban was sitting in his usual chair, behind her and to the left, leaned back and looking relaxed. "I'm always a good girl. Or hadn't you noticed?" The casual banter made her realize she had missed his friendship, despite all the strange events.

"I can't tell. My eyes still haven't uncrossed from you shaking me like a Polaroid picture. How are you?"

"I'm fine. Oh, and Outkast called. They want their lyrics back."

"Wow! Any day you make an obscure cultural reference, you must be feeling fine." Saban pretended to dab tears from his eyes. "And your scalding wit has wounded me deeply."

"I didn't know you were so thin-skinned. You're normally much thicker," she volleyed.

"And I'm not the only one. Did you gain a few pounds over the weekend?" he returned.

Another voice chimed in from across the room. "So that's why all the girls want your phone number. Your smooth way with the ladies." Mikey ambled across the room and sat down behind Margo, high five-ing her on the way.

Margo touched his forehead. "Hey, Mike-zilla! How's your head feeling?"

"Scabbed over fine. My back's better, too. I didn't think those paint ball guns were supposed to draw blood."

"At close range, they do." Saban was rubbing the side of his face that was still bruised.

"Holy crap, Sabe, they nailed you, too? You are so messed up!" He swung one of his huge hands toward Saban, laughing. "Can I touch it?"

Saban reared out of the way. "Not unless you have ibuprofen coming out of your fingers. The guys that hit you were fighting the guys that hit me and Margo. Well, they tried to hit her, but my face got in the way."

"What?" Mikey's expression changed to anger in an instant. "Someone tried to hurt Little Bit?"

"Relax, Zilla," Margo said soothingly. "It's a long story, but in the end, we both lived, and no one got hurt that badly." *Except poor Fax, if she were real.* And then they were chatting about nothing important, all at once, until the professor came in and began his lecture. *Blah, blah, philosophy. Next time, blah, blah, Nietzsche. What's the point to this class?*

Afterward, Saban left quickly, saying that he had to run an errand. He didn't try to pull her aside, didn't make clever quips with dual meanings.

He had been so…unremarkable. Like always. He did say he was still on for their Thursday study session, but so did Mikey, and he didn't stick around either, leaving her alone with her legal pad and her thoughts. Whatever she had been expecting, that wasn't it. She still couldn't decide whether she wanted to kiss him or kill him.

Kill him? Now, where did that thought come from? It sounded more like something that girl Fax would have said. And if she were real, Margo wondered, what had happened to her?

CHAPTER 11: Saban Comes Clean. No, Really! Part I

Saban pulled his Volkswagen into the hospital parking lot and jumped out. The information desk verified for him that Fax had not moved to a different room, and then pointed him to the gift shop. As usual, it took a minute to get the sales girl's attention. It was sort of a game for him to see if he could be noticed without speaking, but finally she took his order.

"A dozen roses for you," confirmed the sales girl. "Red roses, I assume?" She smiled sweetly at Saban.

"Better make those yellow roses," he corrected. She appeared disappointed, but filled the order and went about her business.

He took the short ride up to her room, stopping just at the door. From there, he heard a sound like two tape recorders were being played at a high speed. And they were arguing. Obviously, Franklin had beaten him here. He knocked, and the two voices decelerated to normal speech as he opened the door.

"Hey, keep it down! Sounds like two chipmunks at a helium-palooza. Uhn…is it safe for you to be here now?" Saban's head nodded toward Franklin.

Franklin turned up the bandwidth on his perpetual smile. "Hey, Sabe. It's cool." Dressed in casual beach attire, one would never think Franklin was anything but an easy-going young man visiting his sister in the hospital. Which he was. "Now that the worst of it is over, I'm actually helping."

"For a change," added Fax. Her expression was flat, which meant she was probably in a good mood. *For a change*, Saban thought, but wisely left unsaid.

"Aw, I love you, too, sis. Doesn't it help you to know how much I luuuuv you?" Franklin leaned toward her with his lips puckered up and made kissing sounds.

"Ugh. Stop it! Get away!" Her bandaged hand blocked him, but she wore the barest hint of a smile.

He relented without planting one on her. "I'll leave you two alone. I have things to do, nurses to hit on…. Hey, rocking first mission, dude." Franklin headed toward the door.

Saban wasn't sure if that was sarcastic, so he ignored it. "I kind of thought you guys would be gone by now. When are you trekking back to HQ? Are you waiting for Fax or going tonight?" He was uncertain when to tell them the new plan that he and John had decided.

"We're sticking around for a while. You didn't hear? We got word this morning. Hey, aren't you supposed to be in charge or something?"

Saban's face reddened slightly. Hadn't he and John decided that just a few hours ago? Either John had notified the rest of the team as soon as he hung up from Saban or else John merely allowed Saban to think the decision had not yet been made. Saban considered several angry barrages to cover his ignorance and agitation, but bit his tongue instead. "It all catches up to me eventually, James. I don't have to know every detail. Besides, if you—"

Franklin put his hands up, laughing. "Dude, I'm totally janking you. Lighten up!" He opened the door. "I'll leave so you and Jesse can have fun. Maybe you can take turns describing how the glass really is half-empty. Later!" He stuck his tongue out at his sister.

"I think you're referring to your cranium!" Fax punctuated the comment by sticking her own tongue out. "Creep," she uttered as he left, but one look at her face told Saban she was not the least bit upset with her brother. *Nice to see them back together. I wonder what caused them to stop speaking to each other, anyway?*

Saban sat down and, from habit, began assessing Fax and her surroundings. She was much smaller out of uniform, he noticed, wearing just a hospital gown. Her right arm was in a cast up to the shoulder where she had been stabbed. Her left hand was bandaged with a heplock and a few other tubes attached. Considering all she had been through, she didn't look too bad.

But as capable as she was, she appeared vulnerable. Defenseless. Unexpectedly, she was no longer Fax the agent. This was Jesse, the young girl he had met while she was *becoming* an agent. He saw, for the first time in a long time, a friend—a petite blond who appeared to weigh perhaps one hundred pounds, terribly hurt and in need of a friend herself.

Of course, he had read her file; he knew she was not fragile mentally or physically. And she was certainly much heavier than she appeared. She was all muscle, though one could not tell unless she flexed.

She was also a Talent, like her brother. When she and James were together, her weight would nearly double. Even separately, they were denser than normal people. *Heh.* She hated when he said it like that, he remembered fondly. As for her mental sturdiness—well, assessing that capacity was the only reason he was here, right? *Right?*

"Jesse," he said, not knowing what else to say and unsure what to do with the flowers or anything else.

She looked up. "Oh, just call me Fax. Everyone else does, now. Besides, when James became a field agent and people found out we were siblings, they kept calling us Team Rocket."

"Surrender now, or prepare to fight…." murmured Saban.

"Me-ow, that's right!" answered Fax. "Codenames make it easier in the field, anyway."

"But we're not in the field now, are we?"

"Aren't we?" Neither of them said anything.

She's not going to make this easy on me. And maybe I deserve it. He looked at her, and without meaning to, she began to blur around the edges as he looked past her form, deeper into her. He saw anger, doubt, fear—all of which he expected. He didn't want to put her through any more pain. *Or am I just trying to avoid more pain for my own sake?*

The best thing for the team would be keeping everything professional and detached. Was that what he wanted? Saban was accustomed to thinking communally; that was how he was raised. *You have to think of what is best for everyone when you grow up with nine other guys.* He found it difficult to draw distinctions between Saban the Alpha T-Com, Saban the co-leader of the Ancient, and Saban the person. What did he want? He couldn't decide.

"Maybe I should just go," he finally offered.

"Maybe you should," she said in an inflectionless tone.

Still "reading" her, he saw her fear begin to spike, but behind it, he saw something else, almost obscured by the other emotions. Something unexpected.

He saw love. Romantic or brotherly, he could not tell, but it was definitely there. She still cared about him, after all this time. So what did he want? *Immediate objective: make a decision, make a decision, make a...*

"I'm not going to go," he said. He put the flowers into a plastic cup, placed the cup on the window sill and sat down. Saban saw her relax before forcing himself to stop looking at her so deeply. "Maybe I'm an idiot."

"Maybe you are." She wore that Mona Lisa smile he used to enjoy earning from time to time. Okay, she seems ready to talk about the past.

He, however, was going to need a little time to warm up to it. "So have you guys always been able to do that speed-speak thing?"

"More or less. We didn't even meet until we were seven, but we made up for lost time. It wasn't until we both hit puberty a few years ago that we could really take it into high gear, which we usually save for when we're by ourselves. Plus, it distresses my larynx after awhile." She cleared her throat. "So I heard from Demo and Franklin—excuse me, Bernard and James—that everything turned out well. Why do you call him Franklin anyway?"

"Heh. He thinks it's because he's so good with money and numbers," Saban said. "Like the Franklin Mint. Actually, it's because his mouth is a lightning rod. Like Ben Franklin's kite. It's my little joke."

"Either way, it's a dumb code name."

"Well, it was either that or 'Annoying Lad.' Now I have a question for you." And Saban had an idea what the answer was, but it was better to ask her, since she knew everything anyway. *Or so she thinks.* "What's the deal with you and James being close together? You almost—"

"It's quite simple," she said, cutting him off. "You know that when James and I are far apart, there's no discernable difference between us and anyone else. As we get closer, our metabolisms speed up dramatically, which gives us increased speed and stamina, increased intelligence—not that I need it…"

"Of course not," Saban said with a straight face, "but that's not what I—"

"Don't make me smack you. Where was I? Oh, and due to our accelerated metabolisms, increased healing. 'Increased healing' is a misnomer, however. If there's something malignant in our systems, that can grow, too. The natural conclusion of whatever is in our system happens much quicker. In this case, I developed an infection, and without treatment, the infection would have grown, and so it did."

"Yeah, I know. You got a raging staph infection in a matter of hours. But last time I checked, your rev-radius was forty feet. We had to separate you two by almost ninety feet to get you back to normal."

"Oh, that. I updated my folder recently. When was the last time you looked at it?"

"Uh…couple months ago. Didn't think it changed. But I read James' last week, when he was approved for Alpha."

"Slackers, both of you. I told him he needed to update his dossier. In any event, as long as he stays close to me," Jesse tapped the cast on her arm, "this will be ready to come off by the end of the week. He's an annoying younger brother, but I suppose I'll keep him."

"Younger by two minutes."

"Still," she maintained.

"Still," he agreed. *There was that silence again, darn it!*

"By the way, thanks for the flowers. So let me ask you a question: exactly why are you here?"

"Me? I was…we're…you're on my team, and I was…"

"Don't be patronizing, Saban. Do you feel sorry for me? Is that it? I've barely talked to you in two months, and not at all for over a year before that. The next thing I know, you're all 'Alpha T-Com' and everything. You and James and I are the only Talents still around from our class. I remember your first day; I thought your only talents were being confused and getting angry."

"I got better."

"You were a mess. And now you're the supreme grand poobah? In three years? I think not!" Her face was flushed, looking redder than it probably was against her pale hospital gown.

"Technically, I am." He had wondered where this was going.

"And what about you and me? We're friends one day—more than friends, I thought—and the next thing I know, you're in meetings all day, then you're sequestered...."

Ah, here it comes. "I got busy."

"For a year and a half?" She was almost shouting, with more emotion than he had seen from her ever. "What made it worse was that John sat with me and James and a few of the others and told us to basically forget we knew you."

"Six?" he said. "He spun you? He can't spin—"

"No, no, but it made me think you were in trouble. I worried about you, and I'm not angry about that, but it hurt me that you were so nonchalant about being transferred."

"That's not true," Saban protested. "I was very...very chalant." *Lame.*

"It's not like we were engaged; we were barely dating, but I thought...I thought you and I were closer than that." She looked down at her punctured hand. "You really hurt me. I didn't think you could."

"I'm sorry."

"And it didn't just cost me your friendship. James was so angry at me defending you that we stopped speaking for a year. We only recently became civil to each other."

Wow. How had he not known he had come between them? All he wanted to do today was reconcile with her as a teammate, but he was wondering if the time had come to make some amends on a more personal level. She had been a close friend, and more...but only John knew his whole story. If he leveled with her now...the timing was especially poor, especially with a potential double-agent running around. But for the sake of the team...no, for the sake of his friend....

Margo had been right about one thing: he did have a hard time making decisions. Some decisions, anyway. Why were some so easy and some so hard? "Tell me what you want, Jesse."

"I want the truth!"

"You can't handle the…! Just kidding." They chuckled together. Like old times.

And he made another decision. "Listen, if I tell you, you cannot tell anyone, not even your brother. This has to stay between you and me, okay? I'm being deadly earnest. Well, not lethally, but still very, very earnest."

"Saban, you could have made me believe anything you wanted, for a while. But I trust you. I do."

His heart hurt to hear those two words echoed, but he listened without commenting.

"And I hope you trust me," she said. "So I want to know everything: how you got here, how much older than me you really are—everything you can tell me. You can trust me. And you couldn't spin me when we first met, but now I have to trust you."

"When we first met, I didn't know how to spin girls. I didn't know how to spin anyone."

"That was a long time ago. So," she said in an informal tone that fooled neither of them, "what have you been up to for the past year and a half?"

He took a deep breath. "Okay. Here goes…." He wasn't sure where to start.

This would sure be a great time for Ford to burst in and make with the big distraction. Whatever happened to that guy, anyway?

CHAPTER 12: The Pieces Are Moved Into Place

"Is this more comfortable, Mr. Ford?"

A velvet sack was pulled abruptly off his head, and Devon Ford found himself sitting at the end of a long table in a poorly lit conference room. Despite that, his eyes were hurting, and not just from the fact that he had been in complete darkness for the last four or five days. A small spotlight aimed at his chest prevented him from seeing anyone but the fellow in front of him.

It didn't much matter. He had been listening intently since he was brought in—at least five people were in the room with him. None of them were rushing to greet him, however.

His hands had been cuffed since morning, the same time his captors had placed over his head a bag similar to the one used when he was originally captured. He wasn't sure where he was currently; he hadn't traveled long enough to make it out of the city, but it would be best not to assume anything. No rush. Since he was obviously being prepped for a conversation of sorts, he should get some answers soon.

"You understand why you are here, Mr. Ford?" The handcuffs on his wrists didn't chafe nearly as much as the condescending attitude of his "host." Apparently, they were going to let one person do the talking for all of them.

"No, I'm a moron. I've never been the target of a black bag job before. Enlighten me."

"Very well." Ford was being addressed by a tall, thin gentleman who spoke with the poise and accent of the very British. "Although, given the abundance of evidence supporting your statement, it boggles the mind that I might fulfill your request. At any rate," he stopped to clean his glasses with a small white handkerchief, which immediately vanished back into his suit when he finished, "I shall do my best to 'enlighten' you. You are present at a rare syzygy of international intelligence interests. I have been voted by my peers as most likely to pummel you into unconsciousness should you decide to be uncooperative, and, therefore, best equipped to communicate our desires to you."

"Oooo, I'm scared. Good thing I wore my brown pants." *I've been threatened by some of the best. You're not even close.* "I heard a few accents when you brought me in. I place at least one Mossad agent and somebody's Slavic accent that must be *de facto* KGB. I presume you to be MI-6? Should I call you 'C?'"

Every head of MI-6 carried the nickname of 'C,' so he ought to know when he's being mocked. Let's see what gets a rise out of this 'bloke.'

"My name is Desmond Dewitter," said the man, who seemed unperturbed. "You may call me Mr. Dewitter or Agent Dewitter. You know who some of us are. And now, let me tell you who you are. Devon Ford, aged thirty-six, born in Mission, Kansas, transplanted to a variety of military schools about the country as a young man, and now lead agent of Ford Freelance, a rotating band of B-grade guns-for-hire whose best attribute is that no one will care if you all die. Have I left anything out?"

"Yeah, I also make world-class eggs benedict. If you're trying to psych me out, keep dreaming. I may not have the best guys in the world, but if you know so much about me, then you know I've never been hurting for business. You're not talking to me because you *don't* need me, so just get to it, or kill me now before you bore us all to death."

Let's see what they do with that. "And by the way, if you hire me, this is all on the clock," he added. Emotions were a liability that Ford seldom let interfere, but he allowed himself the tiniest glimmer of satisfaction. Ford thought he heard a muffled laugh from the back of the room.

"Ah, that delightful American braggadocio," said Dewitter. "I was rather hoping I might encounter it once in my lifetime without having to stifle the resultant impulse to gag."

"It *is* sort of our trademark," said an American voice from the back of the room. CIA, Ford would have bet. *That's at least four different agencies represented.* Cooperation was not uncommon between the services, Ford thought, but this level of mutual involvement was highly unusual. *Good. The higher the stakes, the higher the fees.*

Dewitter turned his head to face the speaker. "Bravado will I endure in associates, but in or in front of underlings, to paraphrase Churchill, it is the sort of effrontery up with which I shall not put!" The room became silent, and he turned to face Ford.

Ford was also quiet. If he had chosen to rise up, there was a good chance he could have snapped Dewitter's neck unhindered, even with cuffs on, but he did not. This was an opportunity to negotiate for information, plus it's always bad form to kill a prospective employer. Even a snooty one.

Dewitter collected his thoughts. "Where was I? Yes, we shall cut to the point. You and several of your compatriots recently saw action with another group of individuals calling themselves 'The Ancient.' Like their objectives, the veracity of their *nom de guerre* has yet to be determined. We have gleaned as much information as we could from your synaptically-challenged friend, Mr. Rambeau."

So Napoleon Rambeau is not dead. "And how is he?" Ford asked evenly.

"Deranged, frankly. I would tell you to be concerned were I certain that psychosis is not his natural state. In any event, we have secured him from the local *gendarmes* and learned that, while most of your unit was rendered unconscious from a distance, several—including yourself—were taken down in close combat."

Ford berated himself silently. How poorly trained were his men that they were all taken out so easily? He would definitely want to address this when the time was right.

"None of you remembers a thing except Rambeau," Dewitter said, "and you, presumably. It is the close-quarters fighting I wish to address. While Rambeau seems to be obsessed over being defeated, I am more concerned with the fact that his opponents may have been members of…ahem, 'the Ancient.' What can you tell us? Please note that I have little patience for fools or prevaricators." Dewitter sat down at the conference table near Ford.

Ford was still thinking about Napoleon Rambeau, who was probably not as far gone as he appeared. Acting crazy was merely one way to avoid long interrogations. Why play against type? *Good old Nappy. Bad, crazy Nappy.* Of course, that meant Ford got the short end of the stick. *Time to give them some rope and see if I can avoid the noose.*

"Rambeau and I were beaten by a kid. A male. I think he had his girlfriend with him. He was just a kid. Just a kid…." Ford repeated. *Odd. Whatever.* "If he wasn't an operative, he should be, because the way he moved was unreal. If the girl was an agent, she needs a new career. She was not a factor."

Dewitter peered at him intently. "I see. What else?"

Ford concentrated. "Honestly—and I don't use that word lightly—it was hard to tell in the dark and the mud and the rain. They were dressed like college kids. They may have been posing as students." Ford heard some degree of murmuring. "The kid asked me questions. I can't quite…when I try to remember what he looked like, it's like there's a smudge on my memory." More murmuring. "Her face I can remember. I might recognize her all cleaned up. Him…it's just not there. I do recall his questions. He wanted to know the composition of my team. Who my employer was. Technical stuff."

"Incidentally, who was your employer, Mr. Ford? I'm simply curious."

"I simply can't tell you. Black-Ops professional courtesy. Maybe you should ask some of your friends, here. You're sure they're all on your side?" Ford cast his gaze about the room but still could make out no faces.

Dewitter changed tactics. "And why did you so quickly abandon your team, Mr. Ford? Do you make a habit of deserting your comrades at the least bit of trouble?"

Ford didn't bite. "We were hired for a specific purpose involving non-lethal objectives. We were not hired to engage a possibly deadly enemy. Everyone was aware of that, and everyone knew that another Covert Ops team meant an immediate mission-abort. The fact that the only conscious members of my team decided to work in violation of mission parameters speaks to their priorities, not mine."

"Hmm. All right, then." That seemed to satisfy Dewitter. "I…that is to say, we…have a proposition for you, Mr. Ford." He removed a folded piece of paper from another of his suit pockets and slid it in front of Ford. "We are prepared to offer you the following sum of money to locate these two individuals. They are our only link to this shadowy organization. You will alter your appearance for purposes of close surveillance, and we shall also place our long range survey ops and equipment at your disposal. If the male cannot be identified, we must find the female and use her to locate her partner."

"Why him?"

"Because we think he is a linchpin. Clearly, he is a man of unique capabilities, capable in the areas of armed and unarmed combat. He coordinated a multi-pronged strike that not only achieved its objective but defended a counterstrike from an opposing force. Do you have any other questions?"

"What if I say no?"

Dewitter pulled back his fist and struck Ford squarely in the jaw, knocking Ford to the ground. "I believe I already answered that question. Let the pummeling commence."

"Hold your horses! Geez! I thought Rambeau was the crazy one." *Because only a crazy man would have done that to me.* "Can't you slow down and give a girl time to think?"

"If it makes you feel better, you may have a few hours to decide. As a show of good faith, we will let you continue to live."

The American cleared his throat loudly.

Dewitter rolled his eyes. "And we will return your personal items to you before you return to the holding area. Your handcuffs will remain in place for the nonce. Before you agree, you must determine whether you are up a task you have failed once already. We need to bring this person in or put him down, but make no mistake: he is a serious threat, not to be underestimated. I doubt we will easily catch him off-balance."

CHAPTER 13: Saban Comes Clean, Part II

Saban was completely off balance. Jesse shifted in her bed to get more comfortable. "This is the part where you talk."

"Right. It's just…I feel like I'm in my underwear in front of my doctor and the curtain just opened up with me on stage."

"Hmmm, let me call for a wah-mbulance…nope, no sympathy here. I'm in a hospital gown with the wind touching places the sun has never seen. Trade you!" Her eyes were softer than he had seen in a long time. *Was she this nice before, or was she on a morphine drip?* In any case, he felt this was definitely the right thing to do. Whoever the mole was, it couldn't be Jesse.

"Part of this you already know," he began. "I was dropped off at a boys' home when I was only two, so I don't remember much about my parents. I wasn't neglected or anything, but I was very sick, all the time. Whatever was wrong with me, the doctors never found it. They sure did try. I got violently sick once or twice a year, though as I got older, it became less frequent and less intense. I didn't have much else to do, so I concentrated on schoolwork."

"Blah, blah, blah," Jesse said impatiently. "You're a genius and you graduated when you were fifteen. I know your whole story. I thought you were going to tell me the truth?"

"Hey! I'm trying. I don't go interrupting your secret origin, now do I?" he said, thumping one of her balloons. "And I didn't just graduate," he added loftily, "I graduated with top honors."

"And a massively bad attitude," Jesse added. "That part I know, first hand."

"And my legendary bad attitude. I was angry about being abandoned and about being sick so much, and there was one other issue that was really messing with my head."

“Wait, wait.” Jesse tried to pour herself a glass of water but couldn’t, so Saban poured it and put the straw where she could get it. “What was the thing messing with your head?”

Saban started to blush. “Oh, this is dumb, because at the time I didn’t know that we all went through it.” She stared at him. “C’mon, don’t make me say it…”

“Oh. The delayed…eh, ‘maturation’ thing….”

“Exactly. I didn’t hit puberty until I was past seventeen, just like you guys. No changes, no nothing. But unlike you and James, I lived with a bunch of other guys, and they all knew something was wrong. Some of them had been shaving since they were twelve, and I didn’t have ‘hair one’ until after I left. And the whole guy-girl-relationship thing? I never noticed it. That’s why I could never spin girls.”

“Like trying to relate to an alien life form,” Jesse commented.

“Exactly! I didn’t even drop ‘cooties’ from my vocabulary until after I showed for training. Then puberty hit me like a tidal wave. It all happened at once, and a few months later, everything was fine. But sitting here, talking to you, talking to any girl…sometimes I feel like I’m using crayons to solve calculus problems. I can’t say what I mean, and when I do, it doesn’t get heard the way I said it.”

With a small grunt of pain, Jesse took his hand. “That’s called ‘being a guy.’ You’re not that different from so-called normal guys.”

“At least your changes came before you got here.”

“True,” she said. “But we have more similarities than you think. You and me. James. You know, he never discussed his lack of …development…with anyone. But everyone could see me. I was flat as a board until my seventeenth birthday. I used to cry myself to sleep. And then a few months later…whammo! Check them out.” She looked down and laughed nervously. “I think it’s everyone who’s talented. Are we mutants?”

“Mutation has never produced a generation more robust or viable than the previous,” Saban recited from something he had read. “People confuse it with adaptation.”

“So we’re…adapt-ants?” Jesse said with skepticism. “No one’s going to make a movie about that.”

"We're Talents. John and I and a few others that John talks to—they think the developmental delay is a natural part of being a Talent. It's kind of twisted, really. Our bodies are twenty-something, but our hormones make us act more like fifteen and sixteen."

"Speak for yourself. So why us?" asked Jesse. "Do you think there have always been Talents, or are we the first generation?"

"John says we still don't know. If this were just part of being born in the nuclear age, you'd think there would be a lot more of us, but there aren't. I've often wondered what the connection is between all of us Talents, but John never felt it was important enough to let me pursue it. Maybe now that you and I are on speaking terms, we can compare notes."

"That would be nice," Jesse said, taking a sip of water. "So let's see—you graduated and you were a bit of a jerk. Would you like to pick up where you left off?"

"Not exactly the way I would…never mind. Anyway, I was scrawny and occasionally sick and uhm…immature, you-know-how. I didn't want to go to college and stand out even more. I couldn't leave the boys' home because I wasn't eighteen." He paused. "Also because I kept getting fired from every job—my bad attitude—and I had no money. But a few months passed by, and the local college sent a brochure for career day, and suddenly I realized that I haven't been sick in over a year, so maybe I could go to college."

"But somehow you went into some other agency."

"No, that's when I met John. He talked about a job, a vocation, excitement…. I thought I was signing up for some sort of paramilitary Peace Corps, like we would do good things but be able to defend ourselves. Like the U.N., but with a spine."

"I remember our father saying he had heard about an opportunity with a small foreign service outfit." Jesse was glassy-eyed, remembering. "Our talents were just starting to develop and edge us past normalville. We signed on, not knowing it had something to do with our abilities. So you came into the Ancient…first? Then you trained in some other agency and came back? I'm confused. And when did your spin kick in?"

"Well, I was always able to talk my way out of anything growing up, and I talked my way out of a lot, but after I arrived, that ability took a quantum leap. I learned that there's a certain way that I could talk," he switched modulation, *"so that everything seems reasonable."* He turned it off. "I called it the spin because I could just spin the facts whatever way I wanted. Soft-spin is a gentle convincing. Hard-spin, I can just tell people what to think, sort of like mainstream media, but faster and without commercials. I don't like to do that to anyone."

"Really?"

"Yeah." *So how much more do I tell her? The whole thing?*

"Okay, so you're skipping over where you really got all your training. What happened after we finally met, when we were training side-by-side? What happened then?"

"All I know is that there was some sort of disaster. The Primes didn't go deep cover. They went deep six. John still won't talk about the details. All of them, the higher-ups, were gone, except John. Everything could have fallen completely apart. But John took me aside and told me that the organization had one chance to make it."

"Your spin-tastic super charisma," Jesse guessed.

Saban nodded. "He knew how far my abilities had progressed. I think he knew before I did, somehow. He wanted me to convince all the midlevel agents that there was no need to panic, and no need to vie for a chance to fill the power vacuum, which was the real issue."

"Yes, the food chain of command asserting itself."

"Exactly. We might have destructed from the inside. John prepped me for two weeks, we had a big powwow with the non-prime senior agents and a lot of the midlevel agents, and I spun the whole roomful of them. Just took charge."

"What about the female agents? You couldn't spin females."

"John told me that wouldn't be a factor. I didn't believe him, but he was right." *How did John know that? I never asked him.* "He took care of it on a need-to-know basis."

"You know, I've forgiven a great deal based on those three little words," Jesse observed. "I wonder how much I should question, but I always come back to that need-to-know concept. I guess it's a matter of trust."

"Yeah," Saban agreed, feeling more than a bit hypocritical. *Brave, brave, brave Sir Saban—when danger reared its ugly head, brave Sir Saban wisely fled.* "It bothers me a little when he doesn't tell me things, but I don't think he's left out anything important." *Like I'm doing now.*

"Well, how much could he leave out with you? You two discuss everything."

Yeah, right. "Anyway, middle management bought it, so everyone else bought it. I told them that the Primes were going deep cover, and that I was much older than I looked, that I had been brought in from the outside to learn this operation from the ground up, and that I was ready to assume my role as a Prime. Even John would only be my co-leader."

"Right. But how long ago was that really? How much older than me are you?"

Is she being sarcastic, or does she really not get it? "They bought it, and John reinforced it. The spin is forever as long as it's not challenged. Before long, no one even questioned."

Jesse frowned. "One bad thing about professional soldiers is that they tend not to question orders. There was some general bafflement, but things ran smoothly, then people started getting promoted, and I got a field slot, and…and…life went on. I guess all that questioning was silly."

"Silly?" Saban asked. The way she said it, the word had a curious intonation. Maybe he was overanalyzing, but it felt like she had been spun, and not by him. For whatever reason, if he wanted her to know, he would have to come out and tell her.

"Yes, silly," she said. "Anyway, life went on, and then one evening we got the call to scramble, because all the squads were getting promoted, like they do, and that James would join me as a part of the new Alpha."

"Well, John and I had discussed James being paired up with you, since you two together bring so much to the table. You know you could have been moved up all by yourself, though."

"I never doubted as much. But you know the squad is still too small. And I was surprised that Bernard and Asabi were a part of it, since they have so much experience. And on top of that, I found you had descended from your throne and taken a tactical position as our new Alpha T-Com!"

"I was staking out the campus doing research. John and I discussed the possibility of me taking a tactical slot." *Okay, not really. Just tell her.*

"And it looked like you did it with no prior field experience. If I didn't know better, and no offense, but I would think it should have gone to Asabi."

Saban nodded, feigning confident agreement. "Or Bernard." *I hate this. I hate having to always pretend I'm more than I am. Tell her the whole truth!*

"But then again, you're you. So why are you giving me another part of your cover story? Come on, tell me, where did you get your real training?"

"Jesse, I—"

"Not that Asabi isn't capable."

"Well, John is the expert on her, I guess, and he felt I should be…" *Tell her!*

"But why us! And why now? And why—"

"I don't know!" Saban admitted in frustration, as much to himself as to her. "I don't know, Jess. That's what I'm trying to tell you! I just don't know. About a lot of things. I know how to be an operative, and I'm actually pretty good. But half the time, I have no real idea what our organization is doing."

"I…I'm not getting it." Jesse's face grimaced in concentration. "I never have a hard time getting it. Saban." Her voice carried an accusation that Saban knew was valid.

He swallowed. "I was sixteen when I reported here. Here, nowhere else! For the first and only time. I'm nineteen now. It's not a cover story. It all happened like I said. I was just another agent, like you. Then there was the accident. I did what John asked, and I learned a lot of cool stuff and I tried as hard as I could, but the pressure was too much."

"Too much?"

"I wasn't so much staking the campus as trying not to go crazy. John put me in over my head. He sent me here to do research, to finish what some other agent had started, but it was also to give me a break. I think you're having a hard time getting this because you were specifically spun to believe otherwise."

"Did you do that?" Her voice was accusing.

"No! Last time I saw you, I couldn't have spun you if I tried. I don't know how you were spun, but the only way I can un-spin you is to tell you the truth, and that's what I'm doing. You just have to believe me. I'm sorry."

Jesse shut her eyes.

"And you…you were my friend. And my girlfriend. That was part of what was driving me crazy. But one day I'm nobody, the next day, I've got the fate of the organization on me. I had to think about what was best for everyone. The pressure was just…. I'm sorry."

Jesse kept her eyes shut.

"And I don't know why Alpha is so small. As for the timing of Alpha," Saban said, trying to regain his composure, "well, let's just say I was pretty surprised to see you guys up in the sky. I was with a civilian at the time and never could get her to safety without blowing cover, which I had to do anyway since your brother didn't recognize me."

"You mean the civilian girl who was attached to your hip?" Jesse opened her eyes. "So let me get this straight. You join up, vanish for a year, leave me hanging, come back pretending to be in charge, and the first time I see you, you practically have a war bride. And this apology—this makes it all better?"

"I'm doing the best I can to make it right. I can't make it better."

"So now I should just walk it off?"

"How much do I need to bleed before we're even? If there was any way I could have avoided disappearing, I would have. I'm telling you, it was necessary. As far as the Margo thing is concerned, it's true; I liked her more than I should have—"

"You keep making that mistake."

"Don't worry. It's a mistake I won't make again." This whole conversation was proving to him the liability of personal involvement. "For the sake of the mission, I've spun her out of my life so that I can be joyfully alone again."

"You're only as alone as you choose, Saban," she said softly.

"Says the woman who never asks for help." *Now she reaches out? After she lets me babble on and on?* He was a little ticked. "Don't get all sweet, Jesse. It's out of character. I've tried to even us up—given you more power over me than anyone else has. You're the only one who knows it all. But you can't give me crap about having emotions and then not give me credit for dealing with them responsibly."

"Why do you care what I think all of the sudden?" She had that hint of a smile again.

He ignored it. "Despite my personal feelings and experience, I *am* in charge of this operation. If it goes south, it's on my shoulders. That means that in the big picture, I don't get very many choices. Less than you, in fact."

"Okay, okay! If I had known the apology part would be over so quickly, I would have slowed down to enjoy it."

He took a breath. "Sorry."

"Can I ask one more question?" She didn't wait for a reply. "This is going to sound petty, but may I ask what the attraction was? To that girl? I mean, besides the obvious hormonal appeal."

"Well, Margo was…." *This conversation is taking a really odd direction.* "She's a very nice person, but I think it was…I think it was her spontaneity. I love what we do, what you and I do, but you can quit anytime you want, Jesse. I don't think I can. And Margo—she's like this loose cannon."

"And that's a good thing? You and I run on structure. Why wouldn't you want to keep her at arms length? I would."

"That's just it. In a world where all my decisions are just choosing which obligation to fulfill, being with her was…daring." He was almost glad, though, that things never had a chance to develop with either girl. He stood up and walked toward the door. "Anyway, it's over. I'm just another guy to her. To you. And that's the way it has to be. I'm sorry."

"Wait, Saban." Jesse tried to sit straighter and winced in pain, though she didn't cry out. "Two things. First, I'm sorry I assumed you turned your back on James and me. It never occurred to us…to me…that you had no choices. Or a cost attached. Knowing that means a lot. And second," she said, balling up her bandaged hand into a fist, "if you tell James I still have a soft spot for you, I'll thrash your non-powered body from one side of the room to the other."

"Uhm…thanks?" Saban was unsure if there was really a counter-apology in there anywhere, but he gave her the benefit of the doubt. She had nothing to apologize for, anyway. "And like I said, don't mention any of what I said to Annoying Lad. Or anyone. John will really let me have it if he ever finds out."

"Understood. But I do have one more thought." She drew a breath, and Saban could see without trying that she was nervous. "Don't you find it…wasn't it kind of convenient that there was this big emergency, and you just happened to have the precise talent to set things right?"

"I don't follow," he lied. *Of course it had occurred to me. I'm not stupid. Very often.*

"You just happen to get hired for no apparent reason, with no talents fully manifested, and suddenly you're in the right place at the right time with the right talent? On accident? That kind of randomness makes evolution look mathematically sound."

I know. I know. But I'm not ready to go there. "Hmm…never thought about it." He put forth his best unconcerned face and was considering spinning her when she relented.

"Never mind. I'm not worried. In fact, I feel better right now than I have in a long time. Energized, even. It's been…good to talk to you, Saban. Like old times."

"And yet, not like old times," he said kissing her forehead. "Take care." He walked out the door, barely containing his emotions as the latch clicked behind him.

She certainly raised some big questions. *And why did she have to be so nice?* After all that had happened, it would have been easier if she had treated him like dog-meat. Now, he would have to be careful not to raise her expectations. Or his own.

He walked down the hall and past the nurses' station to the waiting room. James was standing in the doorway, chatting busily with a beautiful red-headed nurse. He excused himself to intercept Saban. "So how is she?" The words were deceptively casual.

That wasn't the question James was really asking. He wanted to know if there was anything between Jesse and Saban. "You should know. Weren't you with her all morning?"

"Uh, yeah. But I'm not the guy who dumped her and disappeared for a year and a half." James' demeanor and stance changed abruptly. Apparently, he was much more protective of his sister than in the old days. And did anyone on his team know how to use tact?

Perhaps Saban would initiate some training when they all got back to headquarters. In the meantime, James needed an answer, but Saban was in no mood to be gentle. "You have no idea what you're talking about. She liked me, I liked her. It ended. If you have any other questions, too bad. All that matters is that she and I are fine, now." There was a quick way to defuse this, Saban thought.

James looked ready to come to blows. "I have a lot more questions. You're going to—"

Enough of this. "She and I are fine. Jesse is fine." He really didn't have the energy to work it out the long way. He was just emphasizing a point, he told himself.

Of course, James accepted it.

"Well, okay then." James was silent, then said, "It took me a while to realize it, but my sister is the only friend I'll always have." He appeared to be in pain at the thought of Jesse's emotional distress.

"Dude. I get it," he tried to reassure James. "I'll be careful. I won't hurt her."

"Then she won't get hurt, because you and I are the only ones who can."

"No pressure, then." They locked eyes and pretended to laugh, but they were both faking. *On to other matters.* "Hey, last I heard, the range where you two start 'revving' each other was about forty, maybe fifty feet. That's increased?"

"My bad." James grinned insincerely.

"Noted. But when the crap hit the fan in the vault, Jesse and I chased Rambeau up to the surface. I'm pretty sure that was a hundred feet away."

"Um-hmm," James agreed. "Bernard and I each took a hit. I think he got more than one, but I passed out as soon as Jesse was out of range. Why?"

"Well, she took a hit, too, at close range. She also took a bullet through her hand and broke her arm. And yet she still saved that civilian's life. So how was Jess able to stay conscious while you were out of range?"

James shrugged. "Beats me. Sheer will power, I guess. You know, she'd die for you."

That was not an answer he had foreseen. Saban felt a lump rising in his throat. "But…I wasn't in any danger. She saved Margo's life, not mine."

"She was trying to be there for you. Once you get past the cold exterior and a few more icy layers, she feels things very deeply."

James was doing his best to lay on the guilt, and even knowing that fact did not allow Saban to sidestep all of it. "So how many of you are staying for the second part of the operation? Are you and Jess going back?"

"Didn't you hear what I said back in the room?" James was still irritated. "We're staying. Too many bogeys in play, too far to scramble from HQ, and you have to stay here to finish out your cover. We begin the installation at the college on Monday is what I heard. Operation "Millennial Eye" or something. We're staying as long as you're staying. All of us. To protect you."

He watched James walk away, only to see him stop and return. This time, there was no mistaking the animosity in his expression. "You say you and Jesse are fine, and for some reason, I believe you. We have to work together, and I'm professional enough to do that."

Professional? Saban stifled a laugh. Instead, he looked at James and then looked into him and past him, making a few quick mental connections. *Oh, I get it. Doesn't he know the real reason he's so angry?* Saban had half a mind to tell him.

"We all have to work together," James repeated. "But stay away from my sister."

Oh, to heck with this. "Reality check, James. I'm not your problem. You are. She was trying to be there for me, but you're angry because *you* should have been there for her."

"Ex…excuse me?"

"You're not mad at me! You're mad at you! If you hadn't been arguing with Bernard about helmet hair and screwing around, you wouldn't have been tagged and you could have followed Jesse topside. With you nearby, she would have been able to avoid the bullet, the knife…everything. But you were careless. Don't lay all this at my feet. I'm not your psycho-baggage valet." *Smooth, Saban. I keep forgetting, brain first, then words.*

James took a quick breath as if to say something, but didn't. His eyes bulged like he had swallowed a live grenade that just went off. When he spoke, he was calm like a gravesite. "Stay the hell away from my sister. Or else watch your back. We both know you don't really have any physical talents, and that Shaolin 'grasshopper' stuff doesn't scare me one bit. I'll make sure you see me coming, and there won't be a thing you'll be able to do about it."

James stalked off toward his sister's room.

Wow. Jesse sweet and James belligerent, and in the same day, too. *When's the apocalypse?* He never thought he would live so long. Saban considered asking James how he could watch his back and still see James coming, but he was pretty sure James would not see the humor in mixed metaphors.

Truth be known, it wasn't exactly cracking Saban up, either. Unconsciously, Saban rubbed the base of his spine.

Well, thank goodness everyone was staying. He certainly felt safer now. Not.

CHAPTER 14: Margo Gets Painfully Schooled

Someone was definitely following Margo.

The sun had long since set, and she had a mile to go before finishing her ten mile run. She wasn't tired. If anything, she continued to pick up speed. The air was invigorating, still not cold enough to hurt, and perfect for running. The back of her shirt was drenched with sweat, but the coolness of the rushing air kept her arms and legs dry.

The path she ran was familiar—a winding route that twisted up and down various streets on the outlands of the city. Mostly, she could run on the sidewalk, but she had adopted this particular circuit because of its lack of constant light, which allowed her to run at her own considerable speed without attracting attention. At the time, it seemed like a clever idea. Even a few days ago, the idea of encountering a mugger of some sort had made her smile. Now it wasn't so funny.

She quickened her pace, concentrating on the rapid thump-thump-thumping of her running shoes hitting the pavement. A sudden gust of wind brought a rise of goose bumps on her legs as she ran, and perhaps it wasn't just the wind. Someone had been following her, but whoever they were, they weren't behind her now.

There was no one alive that could catch her when she pushed herself, she was sure. And she was pushing hard. But her route was not a perfect circle—there were many ways a person could catch her if they were familiar with her routine. Who could possibly know that? She had to be imagining things.

Just because I'm paranoid doesn't mean they're not after me. Still not funny.

She lengthened her strides and kept moving, focusing on her pace and her breathing. The trees and occasional streetlights moved past her quickly, as did the sometimes thickly-lined rows of shrubbery. Her mind drifted to Saban, but she deliberately pushed the thoughts aside. This was time for her—Saban and his drama were not going to ruin it. She had half-convinced herself that Alpha and Ford and all that nonsense really was a dream and the other half dearly wished it were true.

But there was still that nagging feeling that she was missing something—or rather, that something was missing from her. With all the odd, random thoughts she had been having lately, it felt like there were two people in her head, and neither one of them was complete.

She rounded the last corner from the main road and headed up the hill that would eventually yield the back entrance to the college. There were no lights at all. She decided to go for the burn.

About a hundred feet away, through the darkness, Margo could barely see a small figure stepping out from the bushes. If this were a mugger, he was the shortest one in this hemisphere, Margo thought with a smile. She moved to the other side of the road, anyway, just to be polite.

Margo watched with shock as the figure moved to intercept. As she got closer, she saw the figure was dressed entirely in black, including a hood. An excitement grabbed Margo's heart, but not fear. *Why am I not afraid?* She was intrigued more than anything else.

By this time, she was only ten or fifteen feet away from him. She couldn't see the hedge line well enough to know if she could squeeze through, and if she stopped to turn around, she would be giving whoever this was a free shot at her. She could try and barrel through this person, but there was another way out. Or rather, over.

Margo took three more steps and jumped as high as she could, tucking her knees up to her chest. Perhaps, because of the dark, her assailant would think Margo dodged him, rather than sailing over his silly little head.

And that was what Margo thought, until she felt a hand at each of her feet. He didn't grab them, but pushed them up with tremendous force, giving Margo a boost and blunting her forward momentum. She was able to keep her balance and come down as she would have normally, but not nearly as far away as she wanted.

If this person had desired, he could have simply grabbed her feet and held on. Margo would have gone head first into the pavement, and it would not have been pretty. So what did he want? She turned around as soon as she got her balance.

"Okay, you had your shot and you didn't take it." Margo stood with both arms akimbo. "What do you want?"

Her assailant drew himself up into a fighter's stance. *Wait. This person isn't a man. It's a woman!*

"Fight," was all the woman said from behind her cloth mask.

What? "You weren't trying to hurt me. Why do you want to—"

"Belt up and fight!" The ebony-clad woman lunged at her.

"Belt huh? What are…whoa!" Margo retreated swiftly and barely avoided a series of punches.

Her assailant aerialed to Margo's side in one swift flip. For a moment, it seemed that the attacker was open from the left, but she was too fast, too fast. She set her feet for a millisecond before round-housing Margo in the back.

Margo went flying off the road and into the thickets that lined it. The branches scratched at her bare legs and arms. "Stop it!" She was able to brace herself without falling and tried to think of what she could possibly do next to get away.

"Fight me!" The assailant swept Margo's legs out from under her, dumping Margo onto her side as she evaded another set of punches by rolling several feet to the left.

"Why? What do you want?" Margo yelled as she came out of her roll and continued moving away.

"Are you daft? Stop running away and fight me!"

The small but powerful attacker seemed to be getting angrier every time she told Margo to fight. *And what kind of accent was that?* Whoever this woman was, she wasn't going to be content until Margo put up her dukes.

So that was what Margo did, drawing herself up into a fighter's stance as best she could, very much like the one she had seen moments prior, but raising her fists in front of her face tentatively. "What, what, like this?" Margo yelled. "Is this what you want?"

"Oh, sure, if you want to box me," said her assailant, dropping her own arms to her sides. "And if we lived in the 1920's!" The attacker stopped moving.

Margo sensed that whatever was going on had concluded. Was it a test? Did she pass? She didn't think so. "What do you want?"

"What you don't have." The woman's shoulders slumped ever so slightly. "I just had to see for myself. I can't believe it's all gone."

"What's gone? Who are you?" Did she know this person? Was this someone from that night—something she didn't remember? Or something completely different?

"I'm no one," the woman said with apparent sadness. "And so are you. I just wanted to…to…."

"Who are you?" Margo repeated. Then, on a whim, she asked, "Who am I?"

"You…." The woman tensed up. "You stupid…! Why did you have to—" She threw a punch at Margo's face, mid-sentence.

Margo didn't have time to think. She reached out, grabbed the person by the wrist, gave a half-twist and swung her arm down as hard as she could. *This woman is heavy beyond belief!* But her body did two nice pinwheels in Margo's firm grasp before she landed hard, flat on her back.

How did that happen?

Margo braced herself to run away again, but the woman stayed on the ground. Her body appeared to be shuddering, and not from pain. She was laughing. "Maybe not all gone," the woman said softly. Then she popped into a handstand and launched her feet at Margo's head, connecting to her chin and sending Margo to the ground as well.

By the time Margo had gotten to her feet, her assailant was nowhere to be seen. *Great. Do I tell Saban? Do I tell anyone?* Whatever was going on, she was sure she could handle it. Probably. *After all, who could handle things better than me?*

Except that she wasn't handling things. Things were handling her. And all she could do was react, which was as profoundly contrary to her nature as anything she could think of. Something big was happening. Bigger than she could deal with.

A violent shiver went through her whole body. Since she had stopped running, she had become covered with sweat. Was that shudder just the moisture evaporating off her? She wasn't sure.

Margo rubbed her eyes with her hand, shook her head, and continued on her run, her agile mind clicking through all kinds of possibilities, and none of them bringing comfort.

Chapter 15: Mr. Ford Is Put Back Into Play

"All right, here we are again," said Agent Dewitter. "You've had sufficient time to make a reasonably informed decision. Are you ready to help us find the person who took you down?"

"Not so fast." Ford leaned back in his chair. "I do have one or two questions of my own. *Quid pro quo* and all that."

"Your 'pro quo' is the 'quids' we pay you. Nothing more." Dewitter stood up and pulled his fist back, but Ford interrupted him.

"Listen, MI-6. You want the ox to plow, you feed him. You want a temporary operative, you give me the info I need to do my job. Right now, I think you got close to jack-nothing. If I can find one fragment of relevant data, I pretty much double your current knowledge base, am I right?" Ford leaned forward and picked up the folded paper he had left on the table, mentally converting the written number into a bank balance. "So let me ask a few questions, and help me do the job you're about to pay me to do." He leaned back in the chair again. "Or we could just sit around and have a smarm-off."

Ford smiled. It was unsettling to both Dewitter and the others in the room, he knew. Even people who liked him said it was like staring into an abyss. Some people, you just don't want to smile at you.

"Ask," Dewitter relented.

"Question one. If you grabbed me so close to campus, why didn't you sweep in and grab the rest of them?" *That could have saved all of us a lot of trouble.*

"We did not have all of our forces marshaled. The unit that apprehended you was the only one we had in the field at the time. Next question."

"Question two. Why were you not surprised about the gap in my memory?"

Dewitter cleared his throat, but the American answered instead. "That gap is consistent with other encounters. Gaps in time. Gaps in conversations. None of us tend to hire folks who have memory issues, so this reoccurring phenomena stands out."

Whenever the American spoke, the air smelled powerfully of wintergreen. Ford had heard a little tin box opening periodically. The man must have a whole stash.

"Your memory loss proved you were not making anything up," the minty-fresh man continued, "and truthfully, stopped us from disposing of you on the spot. Altoid?" Ford saw a napkin with a mint on it being pushed toward him from the darkness.

"No thanks. Question three. Do you have any strategies or countermeasures to identify or compensate for memory loss?"

Dewitter fielded that one. "Quite ingenious, actually. It's a technique called 'writing things down.' A tape recorder may also serve. We have no way to prevent incidents as yet, only identify them. The incidents by themselves appear to be minor. No one has forgotten their name or anything significant."

"As far as you know," Ford observed.

"As far as we know. There are simply…gaps. Small gaps, to be certain, but taken together, they create a disturbing trend."

No doubt. Even Ford found the notion vaguely disturbing. What if an Ancient operative pumped someone for information and *that* was the gap in memory? "Question four, the bonus question. Who are the Ancient, and how could their presence be missed by the world's top information gatherers for so long?"

No one spoke. Either he had stumped them, or he had pushed his luck too far.

One voice answered from the darkness and in a Slavic accent. "Ve do not know."

Make that a thick Slavic accent, Ford thought, unusual for high-level operatives. *An accent that thick was normally peppered with the words "moose and squirrel."* Perhaps age and other factors had taken their toll on the man.

"Ve have incident that is now like urban legend in higher circles of global spook community. Many, many years ago, there vas problem in vun of the smaller countries of vhat used to be called U.S.S.R. Delusions of grandeur and technology to make reality out of madman's dreams. Ve sent operative to check it out. A friend of mine named Yuri. Best agent ve had. Maybe better than me at time."

The man was racked momentarily by the kind of coughing that only comes from a lifetime of smoking. *The price of being one of the cool kids. Idiot.* Everyone waited patiently for him to continue.

"There vas big explosion, like Chernobyl, but no radiation. After a time, Yuri comes back. Cannot remember what happened. He never recovered and vas just shell of man I knew. Retired from service. A few years later, I heard he had died. I still miss him. This vas almost forty years ago."

The Israeli, from the darkened other side of the table, picked up the story. "As my respected associate said, this incident was decades ago. There were at least six agents on the ground that day, one from each of our six groups. All of them came back with virtually no memory of what happened. All of them slowly lost what little interest they had for life, and all of them died not more than a few years later. All but one…or two."

Dewitter took over. "We only recently reconstructed events. The man who has survived the longest was from British Intelligence, my group. In fact, he was slated to take over MI-6 shortly after his last mission. He would have been the youngest commander in our history, but it…it fell apart. He fell apart. He has since passed off the grid, as they say, but he does pop up from time to time and there are no reports of his death."

Ford found this fascinating. "You said one or two people survived. That's a fairly significant difference. What about the other person?"

"Ah, and that's what everyone wants to know. Including us." The American again. "So before I answer, are you in?"

Ford didn't hesitate. It sure beat being bored. "I'm in."

"Good. I'm Special Agent Bridges." Ford got a good look at him as he walked up and turned off the spotlight. He was younger than Ford, early thirties, with brown hair and wearing a grey suit, one that was practically standard-issue for every government agent. Ford would know—he still had his.

The room lights started to brighten. Ford got his first look at the cast of characters before him. Beside himself and Dewitter, there were four well-dressed men in the room, one elegant woman, and all in their late fifties or sixties. "The list of agencies that could have fielded an agent that day is surprisingly short. We are convinced that if there was a seventh person on the ground, that person had to be an Ancient operative. This sets the timeline of the Ancient's existence back at least forty to fifty years."

Ford felt compelled to speak his mind. "The way everyone showed up at the same time. An agent from each agency. There's no way it could have…it was a setup for those agents. It was a trap."

"Oh, bravo. Bravo, Mr. Ford." Dewitter again. "Your dossier did not mention a Mensa membership. Of course we know it was a setup. Now impress us: who did it, and why?"

Ford was silent for a moment. *Pearls before swine.* But he stated what was obvious to him. "If there was a seventh agent off-grid, an Ancient, there must be a connection, if not outright causality. But I couldn't tell you why."

Dewitter pushed back from the table. "As we thought. Agent Ford, why did we bring you here?"

"I thought you knew," Ford taunted. "That other team I was fighting, the ones in blue: you think they were Ancient. And the kid was fighting on their behalf. You want me to find him."

"Do you think you can?" asked Bridges.

"I have no idea what he looks like. But I remember the girl. Find the girl, and she'll lead me to the guy. Find the guy, and I find myself with a lot of money on my hands. When do I get started?"

"In a few days hence," Dewitter answered. "Let's make sure you appear as if you could be on a college campus in any capacity other than a dropout. This will also give you time to become familiar with your new team."

"I run a new team?" Ford was surprised.

"No, Herr Einstein, you are a part of *my* team. A minor part. And one more thing." Dewitter stood directly in front of Ford. "This group has agents in every country you can spell, and most that you can't. Should you decide to betray us, go AWOL or leave any of us in doubt as to your utter devotion to this task, I shall personally give the order to have you shot. You won't make it two steps."

Ford stood up quickly, and Dewitter jerked backward. "That's fine. I only need to plant one foot to take my own shot. And if you imply I'm stupid one more time, I'll take my chances. You'll be dead before I hit the ground." He held out his still-handcuffed wrists. "Now that we're clear on that, how about showing me some love and getting these things off me?"

Ford heard the rustle of keys, and for grins, he asked Dewitter one more question. "Just out of curiosity, wouldn't it be easier to find that other agent, the one that's still alive? Your last, lost MI-6 agent?"

"Certainly," Dewitter replied. "We'll get right on it. All we need to do is search the world for a seventy year old man named John Smith."

CHAPTER 16: Changes

There were several things Jesse appreciated about this particular satellite location. The full gym was one of them.

Her arms were sore. Her legs hurt. And there was a dull pain where her pride used to be, but she would not effectively finish rehabbing her injuries by pushing past her current limitations. She had just finished ten sets of ten for her biceps. Now it was on to her triceps.

This old warehouse was not in the best district of town, but that meant Alpha had lots of space and very little in the way of prying eyes. Downstairs was an office and a living quarters equipped with two bunk beds, which she often heard referenced as "racks," though they were hardly torturous to sleep in. The weight room she occupied was directly adjacent. Across the way was the combined kitchen and dining area, and next to that was the infirmary, where she might have spent time had she not needed a hospital stay.

Besides the bathroom, the only other areas downstairs were the common areas, two of them, each in opposite corners. Additionally, each common area extended all the way up to the roof, which made the commons feel more relaxed and open. Too much close living was bad for relationships, working or otherwise. Not that she felt she would ever want the chance to find out. Relationships were not her forte, and as her brother might have said, not worth the investment for the probable return.

Upstairs were two more offices and five more living quarters, each with their own set of double racks. At each end of the rectangular-shaped building was a bathroom on both floors, four total. *We wouldn't want an emergency to happen while a handful of agents were queued up to use the facilities, now would we?*

The thought would have made her giggle, but she caught herself long before it might have changed her expression. There had been enough of that already. She was still a little embarrassed about her uncharacteristic openness with Saban in the hospital. *Those must have been powerful drugs I was on.*

No, that wasn't it. There was just something about Saban that made her want to be…open. But being open meant being vulnerable. *A pox on vulnerability!* The barbells hit the guides with a clang. She pushed her uncomfortable thoughts away and concentrated on her workout.

Upper body was not normally a priority, but her shoulder wasn't anywhere near where she wanted it, and she would accept nothing less than complete restoration or better. Low load-high reps were what her shoulder needed. The last thing she wanted was to bulk up, which meant long hours right where she was. Fine by her.

This was another thing she appreciated—not having to endlessly interact with others. It wasn't that she couldn't, and it wasn't that she didn't like the other members of her team. Some people were rejuvenated by the presence of others, like her brother.

Not her. She had very high standards for others, even higher standards for herself. It was easier to avoid others entirely rather than interact and risk confrontation.

She moved to another piece of equipment, toweling off her sweat before starting over. Today was actually a lower-body day, but the injury to her arm and shoulder forced her to work on them every day. The bone had set (and healed quickly, thanks to James being there so consistently), but the muscle needed work, not just healing. The sweat and effort involved helped her relax, and James worried less about her when she was not wired so tightly.

That was another goal—she needed to loosen up. James and Asabi were constantly telling her to relax, but she hadn't felt truly motivated to do so until her conversation with Saban at the hospital. And she was making progress. Just this week, she left her bed unmade until noon one day. A bold move. And she played some kind of video game with Bernard, James and Craig that involved aliens, zombies and a lot of killing.

Boys and their toys. How could they just sit all day and waste…no, they were allowed to do what they wanted in their free time. Everyone was not always as productive as she would like, but that was okay.

"It's okay," she said without thinking, and exhaled deeply. She was not as unwound as she would have liked. She hated to admit it, but she would welcome the opportunity to spar with the others tonight.

Jesse considered herself to be about as feminine as a girl could get, but there was something about the violent ballet of fisticuffs that she found oddly thrilling. And fulfilling, since she was quite proficient at it, though she could not quite give herself emotionally to her pugilistic endeavors. Wanting to improve her skills was enough of a motivator for her—enjoyment was never a requirement for anything.

The good news was that in the entire Ancient there were only three Talents she knew of that could even lay a hand on her. The bad news was that all of them were on her team.

James was as fast as she was (perhaps faster if he would apply himself). Then there was Spar, who had already been an accomplished martial artist even before her agility talents developed. Spar was also incredibly flexible. Sometimes when she fought, she moved in ways that didn't seem physically possible or even "physics-ly" plausible.

And then there was Saban. From what she understood, Saban had the ability to read a foe and know what that person was going to do before *they* knew. He could do the same thing in conversation (what a relief to be on speaking terms again). They had even squared off against each other a few times since she left the hospital, testing his skills and her recovery. Neither had really pushed the other—too much chance of opening old wounds, hah-hah. No, it was alright. Or at least, it was getting better.

Saban had some interesting strengths. In combat, he could hold his own against anyone, except Spar. Of course, he also had his spin. But there was another talent Saban possessed, something almost imperceptible, something Jesse had only recently deduced. It was possible that Saban himself might not even be aware of it.

He was a Revver. Sort of.

Revvers were only a little stronger and faster than normal. Their talent was to impute their energy to any other particular person for a time, leaving that Talent's abilities at two or three times their normal levels. And Saban could do something like that. Again, sort of.

Her first clue had been the fight in the library. After Rambeau had caught her by surprise at the top of the stairs, she should have passed out. Clearly, she had been out of Franklin's range. Instead, she was able to keep herself together long enough to save Margo's life, before succumbing to the toxins in her body. That was an effect consistent with a Revver.

And the hospital visit. Fax had been tired before Saban visited, wired after he left. She did care for him, but not like a lovesick school girl, and so she doubted her response had been purely emotional. And that day, Franklin had already been in range, so the extra energy had to have come from somewhere. Saban was the only common element.

The thing that had thrown her was the nature of a rev. Strength and agility talents were not unusual, but there were only two Revvers that she knew of—a valuable commodity. And from what she knew, a rev was always specific, deliberate and finite in duration.

Saban's rev didn't work like that. To a lesser extent, Saban revved people all the time, not when speaking casually, but as soon as he asserted his authority. He had that special "something" that caused anyone nearby to be a little smarter, a little stronger, a little…better. Perhaps it could not truthfully be called a rev.

It was subtle, but real—a "leadership" talent. As if his mere presence insured victory.

Based on careful observation (the only kind she would accept from herself), Saban generated a field that gave…oh, somewhere between a fifteen to twenty-five percent boost in performance. She hadn't determined the exact range, but she would.

Numbers were comforting to Jesse. They made her world more secure.

But there was no number she could think of to quantify everything that Saban brought to the table. He was unique. No wonder John had required his involvement. And how exactly had John discovered Saban, picking him out from every other boy genius in the world? That was a question that would need to be answered. Saban didn't fool her. He wanted to know, but he wasn't ready for the implications. Well, if he was not ready to pursue an answer, she would be, as soon as they completed this mission.

She finished her last set and wiped the bench, threw the towel onto her neck and left the gym area. Once she was in the open hall, she heard the sounds of attacking aliens from one of the common areas.

"Hey, Fax!" shouted Craig, one of the Standard agents on the team. "Anni and I challenge you and Demo to a death dual on the surface of Mars!"

"Great multi-player!" Bernard shouted with the same gusto as Craig.

More quietly, a woman's voice added, "Uhm…I will if you will." A mousy brown-haired young woman with large spectacles appeared from around the corner. Anni was much shorter than Bernard, but still the tallest woman on Alpha, and almost as slender as Spar. Anni sounded like she hoped Jesse would refuse, because then she could, too.

She liked Anni, who was painfully shy, but knew more about weapons than anyone she had ever met. Fax looked forward to them chatting over security schematics later, and knew that neither one of them had the desire to be drawn into something as trivial as a video game. *Honestly, boys and their toys!*

"Shouldn't one of you be on platform?" Jesse inquired. The "platform" was what they called the master observation post. It was tied to the surveillance system they were installing on campus. Her own shift didn't start for another four hours, but there was one agent on monitor duty at all times when no one was physically near the "rabbit," Ms. Weissmann.

"Nah, Franklin is local in the comm-car, and Spar is on lockstep with the rabbit." The comm-car was an unmarked communications car they used for surveillance. "If Weissmann experiences a sternutation, we could wipe her proboscis—"

"Must you always be in touch with your inner geek?" Fax asked gently.

"—before she reaches for a tissue. She's secure." Craig sounded pretty confident; he took his responsibilities seriously. They all did, with the possible exception of her brother. "C'mon," he said, "what else is there to do around here?"

"Thank-you, but I need to take a shower first. Maybe afterwards." She trotted to the opposite end of the building and up the stairs. *Nice thing about having only seven agents present, everyone gets their own room. But we should have almost twice as many agents here.* She still wondered why Alpha was so undersized.

Jesse opened her door and locked it behind her for no reason other than habit. Maybe she would join them. *See, I'm more easy-going than ever before. Much more.*

Jesse slid her top drawer open. On the left were neat little piles of underwear, folded and sorted by color. On the right were socks, rolled and arranged into orderly rows. Jesse did her own laundry, always. It had been four years since she had misplaced a single sock (and that one wasn't even her fault, she lamented, though the details escaped her).

She pulled one article from each side and closed the drawer. Now for clothes. There were no doors on the two closets; from where she was standing she could see every blouse, dress and pair of pants she owned, organized in that order from left to right, with even spacing between each hanger. She picked an outfit and moved the hangers back to their original positions so they would be there when she re-hung her garments.

Before she left her room, she stopped at a small shelf that contained her hair products and various toiletries (which never varied in brand, shape or size). As she gathered the ones she would need, she noted the circles and squares she had already drawn on the shelf, at the base of each product to denote where each one should be returned. She unlocked her door and stepped out onto the causeway that ran the breadth of all the upstairs rooms.

Her sole hope was that the last person to change out the toilet paper had hung the roll in the proper direction. And maybe, when it came time to shampoo her hair, she would only lather once, and not repeat. *Saban is sure to see just how spontaneous I'm becoming. I'm definitely loosening up.*

CHAPTER 17: The Problem with Power

"Where were you? Mikey and I waited for you."

Margo was out of wind as she settled into her desk in front of Mikey. "Went running," she huffed. She no longer took the chance of running at night. Early morning was the best she could hope for if she wanted to keep her daytime schedule intact, but even running during the day was beginning to make her nervous. "Lost track…of time. Hey, Mike-zilla."

"Hey, Little Bit," said Mikey.

"How far did you run?" Saban asked.

"Maybe…" Margo added it up in her head, "fifteen miles." It was hard to say, since she varied her route daily.

"What? Fifteen miles?"

"I meant five miles," she blurted. *Is fifteen miles more than average? I forget.* "Five miles, five miles." *Which equals fifteen miles, so it doesn't count as a lie.* Her routine had returned to its usual dullness—no more attackers in the dark—but she needed to be careful not to let Saban (or anyone) get too close, know too much.

She was accustomed to keeping her secret, but this new façade felt like a perpetual lie, more so because she was less and less sure who she was. Everything she did felt unnatural, and lately, she was moving and acting and talking on pure habit. When she wasn't, she was trying to determine what she should most likely be doing in any situation. Uncertainty eroded each decision she made, each thing she said. This morning, she had just wanted to run and keep running.

I can do this. I can do this. Act natural.

She continued to catch her breath and tried to put everything except her class out of her mind. As distracted as she was becoming, she needed to concentrate. This was her least favorite class, so she had to make an effort to keep up even under normal circumstances.

As the rest of the students settled down and Mr. Steele began his lecture, it occurred to her that the phrase "act natural" came with its own built-in irony.

Mr. Steele was one of those instructors who was born to teach, not necessarily in a good way. Margo used to fear that if he ever had a different job, he would get beat up by the men and laughed at by the women. Perhaps he did here, too, but he hid it well if so. Despite his occasional creepiness, he seemed to genuinely enjoy teaching. Pushing forty and thin as a rail, his slender face was framed by a sporty goatee and a bad comb-over. The birth-control glasses and bow-tie added that extra-special touch. Fashion was not his friend, but he didn't teach fashion. This was Philosophy 101.

For some reason Margo did not understand, this class was Mikey's favorite. Personally, she wasn't sure what the practical application was of all this head-knowledge, so she had a hard time staying focused.

"Now that we've reviewed the midterm results last class, we are ready once again to make the most of your parent's money in these hallowed halls of academia," Mr. Steele began. Mikey tapped Margo on the shoulder, as he often did.

"School," she whispered to him before he even asked.

"Oh."

"So let's not waste time. We've laid groundwork for the first half of the semester. Now we get to enjoy the fruits of our mutual labors by delving into one of the most fascinating, if somewhat misinterpreted, thinkers of the nineteenth century. Friedrich Nietzsche, 'Fritz' to his family, exerted quite an influence in only twenty years of writings. Some of you may have heard his famous phrase 'God is dead,' but you may not know that he had the intellectual prowess to back up such assertions."

Margo's ears perked up as he continued. She had just been to temple on Saturday, and some days the thought of God was the only thing that kept her going.

"One of his most significant works, Thus Spoke Zarathustra, discusses a mode of humanity beyond what is accepted as normal. The '*ubemenschlich*' or superhuman was part of the inspiration for the 'superman' concept that the Nazis espoused so many years ago. In fact, thirty years after its initial release, the German government printed 150,000 copies and issued it along with the Bible to its soldiers, even though the two works were at most times diametrically opposed." Mr. Steele rolled up his sleeves as he talked, warming to his topic.

"Coupled with his concept of 'master morality' versus 'servant morality' from another work, a seductive idea spread among the Nazis that there were two sets of rules: one for the people in charge, the lions, and another for the people being led, the sheep. The lions could make any rules they wanted to simply because they were lions and had a 'will to power.' Now, you might ask how this could be accepted in a culture where traditional Judeo-Christian values…yes, Mr. Smith?"

Saban had his hand up. "Mr. Steele, wasn't 'will to power' a concept that all beings have an out-pouring of energy that is constantly trying to reshape their surroundings into their own worldview? And that only the strong were able to do this?"

"Why, yes, Saban, I was coming to that. Have you been reading ahead?"

"No, sir, it was in a movie I saw. They called it 'the force.'"

Margo winced, hearing some laughter and a few groans.

"Ah, yes, well, not quite. As I was saying, this did not sit well with the culture of the time. Nietzsche cut the legs out from under this problem by showing that the traditional morals of the time had no meaning, since there is no such thing as absolute values. With no absolutes, morality is free to make itself, which is where we, as an advanced society, find ourselves today. If we…uhm, yes, Miss Weissmann?" Margo was almost as surprised as Mr. Steele that her hand was raised, but this did not sit well with her either, not well at all.

"How can you say there are no absolutes? 'Thou shalt not murder'? 'Thou shalt not steal'?" Margo rarely missed Shabbat service, and though she was no theologian, these were truths that seemed fairly immutable. She was a trifle indignant. "Aren't these the absolutes upon which our society's civil and criminal laws are based?"

Mr. Steele almost sneered at her. Margo got the distinct impression that his comments were merely the bait, and she had just snapped it up. "Miss Weissmann," he said, as if trying to speak to a deaf person. "Would you kill someone to save the life of your parents?"

"I…." She wasn't sure.

"Do you have any siblings?"

"A sister. My little sister." She saw where this was going.

"Imagine now: someone is threatening her life. They *will* kill her…or worse. Will you engage them persuasively in comparative morality, or will you make them dead?"

"They're dead," she said without hesitation. "But all killing is not murder. Killing in self-defense is…acceptable. Tragic, but acceptable."

"Is it? Says who? And what about thievery? If your sister were starving and you had no money, would you steal a crust of bread for her? Is it wrong to keep your sister alive at the expense of a lesser value like stealing? Hmmm?" He had her, darn it.

"That's not…you're twisting…." She knew he was wrong, but could not put her finger on why. She would have loved to jump up from her desk and teach him a lesson about only the strong surviving.

"No, it's you, twisting, twisting in the wind with your so-called absolutes, just as Nietzsche would have said. Come now, let's be clear on this," Mr. Steele said loudly, as if challenging whole class. "Is there anyone else here who believes there are such things as absolutes?"

No one said a word, but Margo desperately wished she knew how to defend her own beliefs. In a flash, she realized that this was the practical application of the class, but it was too late. She could not even articulate the intrinsic value of virtue, and a horribly helpless feeling in her grew until she heard someone near her say in a small voice, "That's enough."

Saban? That was what he said to Rambeau and Ford, in her defense. Margo felt Saban's hand on her shoulder as his other hand slid up into the air. *Stop defending me! I'm the one who is supposed to be defending…I'm supposed to…* She couldn't finish the thought and instead listened.

"You, Mr. Smith? Stand up. You believe in absolutes? This is unexpected. Or are you going to compare absolute values to other great works of Hollywood instead?"

Saban stood as requested. "Let me ask you something," he said. "You're saying you don't believe in absolutes?"

"I think I've made that evident."

"That there are no absolutes," Saban emphasized.

"Again, there are no absolutes," Steele repeated. "What is your point?"

Saban paused. "Do you believe that absolutely?" Judging from Steele's face, he understood instantly, but Margo wasn't following yet. "You say there are no absolutes, and I understand you to believe that absolutely. Correct?"

"I'm not...." Steele fiddled with his bowtie as Margo wished she had a video camera.

"Mr. Steele." Saban paused in the same way Steele had moments before. "You cannot say absolutely there are no absolute values, because that itself is an absolute. Didn't you tell us once that to believe in a contradiction is grounds for insanity?"

"You're arguing theology, not philosophy. Your...your opinion is obviously biased by your arbitrary moral, most likely religious, values. I won't have that bias in my classroom."

"That's nothing but a 'straw man' argument, attacking me instead of my reasoning," Saban responded. "You know nothing about me, but you assume I'm biased because I don't agree with you. I don't even have a religion. And this isn't about morals. It's simple logic. Logically, there must be some things that are always true. The fact that you don't know what they are doesn't mean they don't exist." Saban sat down. "Even if I don't know what they are, I have to acknowledge that there are absolute truths, absolute goods, absolute bads."

"Those are different kinds of absolutes."

"No different than the kinds you set Margo up with. Give me a break."

Margo tried to gently shush him, but Saban was not quite done.

"And isn't it true that a few years after Nietzsche wrote all that stuff, he went insane? Why would anyone listen to the ravings of a lunatic?"

"Well, as you said, truth is truth whether believed or not," Mr. Steele countered.

"True. And garbage is garbage no matter how much sugar you pour on top. So let's put it to the test: if the whole '*ubermenschlich*' thing is true, then we should arm wrestle for my final grade. If I beat you, I get an 'A.' Might makes right, correct? If things don't work that way in real life, why should we study this clown at all?" Saban crossed his arms, fuming. He was actually angry.

No one said a word as all eyes turned to the front of the class.

Mr. Steele cleared his throat, and then spoke calmly and directly. "First of all, let me say that I'm…pleased. You've spoken more today than the entire first half of the semester. Good arguments, and…somewhat valid." He was still pompous, but it was evident Saban had let some air out of his tires, and this may have begat some degree of deference. "Perhaps there are things like absolute good and absolute evil, but I don't see them, and I doubt you would recognize them, either. And as far as power goes, the 'will to power' is all around us. You've just exercised some of yours. And now, here is mine." The room was rapt.

"I don't need to arm wrestle you, Mr. Smith. Just as there is more than one kind of value, there is more than one kind of might. As the instructor, I have the power of the pen, and you know what they say about pens and swords."

Mikey tapped Margo on the shoulder.

"The pen is mightier than the sword," she whispered. "Edward Lytton."

"Oh."

"That was the tactical mistake the Nazis made under Nietzsche's tutelage," Mr. Steele said. "They saw all power as physical might, and by the same they were destroyed. And don't misunderstand; the world is better off for it. But if they had tried harder to capture the *hearts and minds* of the world instead of mere cities…I shudder at the thought."

He turned and wrote, "What is might?" on the chalkboard. "Good leadership motivates the masses to move mountains. *Great* leadership will make those same people think it was their idea in the first place. The ability to persuade others to see your worldview as their own: *that* is the 'uber' they missed."

"Hmpff," was Saban's only response.

"And I would love to discuss this with you further, Mr. Smith. Please see me after class. Now then, turn to page…" and the remaining seventy minutes proceeded without incident.

* * *

"Grounds control to Major Tom." Devon Ford poked a soda can with his brand new pointy stick. An untold number of intelligence agents virtually at his side, and no one could tell him what it was called. "I am picking up my tin can." He scraped the can into his garbage bag.

"Cut the crap, Ford," the familiar voice of a technician replied through his earpiece.

"Just wanted to make sure you were still in range." Even through his Ray-Bans, the sun hurt his eyes. He walked past the library, letting the building block the light.

He heard a few "thunks" over his earpiece, like the microphone had been dropped on the other side. "I assure you," said Desmond Dewitter, "that one way or another, you will never be out of range. Have you seen anyone that looks remotely familiar?"

"Hey, we're only an hour into our little mission. Question: you don't have any other agents on this detail, do you?"

"No," Dewitter answered slowly. "Why do you ask?"

"Well, I saw a guy that looked like a red-headed Fabio and a little oriental girl, wearing overalls just like mine." *And they were arguing like an old married couple.*

"They must be a part of the company that was hired to install the new surveillance cameras. Pity. If they were already finished, we could tap into them and view the entire campus remotely. What is your twenty? You're out of visual."

"I'm in front of the library, about to head over to the gym."

"While you're out there, make a note of any locations where cameras are being installed. That may be useful for our future endeavors."

"Anything else?"

"Yes," said Dewitter with disdain. "Work on your garbage collecting technique. That may be useful for *your* future endeavors."

Ford muttered more than a few obscenities as he passed by Quinlan Hall, where a small hoard of students was exiting.

* * *

After class adjourned, Margo and Mikey sat pensively on the steps of the library, waiting for Saban and Mr. Steele to finish their impromptu conference.

Margo watched Mikey pull a candy bar from his satchel and offer one to her. She waved it away, he tore into his, and a moment later, the whole thing was in his mouth. He looked around for the trash can and caught the attention of a grim-looking groundskeeper in Ray-Bans.

The custodian looked away but pointed directly behind Mikey at a trash receptacle. Mikey promptly deposited his candy bar wrapper bin behind him, and the custodian moved on.

Boy, they take their litter seriously. She was too distracted to think about food.

"Do you know what that was all about?" he asked through a mouthful of chocolate.

"I was wondering the same exact thing during class!" Margo responded excitedly. "Saban hardly talks to anybody except us, then he's, uhm, all up in Mr. Steele's grill, and…" She laughed. "Did I say that right, Mikey?"

"Yeah, you're learnin' redneck real good…but what I meant was: did you follow all that 'pen and sword' stuff?"

"The pen and the sword? Not exactly. I know the quote, but not the context. Maybe writers have more power than fighters? That doesn't make sense."

"Well, who has more power over your life, a policeman or a politician?" Mikey asked.

"The cops can put you in jail. What can a politician do?"

"I don't know. Maybe make the laws that the cop has to follow?"

"Oh! Then it's the politician, I suppose."

"So the power of shoving somebody is nothing compared to the power of deciding who gets shoved?" Mikey's voice had its same gentle Southern cadence, but he was speaking purposefully, as if teaching rather than asking. "Is that what you're saying?"

"Hmm. I never thought about it that way, but exactly."

"Now let me ask you this, Little Bit. Do you remember when we talked in class last month about 'power corrupts, and absolute power corrupts absolutely?'" He made quote marks in the air with his fingers.

"Sure. What about it?"

"So why do many politicians and other leaders go bad? Assuming they're not bad to begin with, that they start out with good intentions." Mikey did this sometimes: sounding very un-Mikey. It was kind of neat and kind of strange, but she connected with the idea.

"Because leadership is a very real power in this world. So the greater the leader, the greater the temptation. I get it. But you know, Mikey, that's why we have to set our standards on things we *know* are true, not just things we *feel* are true. That's why I go to temple. But what I want to know is…shhh! Here he comes."

Saban walked out of Quinlan in no particular hurry and made his way over to Mikey's outstretched candy bar. Margo and Mikey were both staring at him. He quickly checked his zipper and, seeing as it was zipped, blurted, "What?"

"What 'what?'" Margo responded. "What did he say?

"Oh. That." Saban had about half a cheek full of chocolate-covered-something-healthy. "He wanted to know if he could get me to debate with him in class once a week. He's never had so many students so interested. Poor guy. It's been 'Yawn of the Dead' in there since day one." He took a moment to swallow. "I told him 'no thanks,' but I gave him a little pep talk. I can't stand Nietzsche." He took another bite.

"Great. Glad to hear it. Glad you're not in trouble for being disrespectful and all. But what I really want to know is—" Margo waited for the Saban to finish chewing.

"Am I gonna go your way?" Saban popped in the last bite and made a few quick air-guitar motions.

"Uhm…no, what is the big deal about that particular philosopher?"

Saban cocked his head with that far-away tilt that always made her so curious to know what was going on between his ears. "It's not the philosopher; it's the philosophy. It's a manifesto for bullies.

They think they can get away with anything just because they're bigger."

Mikey agreed. "Yeah." He leveled his gaze at Margo. "Intellectual bullies are no better. Pushing their superior thinking over the great unwashed masses."

Margo felt almost like he was addressing her personally. "Me? What did I do?"

"No!" Mikey grabbed her in a gentle headlock. "Not you! You're my Little Bit!"

She wriggled out of his arms. "How about you, Saban? You still carrying a torch and pitchforks for your teachers in high school? You told me about that once."

"I did? Well, no. I just resent know-it-alls based on their own merits. Or demerits, I guess. Anyway, I wasn't about to let him push you around when you're so…so…"

"Stupid?" she finished. Her temperature started to rise.

"No! I was going to say 'nice.' Not sure why, though."

Oh. He really had been defending my honor. Again with the defending her—it didn't feel right. But a lot of things didn't feel right, so what of it? She bit her tongue, embarrassed.

Mikey broke the uncomfortable silence. "I never worry much about getting pushed around physically. But it always bugged me when people think they're smarter than me, better than me…and maybe…well, I can definitely relate." For a moment, Mikey had a curious tilt to his own head, then he was himself again. Margo would have sworn something profound had just happened. "You're alright, Saban," was all Mikey said.

"It's cool. Hey, listen, I have some things I have to get done today. Can we do our study session next Monday? Are you guys free?"

"I'm good. How 'bout you, Little Bit?" Mikey gathered his books.

"I'm fine, too." Margo replied.

"I noticed," Saban threw in.

That flirter. I wish that was all I had to worry about, but my world is turning upside down, and I think I have you to thank for that, Saban. She grabbed his shoulder, pulled his cheek toward her and gave it a kiss. "That was very nice of you to defend me again.

It's a shame the most we'll ever be is good friends." She let him go with a tiny push.

"Uhm, yeah. You're right." He half-staggered away. "But 'friends' is good, too. See you next week," he called out, and then he was gone.

Margo watched him make his way across the field, then turned to Mikey, who was eyeing her suspiciously. "What?" she said innocently.

"You're weird," he said. "But there's something I want to know, too. Did you mean it in there? About killing out of necessity?"

"Yes." She hadn't really considered it before asked, and there was so much inside her that seemed more and more jumbled, but the idea seemed very firm in her system. And she would never intentionally lie—and that was another thing that wasn't up for questioning. "There's a time for words, and a time when words are done. Does…does that seem cold?"

"No, I just never figured you to be so…I mean, you come on strong, but you're such a goody-goody." He threw his hands up, palms out. "I don't mean that in a bad way."

"And isn't it truly weird that being called 'good' nowadays might be considered an insult? But trying to be good doesn't mean being a wimp. True character requires true courage."

Mikey smiled. "Hey, that's not bad. I think Saban's big words are rubbing off on you. Later." And then he was gone as well. *What was that all about? They were all being weird today, not that it made her feel better.*

She pushed Mikey out of her mind and returned to Saban. It was easier than concentrating on herself. She began walking toward her next class.

The way she had treated Saban was probably not fair, shoving his own words back in his face. She knew, really knew, that nothing from last Thursday was a dream, which was ironic, since lately she had been having some increasingly vivid dreams about rivers and monks and…stuff that probably wasn't important. It wasn't laziness that had kept her from making up her mind faster. Rather, she would have been forced to reach conclusions she was not ready to deal with. But now that her potential outrage had been dulled by procrastination, she was left with the task of deciding what to do.

The crux of the matter with Saban, she supposed, was trusting him and his intentions. Even if she trusted him, and it was hard not to, she still resented him for taking so many choices out of her hands and keeping them in his.

Hours later, by the time she made it to her room for the evening, her resentment had subsided even more. She looked at her legal pad and wrote down another line: "Saban defends those whom (he thinks) cannot defend themselves."

She couldn't fault him for that. Like so many other things lately, it was a thought that clicked quite naturally into place.

But now—and here was an odd concept—did clicking something "in" mean that something had to be clicked "out" to make room? She still hadn't figured out why life seemed so vivid now, why every moment had taste and texture compared to…to what? And to make matters worse, though she felt continually "in the moment," her internal ambiguity had grown even more acute. Like she had been given the gift of perfect sight, then forced to look at blurry photographs. She couldn't tell where the problem was. It was maddening.

She wished she knew someone she could ask for some advice. About Saban. About the attack. About why her senses and emotions seemed so sharp, but the facts themselves seemed so nebulous.

Didn't she used to have someone she could ask for advice? This was the longest she had gone without…longest it had ever been since she…since she….

Her face suddenly felt cold as the blood drained away. She couldn't remember.

CHAPTER 18: Games and Their Consequences

John was more nervous than he wanted to admit. The interior temperature of the Boeing 737 was perfect, but he was unusually hot in his grey pin-striped suit. He remembered a movie where the hero had been anxious about being in an airplane and took off his socks and shoes to relax. That would not do here.

For one thing, he wasn't nervous about flying. He had flown many times, and this commercial airliner was surely safer than some of the aircraft out of which he had thrown himself.

For another thing, the British do not take off their socks and shoes in a public venue. Besides, the plane had already landed and was taxiing to a halt. The other passengers were moving like a wave of human chaos toward the unopened exit, snatching their belongings from various compartments, but John did not leave his seat. His briefcase was in his hand, chained to his wrist, and he would retrieve his hat from the overhead compartment in due course.

Several parts to the master plan were open to error and not without danger, but truthfully, this was the one part he felt had the least chance for success. That was why he was going to see to it personally. After all these years of planning, everyone must play their parts perfectly. Including him.

The main door opened and the passengers began slowly shuffling out. He was in no hurry. He strode briskly through the chilly concourse and into the heated terminal, turning on his cellular phone as he did so. Only a few seconds after it was activated, the phone rang with a text message.

John sat down quickly and unrolled his portable keyboard. There was no determining how much time his contact might have, so this would need to be fast. The noise and bustle of the airport faded into the background as he concentrated on the information in front of him.

"New orders?" it said.

"No new," John typed. "You raised a big stink."

"Part of job."

"Not job you are paid to do," John texted back.

"Doing best I can. Dewitter is a jerk."

"I know. Observe. Call if in danger."

"Me or the boy?"

"Either."

"Didn't know you cared. Ford out."

One more person whose part is played out. All the pieces were either moving into position or being removed from the board. Not flawless, but things could be worse. He had known several months ago things were necessarily going to be more fluid than he liked.

It would have to do. He cared about Saban and had great confidence in his abilities and the abilities of Alpha, but John's sights always returned to the big picture. And the mission.

John rolled up his portable keyboard and placed it into his other carry-on bag. After looking around to get his bearings, he made his way to the entrance of the airport. A man was waiting with a cardboard plaque that said, "SMITH, JOHN." The man led John to a waiting limousine, which John entered and began to make himself comfortable. No words were spoken. The driver knew where to go.

As his vehicle left the airport grounds, he read another sign by the roadside: "You are now leaving Washington-Dulles Airport. Enjoy your stay!"

If he were successful, the thing he would most enjoy would be the expression on Saban's face when this part of the game had played itself out.

* * *

"You should have seen his face!" James shouted. Dressed in utility-green coveralls, he and Asabi were working in the nearly deserted hallways of the Quinlan building. Asabi's short 'do fit easily under her cap, but his shoulder-length hair was barely contained. *The only thing worse than helmet-hair is cap-hair.*

He was having a hard time balancing the equipment he was holding and staying on top of the ladder. His ability to talk, however, was not impeded at all. "I thought he was going to jump through the roof."

"It wasn't funny, mate." Asabi was holding the ladder steady, her overalls and golden skin smudged with dirt and debris from the plenum space above the ceiling panels, where they were working.

"Craig thought it was funny, too. Guess you had to be there." The hallways were empty except for an occasional custodian. "Hand me the whatchamacallit, will you, Spar?"

"Shhh! It's an inductive amplifier," she scolded. "And don't call me that out here. It's Asabi. Can't you ever remember?" She handed him a device that looked like an over-sized thermometer with a speaker at one end. It emitted a loud electronic trill as he passed it over various wires.

Several cardboard boxes of equipment were strewn around them. A large reel of cable was beside them as well, with part of it stretching up into the ceiling over James' head. He was trying to pull a length of cable over to the next hallway, but having a difficult time. "Since you're so smart, explain to me how we landed this gig and why we're doing this? I'm used to crunching numbers, not cables."

"Ugh! Will you just let me do it myself? For someone so quick, you're awfully slow."

"You're not the brightest torch on the island, either." *It's not like I'm an idiot.* He came down the ladder, deliberately waving one foot in the air as if trying to find the next step, then hopped lightly to the ground.

Admittedly, he was smarter around Jesse, at least regarding the ability to mass-process information. But one thing he could not understand, by himself or with his sister, was Jesse's fascination with Saban. James used to love him like a brother. But he had meant it when he said he would take Saban down if he and Jesse got involved again.

James smiled, remembering the way he had "punked' Saban a few days ago.

James had been moving a light fixture in the cafeteria when Craig told him to stay up in the ceiling. Margo had walked into their work area, and she might have recognized James even with his hair up. He would have waited patiently had Saban not walked in shortly afterward, tailing Margo and trying not to be seen.

James had looked at the light bulb in his hand and the temptation was too much to resist. He waited until Margo was in proximity and threw the bulb to the floor. It hit the ground just right, sounding almost like a gunshot—pop!

Saban was all over Margo in a flash, then saw they weren't under attack and moved away quickly. James caught a glimpse of Saban's face as he was leaving the cafeteria.

Saban mouthed the word "professional" while giving James the evil eye. Whatever. He was pretty sure Saban didn't have any kind of evil eye talents, anyway. In any case, James had his own agenda, and if making Saban uncomfortable dovetailed into that, well then, so much the better.

Funny, as promptly as Saban had reacted, Margo had barely flinched. Either she had nerves of steel, or she was zoned-out in the land of deep thoughts. Probably the second one—whenever he had monitor duty, he almost never saw her smile anymore, and half the time she seemed oblivious to anything that wasn't directly in front of her. She definitely was not the same perky vixen from a few weeks ago. At least they didn't have to worry about her fifteen-mile runs anymore—*I wonder why she stopped?* She hardly left her room for anything but classes.

He felt a tug on the cable in his hand.

"C'mon, then, pay attention," said Spar. "I'm sweating right through my boiler suit. Faster we're done here, the faster we're back to the maisonette."

"Don't you call it a 'flat?'"

"The warehouse has two floors, twit. Flats have one." Asabi was atop of the ladder and pirouetting like she was standing on a sidewalk.

"Hey," he said, rocking the ladder violently, "weren't you gonna tell me something?"

Asabi adjusted her balance absentmindedly. "Stop that. Oh, yeah. Do you remember when Bernie and I deployed together a few times before Saban vanished?"

"Yeah, I think so."

"Well, this university is where we were. They weren't tactical missions; they were logistical. We were setting up for this. Bernie and I came with a proposal for a state-of-the-art security system for this college. John got us some face time with the college president to make a presentation, and surprise! On one of those missions, Saban was waiting for us."

"So you knew Saban was our mystery date the night we all dropped in!"

"There was one other person it could have been, but yes, I did. So the three of us went in, and Saban convinced the fellow into admitting us to the bidding process. Bernie and I met with the president two more times, and we won the bid, but it was ours to accept or decline."

"Does Saban mojo his way into all our contracts?"

"I don't think so," she replied. "If he does, I'll tell you straight up I have a problem with that, but I'm done arguing with people about what I can't change."

"Well, it *is* his talent. In a way, his mojo isn't much different than being extraordinarily handsome. And who am I to deny my own gifts?"

"Now I know you're off your trolley. Anyhoo, John and Saban were waiting to see how things played out here as to whether we would go through with the job. Since we needed a reason to stay in town, we accepted. Now we just have to deliver the system, train the people who will run it, and hand them the keys. In the meantime, we have an excuse to keep our people closer than the maisonette downtown."

"So, we had a contingency plan that required months of prep work, and we might not even have used it?" The accountant in him said it was too much work for possibly no return.

"Well…there was a good chance we were going to need to stay."

"And why is that? How did you know what the grand and mysterious Saban didn't?" His hands fluttered about his face for effect.

"That's 'need to know,' Frank…James. Look, you've got me messing up, too. James, I have had to accept the fact that everyone does not always know everything. Part of that is for safety. There are a lot of moving parts to this operation. If any of us get taken, we won't say more than we know."

"Know? I don't know anything! How could I say anything if I don't know anything?"

"Brilliant. Very good. Hand me the crimpers." Asabi tossed the inductive amplifier down to him.

"That's not how I meant it, Spar!"

"Asabi! It's Asabi!" Her head came down out of the ceiling and she looked around, making sure nobody was near. "Don't force me down there to bash your blonde bum."

And she probably could. There were agents with strength talents and agents with speed talents like him and Jesse. But nobody, nobody could take her down in hand-to-hand. Maybe he and Jesse together. *Maybe not.* "I'll have you know that every hair on my butt is distinctly red."

"Thank you for that disturbing mental image. I know what you meant. The thing is, you do know a lot. You know more than most about the real-world financial structure of our operations. You know some of our financial goals that I don't know about. But the only one who knows it all is John."

"And Saban," James added.

"Right, and Saban, of course."

"Even so, don't you get the feeling that whenever you talk to Saban, he's holding something really huge back from us? How does someone in his twenties get to be the co-head of an operation that's half a century old? How much older than he looks could he be? I know he's got his mojo and all, and I know he can hold his own in a fight, and I know he's smarter than most of us." James considered his own words. "Okay, maybe I do buy it. I don't know." There was something else that bothered him, too, but he couldn't quite put his finger on it.

"Age is a non-factor. Napoleon was a brigadier general by the time he was twenty-four, and by the age of thirty he was the *de facto* ruler of France. Alexander the Great was—"

"That's what it is," he said. "Doesn't it bother you that all of us field agents are so young? Even Bravo and Charlie teams and the rest of them are only a couple years older than us. We're like rejects from a casting call of *Logan's Run*! And the only ancient Ancient I've ever seen is John—"

"—who will also bash your bum if he hears you calling him 'ancient.' Stop throwing that word around!"

"And the way John calls Saban 'Master Eight' is ridiculous. Makes me laugh every time I hear it. It sounds like he's saying—"

Asabi pulled her head down and interrupted. "If anything except the word 'masticate' comes out of your mouth, I will put my size six foot straight up your—"

"Asabi! Of course that's what I was thinking. 'Masticate.' What else could I be thinking?" he said unconvincingly.

She popped her head up into the space above the tiles. "I swear, how did you ever make Alpha, anyway?" Asabi was dripping sweat from being in the ceiling for so long.

"I ask myself the same question. Yet, here I am. Don't worry; I won't embarrass your brother. Or my sister. Is a sense of humor against regulations?"

"Sorry. I've got a lot on my mind, and I'm just a bit testy. I need you to be serious, sometimes," came her muffled voice. "We're going to finish putting in this system, nobody is going to get hurt, the semester will end, and then we'll get to leave. All of us," Asabi said with an emphasis that James found curious. "And Margo can go back to her old life."

"I still say this is an awful lot of effort over some dumb girl. You want to get something to eat?" James turned in a circle to see if there were any vending machines nearby. When he looked at the top of the ladder, Asabi was no longer there.

The lapels of his overalls took on a life of their own—small but powerful hands clutched them in white-knuckled fists, and suddenly he was face to face with a snarling Spar. "Whoa, GI Jane, what's with the Kung-Fu grip?" He didn't think she had much in the way of strength talents, but he could not squirm free, and Spar would not relinquish her grasp.

"I think I'm quite done being nice. Pay attention, you air-headed git," she said through clenched teeth. "I've enjoyed being your colleague for the last few weeks, so I'm going to give you some information directly, instead of having you sacked for your constant disregard of protocol and authority. Are you listening?"

James nodded.

"Margo—that girl—is in harm's way, and she has no idea how much. If a bullet comes at her, I will put you or me between her and it." She let go and pushed off him. "She's not dumb, and…and…she's worth defending. If necessary."

"Are you done?"

"Yes. No, one more thing. Saban is your superior and mine as well. You may not like him…hell, I may not like him, but he has earned, and continues to earn, his position. Better than you are, I'll add. He has more on top of him than you may ever know. I don't agree with everything he does, but I would appreciate it if you showed him a little respect."

"Okay!" said James. "Didn't know he was your boyfriend! Whatever!"

"Super. Now bung me that ball of string, and let's run these cables. And stop messing around. I really do enjoy your company," she smiled as she took the ball of twine from his hand, "when you're not being a twit. Even if I wasn't a squad leader, I'd take a bullet for you, too."

Women. They should come with wo-manuals. He could barely keep track his own thoughts, let alone hers, but there was something else going on, he was convinced. Did it have to do with Spar and Margo or Margo and Saban? Or all three?

What was the big stupid deal with that Margo girl, anyway?

* * *

Saban's knuckles hurt from knocking, but Margo finally opened the door, still in her bathrobe, though it was well into the afternoon. Her eyes were puffy. *Had she been asleep, or had she been crying?* He tried to look deeper, but all he could see was that she was tired. "Are you okay? You missed class again."

"I did? I'm sorry. Did you take any notes? I'll try to catch up." Her gaze was not quite on his face.

The last few times he had seen her, she seemed a bit sullen and stooped, which was odd, because for a while, she seemed ready to take on the world. That version of Margo had left the building—and this one never left her room. "You weren't hit by that light bulb that fell the other day, were you?" *Stupid Franklin and his not-funny sense of humor.* "You don't look so hot."

"Still the smooth talker, aren't you?" Her smile was painfully thin. "I'm sorry."

"Stop saying you're sorry. Mikey is worried, too."

"I'm sorry. Please don't worry about me."

"Are you getting enough sleep?"

"Hardly any, and still too much, I think. These dreams…." Her eyes focused on him nervously. "I mean, yes, I must have the flu or something."

"Well, maybe you could see the nurse. Or if you're blue, maybe you could call your parents and they could—"

"Parents!" She perked up and glanced at him nervously. "Yes! My parents! Of course. Thank you, Saban! Good idea. I'll do that." She pushed him back like he weighed as much as a sparrow and closed the door in his face. "Tell Mikey I'm sorry!" he heard her say over the ruffle of flying papers and books.

This was not going well. He needed to talk to John.

CHAPTER 19: Things Fall Apart

Several weeks later, at seven-thirty on a Thursday morning, the day the mission fell apart, Jesse picked a random number between five and ten by rolling a die and adding four to that number. This was the number of minutes early she reported for her shift. She wore blue jeans and a blouse she hadn't scheduled herself to wear until the weekend. She felt confident she would soon have this "being spontaneous" matter down to a science. "Status report. What have I missed?"

"Plenty," Craig replied. "I think Saban and John were arguing last night. Again. About Weissmann, again. Saban still thinks Weissmann is destabilizing, maybe an adverse reaction to being spun. Do you remember reading that report he filed three weeks ago, where she jumped on the word 'parents' like she'd just won the lottery?"

"I remember. Did she stop going to classes again? Saban needs her to act normal—we don't want her to attract attention."

"Oh, attention isn't the problem. She's as quiet as a little mouse—reticent to the extreme. Hard to believe this is the same girl as when we started. All she does is write in her pad, read her bible and argue with herself. I think she's nuts," Craig said, crossing his eyes and letting his tongue hang out of his mouth. "But last night—"

"Grow up," Jesse snapped. "I mean…so what happened?"

"She took her pillow and blanket and slept half the night in the middle of the soccer field." Craig grabbed one of the logs they filled out hourly. "It's all right here. Freaky-deaky."

"So what was the outcome of John and Saban's conversation?"

"Same as always. Saban wants her out—John said no." Craig cupped his hands over his mouth. "I didn't think they ever disagreed," he whispered.

"Well," Jesse said, careful not to sound too interested, "it probably happens more than we know. How's the M-Sec project coming?"

"All the cameras are connected and online. The control center is almost fully functional, and Anni is doing more training in about an hour. We'll be completely done by tomorrow."

"Hmm. Forty-two days from start to finish. Any word on Ford?"

"Not a peep. I think he left town that night. Of course, we still don't know who hired him, but I think something else is up."

"Why is that?"

"Check out the surplus of supplies in the kitchen. We're expecting company. Bravo or Charlie team, I would surmise. I wonder why? The semester is over tomorrow, then finals, then we all depart."

"How is, uhm…" There was no way to ask without sounding like she cared, but she supposed it was allowed. On a strictly business level. "How is Saban taking the, uhm, Weissmann situation?"

"Cool as a cucumber. I've never seen him sweat. I don't think he cares one way or the other."

Jesse knew better, but kept her opinion to herself. "I suppose you're correct." Quite involuntarily, she felt bad for both Saban and Margo. They used be to friends, and now they were not. She knew how it felt, and the feeling wasn't pleasant.

Craig continued on, oblivious. "Hey, I don't care, either. But I can't comprehend the source of her distress. I mean, extra strength aside, she's just a college kid. What does she have to worry about? How bad could her life be?"

CHAPTER 20: Two Minds Are Worse Than One

Margo's own cry almost caused her to wake up. As she slept, her head would occasionally jerk from one direction to the other like a spastic metronome, and her eyes flashed back and forth under her eyelids. She was having the dream again. Not the one where she was diligently gathering information. No, the other dream. The scary dream. The story.

The village had been built long ago by a fast-flowing river. The river was…*the Sangra? No, the Sangro.* On the other side of the river was a large hill, more like a mountain, really. And the village at its base was new. She was seeing it before it got old, when the town was freshly built.

The pictures of the village and the mountain changed like a slideshow in her mind. And viewing the pictures, she was there, in the village. Seeing the people. And listening to the story.

The tale was of monks. And magic. And an evil man (but not really a man) with long, long limbs and bony hands. The monks claimed to follow God, yet did not rely on Him when faced with a calamity greater than their abilities. .Regardless, they did the best they could, with good intentions. And with those intentions, they paved a road to hell. A two-way road.

An evil man (not a man, but the shell of a man) had been causing great harm. To end his terrorizing rampage, the monks made a Contract with a much greater evil. And so, the essence of the evil man (the essence which animated the shell) was captured and divided, placed into five ordinary shards of glass. The shards were cursed such that men would never seek to destroy them, only possess them. Protect them. And the shards of glass, filled as they were, became something else: crystals, unremarkable in appearance yet somehow mesmerizing.

For their part of the Contract, the monks were required to document what they had done, along with instructions as to how the evil man (the essence and the shell) could be brought back to this plane. The crystals were required to stay where they were, in a vast basement under the monastery. The instructions would be guarded by the monks. It was part of the bargain.

But the monks were clever. The bargain required the crystals to stay where they were—not the monks. They filled in the basement and razed the old town, moving it in its entirety across the river, at the foot of the mountain. They took the instructions with them. No one would ever know where the old town existed, and so no one would find the crystals or the instructions, they reasoned.

And normally, for Margo, here the story ended. Normally. She had dreamed all this before, many times. But this particular morning, she saw something new.

She watched the seasons pass. The trees grew and so did the new village. Three and a half centuries later, an army of evil men with tanks and flags and swastikas would find the monks' instructions and a history of the village in a document called the Kronicon Vulternense. They separated the instructions from the Vulternense, studied the excerpt, and when it was understood, the evil men contrived a plan.

The five shards, the crystals, were found. The men called them "uber-chrysalis," or u-crystals, for they were thought to unlock the power of the *ubermenschlich*. They spared the town by the river so as not to disrupt the…experiment. Ironically, the experiment lasted far longer than the Reich that commissioned it.

But when the time came for the experiment to be tested and the power to be utilized, the tome was stolen. The woman who stole it was adept but inexperienced. Able to be traced. And so a trap was laid for that person, that agent—a trap that snared not only its intended target, but several other individuals from around the world. Covert agents.

Margo could see some of their faces as they were only a few decades ago: a slender woman with fiery red hair, a brown-haired Russian, a handsome young black man with impeccable manners, a gentle wit, and….

It was a trap for one person that snared six others. But the trap backfired, destroyed by the agents it had ensnared. The experiment was no more. And the evil men never again recovered the instructions, which were labeled "Nos-fera-tu."

No, no, that wasn't it. Margo remembered reading that phrase in the underground room, but she had read it wrong. It wasn't a phrase. It was a name.

Nosferatu.

With that, her mind was filled with the face of the evil the monks had banished. The slideshow changed, became more like a movie than snapshots. She saw the man-that-was-not-a-man facing away from her, his gaunt shoulders covered by a black shawl. Slowly, his bald head rotated toward her. She could see a vein running from one side of his forehead to the other, but it was his eyes, like cats' eyes, that drew her attention.

Until he smiled.

His teeth were bright white. Two of them extended from his upper jaw like the ivory thorns of an albino rose bush. She looked up at his eyes, and suddenly he was looking back at her, just as he did when she found his face at the center of the crystal.

His face was for anyone who looked deep enough, but his smile was for her alone.

She screamed, and this time she did wake up. She checked the clock next to her bed; it was just after eight a.m. Her sheets were soaked with sweat, despite her dorm room window being open to let in a chilly December breeze. She didn't like the cold, but her room was so tiny, she had to have the window open or else sleep outside. The last time she did that, she had woken up covered in dew, freezing, at three in the morning.

Margo had no idea where these images were coming from, but they felt more like memories than random thought. At first, she had dismissed them as imagery from the pictures she had seen in the underground room, but she looked on the internet and there really was a river Sangro in Italy. How could she have known that?

She would have loved to call home to hear a reassuring voice, but she couldn't, and not because it was too early. She couldn't remember her own phone number. She had searched her room ten times. She couldn't even find any family photographs. *What kind of terrible person goes to college and doesn't bring any pictures from home?*

There were other gaps in her memory. Unfortunately, she didn't know what she had forgotten until she tried to remember it. Some things, like her class schedule and her subjects, were no problem. Other things were complete blanks. She knew she had parents, but couldn't remember what they looked like. She knew she had a sister but did not recall her name.

She located her journal, the one she used to sort her ideas about Saban, now the sole repository of her failed memory, and began leafing through it absently. When she started it, all she wanted was to figure out Saban's game. He seemed like he had her best interests at stake.

Could he be responsible for this? He had to be. Saban. This all started with him.

Try as she might, she could not fill in her missing past. And she couldn't go to a doctor. What if the doctor found out how abnormal she really was? What would happen then?

She wished she could talk to her father. She wished…she wished she could remember what he looked like. She wished she could talk to Saban…*well, not Saban, stupid Saban, but Mikey or anyone*, but where would she start? What would she say?

She wished she could remember a time that she did not feel irreversibly miserable. For an extrovert, there was no greater pain than feeling utterly alone. She placed the journal carefully on the sheets beside her, hugged her knees to her chest, and began to weep.

* * *

Their last class together would be over just before noon, only a few minutes away.

Saban had watched Margo, listless and puffy-eyed, slouch her way into class just as it began. He had done his best to be funny. The mood was fairly relaxed, so he was free to make smart comments and witty pop-culture references. Nothing made a dent.

He and Mikey exchanged several pained glances. Sadness was etched in Mikey's face every time he looked at her. Poor Mikey. He was doubtless sad for his Little Bit, not knowing what to do for her.

Saban didn't know what to do either. He did have some questions for her—some serious questions—but watching her, remembering the dynamo he had met and nearly fallen for at the beginning of the semester.... "C'mon, Mar. Last day of school. Christmas break—you get to go home!"

"And that would be?" she said. "I'm sorry. Yes, that's good. Sorry."

"Mar, can you at least stop apologizing for everything all the time?"

"Sorry." She was looking at nothing in particular.

Suddenly, Saban realized she was looking at him.

"Sorry, sorry, sorry!" she cried. "I'm sorry I met you. Can't you leave me alone?" She turned away from him.

He wasn't offended. He half blamed himself, anyway, but whatever was going on, she had it bad. There had to be something he could do. Why wouldn't John let them pull her out? He had to have a good reason, but this girl was going to need therapy if they couldn't...*where's everyone going?*

Professor Steele had finished up and dismissed the class while Saban was thinking. Margo was gone in a heartbeat. Saban bolted out the door and down the hallway. He went through the double doors of Quinlan at a full sprint, only to plow directly into one of the custodial staff. They both tumbled to the ground, books and garbage bags flying.

"Are you okay?" Saban asked, gathering his own belongings as quickly as he could. Maybe he could still catch her if he hurried.

The custodian found his Ray-Bans and stood. "I'm fine, kid. I wasn't watching where I was going." He glanced at Saban, eye to eye, before repositioning his sunglasses.

No.

No! The hair was different. The coveralls were distracting. But the eyes were Ford's.

Saban quickly averted his own. "No, it was my fault," he mumbled. "M'late for a class." *Oh, God! Oh, God! We were so close to pulling out undetected!* He reached for one last fallen book and walked swiftly away, pulled out his cell phone as he rounded a building, then headed to the parking lot at a gallop.

"Patch me through to Six." The usual bleeps and bloops were hard to hear as he started his car. The other end picked up. He didn't even wait for John's greeting. "Six? We have a problem."

PART THREE:

The Final Evening, When the Game Became Real, and Some of the Pieces...Stopped Playing...

CHAPTER 21: One More Day

The past weeks had fairly flown by. John was sitting in his office, taking a break between various status reports as they rolled in. It had been almost two months since the chaotic evening that ended with Fax's injury. *Happily, she has made a complete recovery of body and spirit, with perhaps partial credit to her rekindled friendship with Saban.*

Saban. Many months ago, John had asked Saban to pursue a rigorous and formidable training period. He was required to separate from his new friends, and John remembered advising a clean break—that was what John would have done, what John knew how to do.

But Saban wasn't John. The training alone pushed Saban past his limits, though he persevered. John could not have been prouder. And Saban had also been asked to almost single-handedly carry the weight of the entire organization's structure.

Saban had carried his new responsibilities well. But it was his prior obligations that almost caused him to crumble. So John had sent him away, forced him to take a break, doing research at the college.

He had soon come to appreciate just how firmly Saban grasped the reins of leadership. The various other officers checked in with John, but they were always mindful that Saban needed a report as well. John was the one who had to remember to keep Saban in the loop.

Is Saban even aware of how effective he is? What began as a necessary charade had morphed into something John had not expected.

John shook his head to clear his impromptu reverie and turned his full attention to the stack of papers from the nearly concluded the Millennial Eye operation. Most reports from Alpha had been positive, and that was troubling. Time was running short, and he was no closer to discovering the betrayer in the Ancient. John had allowed Saban to believe they were looking for a mole, a mere informer, but the stakes were much, much higher.

Perhaps it would be helpful to review the progress on each member of Alpha.

Demo had spent enough time in the field that John trusted his judgment, and his speech impediment was barely noticeable anymore, thanks to the constant encouragement and support from his sister.

Spar had been in the field much longer than Demo, and her leadership was solid. John trusted her implicitly, having known her longer than any other person on the team.

Fax was maturing into an excellent agent, but she was wound so tightly, she almost made John himself appear frivolous and unfocused by comparison.

And Franklin. John worried about him most of all. He was a good agent, but only time would tell if he could be a great one. Franklin's continued obstacle would be to move his own resentments out of the way. No telling how such resentment might manifest itself if it grew unchecked.

Subnet was still too pre-occupied with himself. Anni was too reserved. But ultimately, they were all still suspect. If a member of Alpha was a mole, he may be waiting for the best time to implement maximum disruption. Or perhaps whoever it was had a change of heart. These affairs seldom happened without some degree of bitterness or resentment. So who could it be?

If Becca were still alive, or any of the others, he could just ask them if he had handled this correctly. Oh, how he missed her purity and their guidance.

But she was not. They were not.

Ironic, was it not? Two explosions—one, several decades ago, that inadvertently birthed the Ancient. And another, several years ago, that nearly destroyed it. John had done what was needed to ensure the survival of the Ancient. They had invested too many resources to start over, and there wasn't enough time to begin again.

And Saban's contributions had meant not having to start over. In fact, when Saban began growing more competent, those many months ago, John had finally been left with enough time to concentrate on finding out what went wrong. John remembered his dismay after going over the logs again and again and realizing when the facts were examined, only a handful of people were unaccounted for in the disaster that took the lives of his friends.

Compounding John's misery had been the knowledge that Saban was on that list. And the only way to determine the mole's identity was to gather all the possible suspects….

John sighed, a deep and weary exhalation.

Perhaps there was no mole, no betrayer. Yet until John had conclusive evidence one way or another, he would pray for assurance that this had been the best course of action. Perhaps he should have placed Saban in that loop from the beginning. But he could not—for the same reason Saban himself was in Alpha, despite the level of trust between them. Yet if Saban deduced the real reason why John had brought Alpha together, the real reason these particular agents had been chosen to form that squad….

One more day.

He stood up and faced the large window that overlooked the cavernous underground room that housed the majority of their resources. The bustle of activity in the mammoth central column, and the sporadic appearance of lab coats near the testing facility, reminded him of all the work expended to make this operation viable. So many ways this could all fall apart.

Sadly, these were precisely the words used to describe the marked change in behavior of one person that Alpha was ostensibly attempting to protect: Margo Weissmann.

She had been becoming alternately surly and unresponsive, having distanced herself from Saban and any other companions. His reports also stated that she frequently seemed to argue with herself and was often close to tears. But the time was rapidly approaching when the matter would be dealt with. She was a dear child, and heaven knew there were more ways for harm to come than corporeal.

Fortunately, Saban never mounted a serious challenge as to why Margo had not been extracted. Saban was a good lad, but John wished he could teach Saban one more thing: the value of thinking for oneself rather than thinking in the best interests of the group.

Perhaps John would help Saban see that—after they finished up the current assignment.

One more day.

He perused an interesting report from the platform regarding recent COMINT, the general buzz in the intelligence communications. Some of the chatter mentioned Ancient operatives and the possibility of apprehending one or more of them. There were several hotspots John could think of, but this buzz originated within North America. Saban's watcher team was the Ancient's only overt stateside operation. All indications were that they were close to being discovered, but in twenty-four hours it would be moot.

They would have to hurry. In one more day, the scholastic period would be over, the civilian children would depart for holidays and semester break, and John would have to extract all his agents from their assignments. Their opportunities would evaporate in twenty-four hours.

One more day to see fruit from his hiring of Ford's assault team, many weeks ago, to put pressure on Alpha team.

One more day to see if his own mole, Ford, might still be able to expose Alpha's mole.

One more day to try and force a confrontation, force the traitor who killed his wife and friends to reveal himself.

Only a day. But a lot could happen in even a few hours. That was all the time he had needed to spring the new Alpha on Saban and keep him mentally askew. John did what he had to do for the sake of the mission.

But after so many months of using Saban for his talent and working with him, John was now convinced Saban truly was the solution—or not the traitor, at any rate. Saban had proven himself a dozen times over. And as soon as this was over, John would set Saban down and tell him everything. With the two of them working together—truly working together—they would be able to…. His phone rang.

It was Saban. "Six? We have a problem."

"Master Eight. How good of you to call, but your next report is not due for another—"

"This can't wait," Saban blurted. "They're on to us."

At last! Ford must have finally manufactured a way to motivate his other employer to engage in a non-lethal manner. John's heart soared as he listened to the rest of what Saban said.

"I just had a brief encounter with one of the creepy new custodians, and I'm sure it was Ford. I think he made me, too. Darn it, we were an inch away from getting out clean, and now there's no telling how much we're about to get compromised." There was a heavy sigh, one that sounded for all the world like one of John's. "I'm…this is entirely my fault."

"Tut, tut, my boy. I knew this might happen, and so did you. You were made two months ago when you fought him, so it was just a matter of time before he found you. I'm surprised it took this long to get burned. You know what to do now. Break off the platform as soon as you're sure the rabbit won't be in the wind. Repro the pertinent records. Exfiltration at…twenty-three hundred hours?" That might be too long. John considered revising the time but held his tongue.

"Better make it twenty-one hundred hours, our time. We can still roll up smooth. I feel bad for Margo. We were so close. This will not be fun. For us. For her."

So young to carry the burden of everyone. He's a good lad...a good man. "This too shall pass. You may have some contact tonight, so if the schedule is too tight, suit her up and zip her out. Be careful, Master Eight. Oh, and Eight?"

"Yes?"

"Moscow rules." John did not lightly give the traditional warning that they were embarking into a tremendously hostile environment. Saban was too young to remember the Cold War, but he would know that this was notice to be at the top of his tradecraft. With John controlling as many factors as he could on one end, and Ford controlling things from the other, the confrontation should not be too terribly dangerous. But it would be appropriate for everyone to be at their best performance, as it were.

"Yeah, you're right," Saban agreed. "Don't worry; we'll all be fine. It's her I'm worried about." The line went dead.

John stared at the phone before placing it back down in its charger. *Godspeed, my good man. When this is done, I will at last have a trustable ally, and perhaps…perhaps a friend, even one so young. But for now, you have another long night ahead. We all do.*

John assembled his phone and keyboard to make sure things were as they should be on Ford's end. It appeared that everything was going according to plan, as long as Ford was still in control of his assault team.

* * *

Ford sat down on the toilet, but he didn't have to use the bathroom. He had to fulfill, as best he could, a contract to someone he only knew as Mister Six. He attached a special keyboard to his cell phone and pressed a familiar set of keys.

"Strangers in the night," Ford sang softly to no one, "exchanging ASCII…." Before he typed anything, a few words came up on his tiny screen.

"Heard you made contact. Finally."

"Wasn't my choice. Was never safe," Ford typed back. "Still not."

"Explain."

"DD saw me see kid. Nothing I could do."

"What? This contact will not be controlled?"

"No. Trying to warn you. DD is out for blood."

"You must disengage immediately."

"Cannot. Either my blood or the kid's."

"Try sabotage! Will double my price. No fatalities." There was a pause. "Will triple."

"Cannot spend money if dead," Ford typed. "Bumped the kid on purpose, to give him heads up. Giving you warning, as promised. Out of my hands now."

Nothing appeared on the screen for a few seconds. Ford was about to pack it up, when a few more words appeared. "Understood. Moscow rules."

"Always," Ford typed back. "Why kid so important?" It was worth asking.

"That is need to know. But they are ALL important."

"Ford out." Oh, well. Devon Ford could hear Dewitter calling for him, and it was time to go. Time to take out some Ancient. How in the world was that kid mixed up with them? It didn't matter. As of thirty seconds ago, Ford had only one boss, not two, and that boss said it was time to go.

Maybe no one would die. Whatever.

“Strangers in the night,” Ford sang softly, “exchanging gunfire….” He poked the thin keyboard into the back of his pants, flushed the toilet, and left.

* * *

The sun had set fully an hour ago, but from her bedroom window, Margo could see shadows moving in the tree line on the other side of the campus.

They’re coming.

Exhausted as she was, she was not too tired to see and hear the truck as it rolled across the soccer field and came to a halt at the other end of her building. She leaned out of her window to see what was happening. A mechanical arm extended up from the rear of the truck, the carriage moving all the way to the roof. A shadowy figure hopped up and out. Then the arm retracted and the truck started moving again, coming to rest under her window. She stopped watching. She didn’t need to watch. She knew what was happening.

They were coming. For her.

One if by air (or was it by land?); two if by sea; three or more if by force. Was that how it would go down? She didn’t care. She couldn’t think straight and hadn’t had a decent sleep in forever. She just wanted it to be over.

Her room was already clean. She had finished packing and only needed to take down her posters, unhook her computer cables, and make a few more things ready. She was tired. She would not make it difficult.

They were coming for her tonight, and she would not resist. They would take her, whoever they were, and she would go with them. At this point, if they could make the dreams go away, she would go with anyone.

Anyone at all.

Anyone but Saban.

CHAPTER 22: The Confrontation

Saban walked briskly along the path toward Margo's dorm at just past eight-thirty p.m. Less than a half an hour to get her out—not much time left and much to do. But most of what needed to happen should already be done. What did John say? "Break off the platform…"

Check. They had retracted their feeds from the data trunk of the college's newly installed security system almost as soon as Saban was done talking to John. They still had one active data feed, but as soon as it was terminated, there would be no reconnecting without some major backdoor action. The college would then be on its own, a turn-key operation with all the local personnel fully trained. And no strings—the equipment had not been created by M-Sec, only brokered, so tech support would be farmed back to the manufacturer. Alpha probably didn't need to jettison their link, since Saban was the only person 'made,' but better safe than sorry. He didn't want anything traced back to the Ancient.

What else? "…as soon as you're sure the rabbit won't be in the wind." Check. Margo was still the rabbit, and "in the wind" was an expression describing a rabbit on the run, as opposed to "in the dark" or "in the gap," where the rabbit is out of sight for short periods of time. Saban felt like their luck might run out soon, so part of Charlie team had shown up at the safe house last night in response to his call, and they were ready to engage if need be. That should prevent Margo from being anywhere except where she should be.

"Repro the pertinent records." Check. A simple-minded buffoon might be tempted to destroy someone's records, but that would set off red flags in the real world. Better to simply replace her records with bogus information, a "repro" operation. Subnet was taking care of that right now, but based on the information they had gotten about Margo, it appeared someone may have beaten them to it.

That was one of the things he would have to ask Margo about.

Still, they would re-falsify her records for procedure's sake. It would buy more time while they decided where to put her, and this was a significant issue: what to do with Margo once they removed her from this potentially hazardous environment. They were not the government and they had no "witness relocation program." The Ancient were not in the business of housing guests, willing or unwilling. So where did John think she would go after they brought her in?

It made him tired just thinking about it. Most of Saban's ideas involved him doing a major spin on her, giving her a scholarship to some other college, and letting her pick up the pieces of her life. For some reason, John wasn't concerned with relocating her. Normally, Saban found it comforting that John knew things he did not, but there was a growing list of things that Saban didn't know about, and it was time for that to end.

Too much to think about for now. Immediate objective: get Margo somewhere safe. *Heh. It's déjà vu all over again.*

"Exfiltration at twenty-one hundred hours," they had agreed. Check. They were on target to get her out by nine p.m. He needed to be at her door in the next six minutes if they were going to make the deadline. He quickened his pace.

Beneath his tan trench coat, he wore his full Ancient attire and carried a second helmet and an additional set of CDUs with it. He hadn't worn his own CDUs, or Camouflage Dress Uniform, in quite some time. The exterior was a unique mesh of magnetized fibers that could change color, depending on an electrical charge applied anywhere on the surface of the uniform. As such, they had to be tight in order to be conductive. His seemed a little extra snug, however.

Did I finally put on some muscle? Either that or he had picked up a few first semester pounds like every other freshman. *Well, any sacrifice to keep from blowing cover. That's the kind of guy I am.* He smiled grimly beneath his helmet. The helmet had the same coating as the mesh, and was linked to the rest of the uniform over the same wiring that connected the radio headsets into the slender battery pack he wore on his hips.

Just before entering the building, he noted a black SUV with a mechanical arm perched above its roof, parked under Margo's second-story window. That had been Demo's task, which meant Anni was already on the roof. Some of Charlie team was back at the platform, monitoring the cameras on that one last feed. The others were en route, which was according to plan, but if anything happened in the next few minutes, Alpha team was on its own. *How do these things keep happening just a little too fast for everyone but Alpha?*

Two minutes to be at her room. He was keenly aware that he would alarm any casual observer, but he could not risk being unprepared if any action started. He entered the dorm, raced up the stairs, took a deep breath, and knocked on the door.

"Mar?" he called out.

"Go away," he heard from behind the door.

"Margo, it's me. It's Saban. I need to talk to you." He looked around and knocked again. "C'mon, let me in."

"Oh, I'm sorry; I meant to say 'go away now!'"

He heard something being whacked for emphasis and was glad it wasn't him. "Margo, this is Saban, and I am your friend. It would be a good idea for you to open the door and—"

"Oh, for heaven's sake, stop that. You sound demented. If you're not going away, just come in and say what you have to say. That's what you do, isn't it?"

Hmpph. He had never received that kind of response to a spin before, but he got the desired outcome, so he guessed it was fine. No telling how on-the-edge she was. He pulled the release lever on the helmet fastener, and for her sake, pulled off his helmet before opening the door.

The lights were out in Margo's room, but the window was open, and the moon was full and bright in the sky. He could see her silhouette in front of one of the windows, could see the breath coming out of her mouth. How could she stand it so cold in here? Had she seen their truck sitting two stories below her window? Did she care? She hadn't even turned to look at him yet. He wondered if she was depressed, in an official somebody-needs-a-pill way.

If only he could read her better. Saban remembered how easily she had picked him up the last time she was angry. He knew he would have to tread carefully, walking the line between not hurting her and not getting physically hurt himself. But as fast as things were moving, he could not afford to go very slow.

"Margo," he began, "do you remember that night when you had that, heh-heh, that nutty dream where we were being chased by mercenaries?" *I told her to forget it, so it's possible she doesn't even remember.*

"You mean the night you helped me get back here after somebody drugged me?"

That was encouraging. "Yeah, that night."

"The night I dreamed someone spit tobacco near my ear and there just happed to be some in my ear the next day?" Her voice rose a few notes.

Whoops. That was…the opposite of encouraging. *Warning, danger, Will Robinson!*

Margo kept going. "The night when Fax took a knife in the shoulder for me, and you had people stage a paint-ball war as window dressing to convince me that I was insane? That night?" She pivoted in her chair ever so gradually. Tears were running down both her cheeks; she looked as if she had been weeping for some time.

Bad. Hugely bad. Did the spin wear off? Was she ever spun?

She wiped her eyes with her flannel sleeve. "I knew someone was coming, ever since I saw the truck thingee down there. But there was only one of you. I thought you might float down from the sky." Her hands made fluttering motions.

Crap. Should have thought she would see the truck. "Margo, I know this is a lot to take in, but your life is in jeopardy."

"I'm sorry, then, your answer must be in the form of a question."

Is she losing it, or is she joking? "We need to get out of here and get to a safe place. I brought some…some…." *No, she's losing it. She's not even paying attention.* "Margo, there are people who are out there who—"

"Do I know them?" There was an odd expression in her voice. She sounded eager. "Do I know those people? Do they know me?"

She stood up. He wasn't sure, but it looked like she was holding something behind her back.

"Well, no, I don't think so, except Ford, you helped tie him up, and Fax and Franklin, and I don't know who else—"

"Ford. Yes. I remember Ford."

Her voice had a warbling lilt, the kind heard in movies, he thought, just before someone whips out a butcher knife and tries to stab everyone.

"And I remember Fax," she said.

Instinctively, he took a step back and bumped into the door, accidentally closing it and cutting off his best path of escape. "Uhm, yeah, I remember all of them, too. Listen, I'm sorry to be so sudden, but there are good reasons why I had to—"

"And I recall Franklin. I remember them all. But do you know what I don't recall?" The tone and volume of her voice rose again slightly.

"Central Park in the fall?" It slipped out before he could stop it. *Stupid mouth.* He only hoped he would see the butcher knife before it made contact.

"No, you jerk! Everything else!"

Her hands became a blur. Out from behind her back, death flew directly at him in the form of a…spiral notebook? He caught it in mid-flight.

"Open it!" she demanded.

He did so. "Margo, what is this? All I see is stuff like…your parents' names. Your favorite color. Your hometown. You have a sister…with a question mark? I see you wrote your parents' names, but why not Nicole?" *This was how she spent all her time?*

"Nicole! Nicole!" she repeated triumphantly. "Give me that!" She rushed forward, ripped the notebook out of his hands and wrote down her sister's name, then fell to her knees and began to weep again, great wracking sobs. She looked up at him. "What did you do to me?"

"What? Me? I didn't do anything! I mean, I thought I did, but I think you're immune, so I guess I tried to do something, but no one has ever had a reaction like this, and besides, I don't think it worked, and what's been going on with you?" He gasped for air, but it was his mind, not his lungs, that was reeling. "I don't understand."

"*You* don't understand? Oh, boo-fricking-hoo!" She took a few moments to compose herself, wiped her eyes, and tried to speak calmly between gasps. "I didn't notice at first. I was concentrating so hard on why you would spin me into thinking that night was a dream. Why you would go to all the effort of covering everything up." She pulled out a tissue and blew her nose into it. "One day it occurred to me that something valuable was at stake."

"Yeah, your life," Saban filled in.

"No, I mean the things everyone was looking for that night. The crystals."

"The U-crystals," he corrected without thinking.

"If they were that valuable, and they couldn't be retrieved by the bad guys, then the next best thing to getting them would be finding the people who took them."

"Yes."

"So you tried to spin me into thinking it was a dream, so I wouldn't draw attention to myself. That meant you had to stay, too, because your absence might draw attention to me, and you probably to needed to monitor how well your spin 'took.' Am I right?"

"Yes." *How had she deduced all this?*

"And you couldn't just hide me or move me somewhere, because if one or two people suddenly vanished from a school this small—two people whose descriptions match the people who kicked Ford and Rambeau's butts—it would allow them to trace everything back to us. Well, me, anyway. You probably enrolled under a fake name."

"Real name, actually. Everything else is kind of fake."

"So you stayed. You could protect me, but you couldn't protect my family. The bad guys would never see anything suspicious. Extended perception management."

"Yes." *An odd choice of words.* Another red flag was inching up in his mind.

"You were going to leave for good after the end of the semester?"

"Yeah. Tomorrow afternoon. The semester would have been over, we would have left, and that would have been the end of it. At least, that was the plan." Not a great plan, but it was the one he and John—mostly John—went with for reasons that didn't seem as clear as when they started. Flawed reasoning that she had somehow followed perfectly.

In his earpiece, he heard a report of some movement. In all likelihood, there were foreign agents, or whoever Ford was with, here for Margo. He had to take this conversation as far as he could, though, because what he learned in the next minute or two could be crucial.

"Besides classes," Margo said, "you were all I could think about for a long time. One day, I was thinking about going home. That was when I discovered I couldn't remember where I grew up. I remembered the name, but not the town itself, and not the state it's in. When I realized what was happening, I wrote down everything I could think of. I even forgot I had parents until you reminded me. But everything I've written looks unfamiliar now. It's like someone else's words, someone else's life."

Saban become conscious of his mouth hanging open, but said nothing.

"The only things that seem real are things that happened since the beginning of this school year. Everything else is a big white blur." She sat back down. "I don't even have any pictures. Nothing! What kind of daughter am I? My family could be standing right in front of me, and I wouldn't know."

"What about the phone number in your student records?" he asked. He already knew the answer, though, because he had tried it himself.

"It's disconnected!" she wailed. "Maybe we moved before I got here and I had the new number memorized, but I've turned my whole room upside down and I can't find any phone numbers. I think they always had me dial collect. One day, I just couldn't remember the number, and I still don't know it."

"So why didn't you come talk to me?"

"Talk to you? I don't want to even be near you! My life was fine until *you* came charging through it. I don't want to lose what little mind I have left!" She glared at him.

There were so many pieces to this puzzle, and he would have loved to try and make them all fit, but they were running out of time. He would need to make a quick decision. *Why always me?* But he still didn't have enough information. John always said that the best way to fix that was to apply some pressure and see what popped out.

Actually, John didn't say it quite like that, because that sounded more like treating a pimple than covert ops, but the principle was similar.

"Well, you're not going to like this then," he said, deliberately brusque. "Alpha team has been watching over you for the past two months to keep you safe, but we're leaving. I'm leaving. And you're coming with us."

"With you?" She laughed, and it was not a pretty laugh. "Are you prepared to make me?"

"Yes. Yes, I am."

"You and what paramilitary force?" She stood up, sober, fists at her side.

"Listen, Mar, I don't know what's going on in your head. I'm sorry for your lost memories, and we have some outstanding scientists at our home base, guys who might be able to help you. But there are men on their way to either capture us or make us severely pulse-challenged. You have to stay alive in order to be helped.

"Stop trying to confuse me! I'm not going anywhere until I get some bona-fides." She crossed her arms.

That was it. The mental red flag was firmly in the air.

Over the radio, he heard someone at the platform report more suspicious movement near one of the choke points, one of the three entrances to the campus. The bad guys were here too early! He would have to tackle this problem with Margo head-on, and that meant confronting her about suspicions he hadn't even shared with John. He simply did not have enough time to do anything else.

"Margo." He paused to make sure his tone did not betray his racing heartbeat. "What is a bona-fide?" He kept his expression flat.

"Your intentions, your affiliation." She looked puzzled. "Is that too much to ask?"

"It's not what you asked; it's how you asked for it. I've never heard anyone ask for 'bona fides' in that context except another operative."

"You're crazy! I'm no spook! I'm just a girl from…from…." She flipped in her notebook. "Austin! I know one spooky word, and now I'm some kind of spy!"

"You also used words like 'window dressing' and 'perception management.' And 'spook.' These aren't just words. These are trade phrases."

"Like you're the only one who's allowed to read?"

"There's more. I asked one of my co-workers, a man I trust…have trusted…with my life, to check out your background. You listed Austin, Texas as your hometown, but one time you told me that you were actually from a smaller town nearby called Salinamas."

"Salinamas!" she cried out and flipped through her notebook to find the right page.

"Don't bother writing it down. It doesn't exist."

She froze like a deer in headlights. "But…but…maybe you got the state wrong!" Was she busted or just surprised?

"They're your words, not mine," he said. "Anyway, I googled it, too. There's not a Salinamas on the entire planet. Your social checks out; you were registered in Texas about nineteen years ago. You used your real name to register for school, like you said. But you've never showed up as a dependent on anyone's tax return, never been registered to go to any other school, never showed up in any pre-HIPAA medical records that we could find. You exist, but 'just a girl' is almost all I know about you." *She was an operative, no doubt about it, but whose side was she on?*

Margo listened, but said nothing.

"And anyway, you're not even 'just a girl,' unless every girl you know can do a six foot standing jump."

"Okay. You knew all this before you knocked on the door, but you're still here." She stood on the balls of her feet, shifting her weight nervously. Her fists tightened. "So what does this mean?"

"It means right now, I trust you less than you trust me. For all I know, you could be some kind of sleeper agent, ready to kill me when my back is turned. I'm trying to protect you, but I'd rather not die if I don't have to. Especially at your hands."

That affected Margo like a pail of cold water and in a good way. Her fists unclenched. Her back straightened. Even with his limited ability to read her, he could tell she was pulling herself out of her mild hysteria. “Kill you?” she said quietly. “All I’m trying to do is hang on to my sanity. Yes, I’m angry. And confused. I admit it. But I could no sooner kill you than I could kill myself.”

“So you say.”

She sighed. “It’s my memory that’s a mess, not my morals.” She said calmly, “I tried to pretend that you spun me, because I came to trust your intentions. I tried to pretend things were okay. But I never lied to you.” Then she added, “As far as I know.”

He did believe her. Mostly. “I don’t doubt that you believe what you’re saying. There’s something going on with you, but I don’t think I caused it. Right now, though,” he said, putting his helmet back on, “it doesn’t matter. You’re in danger. You can’t stay here, and you don’t know how to get home. You have to come with me.”

“Danger?” she said, as if hearing it for the first time.

“Geez, you don’t listen! That hasn’t changed. Remember the U-crystals? You were right; people want them! They found me, and now they found you.” More reports of activity through his headset. Everyone on both sides was getting into positions. A firefight was in the making, and it would be colossal when it blew. “Agents are on their way over here right now. Some are ours. Most are not, I think.”

“I still don’t know who you are. I’m not going anywhere.”

Saban ignored her comment. “I brought an extra suit and a helmet. You need to put it on, and then we’re gone.”

“And if I don’t?”

“Wake up and smell the bullets!” he screamed. “If you don’t come with me, then you’re gonna die, and you’re never gonna see your parents again. Or Nicole, if she exists. Or find out what caused this. And I’ll probably die, too, because I won’t leave you. Be upset if you want, but I’m telling you, we’re out of time!”

He would not have been surprised if heat vision came out of her eyes and burned a hole right through him, but fortunately, it did not. She muttered a profanity under her breath. “Why do I have to wear the suit?”

"Because it's made from a flexible Kevlar polymer that will protect you from small arms fire. It also gives us radio contact. Any other questions?"

Margo looked up at the ceiling and shook her head, then said with resignation, "Yeah. Will you turn around while I change?"

"No. Like I said, there's something about you that neither of us fully understands, so I'd rather not get a knife in the back for the sake of modesty. But," he said forcefully, cutting off her objection, "I will look away, and you can keep your…your undergarments on. And your tee-shirt, too; it'll keep the top from chafing your armpits." He tossed the extra suit on the bed and turned his head far enough away that she was just in his peripheral vision.

Margo seemed to be done arguing. She changed into the suit wordlessly and pulled on the boots. With the helmet under one arm, she asked, "How did you know all my sizes?"

"Measured you when you were unconscious two months ago." He held up a hand and quickly added, "Not me! I wasn't even in the same room with you. Anni and Spar. They're girls."

"How wonderful for them. What else happened to me while I was unconscious?"

"Nothing. They washed your clothes and re-dressed you. That's it."

"That's it?"

"It's all documented. You can go over the logs yourself if you want. But first we have to get our butts out of here. Every minute we stay is putting the whole team in danger, and the only reason we're here is for you."

Margo nodded. "Okay. For now, we do it your way. What next?"

Finally! "Let's fasten your helmet so you can hear me and the team. You can listen but don't talk. Leave everything and follow me."

"Wait! What about my stuff?

"It's going to get cleared out as soon as we leave."

"I'm bringing my notebook," she stated, then cleared her throat. "May I bring my notebook?"

"Fine," replied Saban, choking back his shock. "Tuck it under the suit and let's go."

As they were leaving, they passed by the mirror; Margo caught her reflection and stopped to stare. Once again, he tried to empathize with what must be going through her head. But this time—how she dealt with change so well, just questioning for a few minutes and then moving forward—her ability to adjust to the bizarre was bizarre in itself. He hoped to explore that someday, as long as she didn't do anything rude, like kill him.

Concentrate! Stay focused on her to keep her from hurting me. Keep her focused on me, to keep her from hurting herself. What a tightrope. "Margo, can you hear me?" he said though their two-way radio. "Just nod your head up and down."

She nodded her head and inched her way to the door, still mesmerized by her reflection. His mild distrust could not prevent him from feeling compassion for her. If she was acting, it was a good act. He put his arm around her. "It's going to be okay," he said, and gave her shoulder a gentle tug.

"You are now entering another world," he heard her say. "Please keep your arms, legs and lucidity protected at all times."

She doesn't seem like an enemy. Had she been a sleeper for Ford and left out in the field? Was there some other entity? He didn't know, but he trusted her. Sort of. And she was still impressive. After all, she figured out why he tried to spin her. And she figured out why he stayed with her. Nothing to do but keep moving forward and try to stay alive. *I know I've missed something...something.*

Unexpectedly, one more thought flashed through his head—an inconsistency that he had missed. *I've never used the word "spin" in her presence. But she used it with me just now.*

He shut the door behind them.

CHAPTER 23: Margo Unbound

Margo trailed Saban closely in the hallway, occasionally glancing at her new second skin. The outfit was very similar to the ones she had seen on Alpha team months ago, sleek but darker. She found the torso to be a little tight in certain places, as it was almost a solid unit. The arms and legs were independently plated to cover the larger portions. And some parts, like directly under her arms, were not really armored at all, so that her arms could relax naturally and not stick out like a primate's. The dark gloves also had no shielding, and additionally her index finger and pinky were uncovered.

A black utility belt, two inches wide, kept the upper and lower portions seamed. The black boots were sturdy but not cumbersome, and a side zipper meant they could be taken on or off quickly. As soon as she had zipped one up, muscle memory told her she had worn boots like these before, but she could not recall when or where.

Saban looked at her, but it was impossible to tell what he was thinking with his helmet on. They walked down the hallway to the stairwell. He put his fist up in the air and held it there. She knew that gesture meant stop, familiar in a way she could not place. He peered down the circular stairs before motioning her to follow.

Seeing the world through the wraparound visor took a little getting used to. The visor was opaque from the outside but surprisingly translucent from the inside.

He stopped her at the bottom of the stairs and pointed to the side of her head. "There's a button at the base of your left ear that activates the night vision," she heard him say through the radio transmitter. "At the base of your right ear is a zoom lens with three progressive settings. The fourth time you hit the switch, you're back to normal—such as you are."

"Ha-ha. What about the buttons at the top of my ears?"

"The top button on the left scans several preset channels on which we communicate, five settings altogether. Four are selective, the last listens to all of them at the same time. Don't touch it. The button top right is the comm-link—a microphone that shuts off after thirty seconds of non-usage. The link has three settings—listen, listen and talk, and off. Don't touch that one, either. Please."

He pushed the control button for her night-vision, making her world over with a greenish tint. "That will keep you from running into trees tonight."

Then he touched his own comm-link. "Eight here," he broadcast. "I have Ninety-nine."

She looked at the patch on her shoulder. "Ninety-nine? I'm Agent Ninety-nine?" *That was so Saban.* If she wasn't part of some plan to kill him, she was becoming sympathetic to the idea independently.

"Coincidence, I'm sure." When they reached the exit, he paused to listen to his headset.

"Hey!" she whispered. "The gloves. How come the index finger isn't covered?"

"So you can feel the buttons as you use them," he whispered back, still listening.

"How come the pinky isn't covered?" This all felt vaguely familiar. She knew the answer before he said it.

"In case you lose the index finger," he answered distractedly. "Okay. I've got reports of multiple sightings of hostiles. I'm going through the door first, to draw fire. I want you to count to five and follow me. Run as fast as you can, and I mean it, Mar, don't hold back. Fax and Franklin will flank you and take you to the evac point. Stay between them and stay close. Ready?"

"Run. Stay close. Got it. What's after that?"

"Don't know. Making it up as I go. Try not to die. Also, don't kill anyone. See you!" He raced out the door.

Five, four, three… She heard a "chink chink" outside, like someone throwing rocks at the building. Two…one. She took a large breath of air and ran out the door into the clear, moonlit night. She knew that looking through the goggles would give even the most familiar sights an otherworldly flavor, but she was still surprised by what she saw.

Nothing. No movement, no bad guys. There wasn't even much of a wind. She looked around, but Saban was gone. She wasn't sure what was going on, and she still had that image of losing a finger in her head. "Chink" went a bullet into the stone wall behind her.

"Get moving!" she heard Saban cry through her headset.

She ran.

In front of her was the soccer field she used to play on. To her left and right, as she ran, there was a "whhzz" of bullets and an occasional spray of dirt close to her feet. The setting seemed unreal, until one bullet grazed her shoulder, throwing her off balance and nearly making her stumble.

Across the way was the row of trees she and Saban had once traveled so stealthily, trying to make their way to an injured Mikey. That night seemed like a long time ago. She knew she would need cover, so she made for the tree line. Were those lightning bugs off in the distance in front of her? No, muzzle flashes. She needed to….

She had barely run eighty feet when she felt hands on either side of her, changing her direction to run the length of the field rather than the breadth. There was an Alpha agent running on either side of her. Amazingly, they were matching her pace, step for step.

"My, you *are* fast. Saban was right," she heard through the radio. It was Fax's voice. "Let's not run directly into the gunfire, shall we? Didn't you see the muzzle flashes? We need to cross this stretch quickly, so let's see what you've really got."

"Yeah, try to keep up with us!" The other agent had to be Franklin.

Margo kicked into high gear, and they ran almost the entire field in under five seconds. Everywhere she looked, there were skirmishes breaking out between blue-teamers and camouflaged agents, or the flash of a muzzle followed by return fire. In her earpiece, she heard several segments of high-speed gibberish, like a phone message played at fast forward. Then she heard Fax's voice again.

"Right," Fax said, as if finishing some other conversation. "We didn't know you could keep up like this, so we've changed plans. This field dumps out into the road that runs behind the whole campus. If we go to the left, there's a low point in the wall that surrounds the campus about a half mile up, where the cemetery is. Don't go the whole distance to the exit—there's four mercs waiting at the end, where the school road meets the highway."

They made it past the field and turned as a unit onto the road. She heard another high-pitched segment as she saw Franklin pointing to the right, near the wall. "I see them, too," she heard Fax say. "Keep going," Fax ordered her. "We'll catch up at the cemetery."

The twins veered off to the right, zig-zagging until they reached the wall. Franklin began to grapple with a merc at the base of the Great Wall, while Fax jumped, used her brother as a springboard, and fairly flew twelve feet up into another agent perched atop the wall.

Margo kept running. The road ahead had a few turns, but she stayed in the middle, hoping that her speed would make her less of a target. She saw no one around, and the graveyard was coming up fast, so she slowed down to a normal pace and eased in beside it, stopping at the wall. The night was quiet; she could hear only her own breathing and the crickets.

The cemetery was very old, harkening back to the days when the college was a simple monastery. The edge of the burial grounds came close to the road and ran alongside it for maybe a hundred and fifty feet, and was perhaps half as wide, with the other edge butting up to the Great Wall. There were mostly headstones and shrines, though she counted at least four of those small buildings where whole families were often buried. *What do you call them? Mausoleums.*

She cautiously made her way along the Great Wall to the middle of the grounds. The graveyard held no fear of the dead for her; she was more concerned with the living. She heard something snap nearby—a stick or an acorn. Fax and Franklin hadn't taken very long at all.

"I was wondering how long you would be in getting here," she said, turning to greet them. But it wasn't the twins.

"Well, we were wondering the same thing," replied a man dressed in camouflage from head to toe. He did not wear cammo make-up like the men from Ford's team. And there was something more professional about his bearing. He was composed and attentive, not a paid thug like Rambeau. This was a real soldier.

"Turn around and face the wall," came a second voice. "Place your hands over your head, sir, and you won't get hurt."

"Hey! It's a female!" A third voice. *Great.*

She froze. "I'm unarmed," she said slowly, keeping her hands to her sides. Two men came out from behind headstones, and all three closed in until they were seven or eight feet from her. She was encircled, having walked past one and right into the others. They all had rifles at their hips, and they were all pointed in her direction. Her back was literally against the wall, and she doubted the light armor would stop a bullet at point blank range.

The first man spoke into his two-way. "We are securing one enemy combatant and will continue to be on alert for the civilian girl."

"Don't kill that agent if you don't have to. We have several others pinned down, but we need as many of them alive as we can," came a voice that sounded just like agent Ford. *That snake.* Margo began to seethe with anger. Not, not anger. Something else.

"And if you see the young man with souped-up fighting skills," came a different voice with a British accent, "don't take any chances. We don't need him anymore. Put him down hard." That had to have meant Saban. They were going to kill him on sight.

"Copy that." The soldier placed his two-way into a holster on his hip. "All right, you. Nice and easy. We don't want to shoot you if we don't have to."

Margo's adrenaline was pumping, perhaps more so than in her entire life. Something was burning inside her, like she was being refined. Or redefined. Her tiredness was gone. Her skin fairly tingled, and she had the vague sensation of cobwebs being pulled away from her skin. Where had she felt that before? No matter.

She looked at the soldier and suddenly felt like she knew him, not from her past, but as if his emotions and values were an open text for her to read. She had trouble interpreting it, but the knowledge was there for the taking.

She could tell the soldier was nervous, probably because Margo was a woman. Aiming a weapon at her caused stress to his sense of honor. She glanced at the other two and saw they had similarly chivalrous reservations. How did she know that? Regardless, she would use it.

"I'm unarmed," she repeated with a deliberately trembling voice. "I'm turning around." She saw them…no, she *felt* them bring down their guard. *Sweet.* She would get one chance.

As she faced the wall, she brought her arms up quickly to help her jump. Midway, she curled up into a tight ball and pivoted her body before bringing her feet to brace against the wall, then pushed off and dove into one of the men before he could do anything. They hit the ground together, and before he could orient himself, she had already popped him in the head with her fist—a Ying Mien Jik Tong. *That's what the move is called*, she thought with astonishment.

He was out cold.

She rolled off him and threw herself into walkie-talkie-man, who tumbled backward but kept rolling, so that when they came to rest he was sitting on her stomach. He was a pro, and she had surprised him, but only for a moment. His hand darted toward her throat, but she moved her head to one side, wrapped his arm around hers and threw him. It was a modified Chor Yau Seung Gwan, a hooking attack that wouldn't have worked for anyone except her, because of her strength. Sure enough, he went up in the air and came down hard. She never let go and used his own arm to pull herself over and straddle him, striking him in the face repeatedly with her free hand until he was out cold. Two down.

The third soldier came in fast but stopped just out of arms' reach and popped a kick to her head, connecting hard enough to hurl her off her unconscious foe and into the dirt. Her face smacked into a tombstone on her way down, and though the blow was blunted by her helmet, it was hard enough that she lost track of her opponent.

She had gotten to one knee when a whooshing sound from behind gave her just enough time to block the kick. She pushed his leg upward as hard as she could, which allowed her to get to her feet and face him. He glanced at his rifle several feet away and judged, Margo "saw," that pursuing it would leave him vulnerable. When he took a stance very similar to hers, it made Margo understand that she might have a serious struggle on her hands. He was definitely the most poised and confident of the three. He came straight on.

Four kicks and three attempted body blows later, he had yet to connect, as Margo moved out of his way with an almost supernatural combination of reflex and grace. Frustrated, he planted himself in front of her and threw everything he had as rapidly as he could. Her arms moved with a mind of their own, faster and faster, blocking each blow before launching a counter strike. More effortlessly than she would have thought possible, she slapped one of his hands away and planted a Hoy Sao Yee Dip Sao, a palming attack, to his midsection, knocking the wind out of him.

Gasping for breath, he snatched from his belt a small canister that was probably pepper spray. She didn't want to find out if she was right. She marked his position mentally before whirling full circle in a Seun Fon Towie kick that separated his helmet from his head. The helmet sailed into the air before coming down into the waiting hands of Fax, who was standing next to a headstone a few yards away. Franklin was nowhere to be seen.

The only noise to be heard again was the soft chirping of crickets and an intermittent unseen frog. Fax said nothing, nor did Margo. She was too stunned to put anything into words.

She had used some very unique moves. She knew what they were called, but this knowledge was different from knowing the history of some monks, like in her dreams. That information was a book she could take off a mental shelf, browse, and put back.

Her knowledge of combat, however, was like a story she had been told long ago and was only now beginning to remember in glorious detail. And frightening as it sounded, she knew that her performance had been rusty, that this was not even her best.

As far as she could recall, she had never taken a martial arts class in her life. But then, there was very little about her life that she remembered. It was all slipping away, except for the tiny portion she had managed to save in the notebook pressing against her stomach.

"Makes me wonder who should be protecting who from whom," Fax observed.

Margo surveyed the fallen men with a mixture of abhorrence and fascination. She was an English major who liked soccer, and she had just taken down three grown men in hand-to-hand combat. Saban was right—there was something freakish about her, and it wasn't him, not at all. It was her, and it was all too much. Her lungs felt tight, and she couldn't breath. Kneeling down, she put her head into her hands, not knowing whether to cry or cheer. She hated this feeling, like she had done something wrong, but not knowing what the wrong thing was.

"Whoa! Whoa!" said Fax, who approached and dropped down beside her. She felt Fax's hand on her arm.

"I don't know what's going on," Margo coughed out between breaths. "I don't know how I did that. You're all trying to protect me, and I don't even know who I am. Or what I am." Margo was almost overcome with a wave of self-loathing.

"Stop that," Fax said. "What you are is a Talent. I saw the whole thing as I was running up, and I'll tell you, I've never seen anyone this side of Spar move like that." Fax's voice became gentler. "Miss Weissmann, you have a gift. Several, actually. Are you telling me you've never used them before?"

"I don't know. Like I told Saban a few minutes ago, I can't remember anything. Since that night we all met, I've forgotten everything I ever did before coming to school here. No family, no childhood. Nothing. And Saban thinks I'm something called a sleeper." She looked at Fax's arm, then at Fax. "It's all better," she said with surprise.

"What, my arm? Yes, yes, I'm a fast healer. Miss Weissmann, listen to me. I don't think you're a sleeper. Not the way Saban means. It doesn't add up."

"What do you mean?" Margo sniffled and forced herself to dry up.

"You have gifts, or what we call talents. Lots of people in the Ancient have talents. And you definitely have some skills that were learned somewhere. But sleepers live their lives and forget their objective until needed. When the mission comes, it's like they're in a trance, and you weren't fighting like you were in a trance. And you got better the longer you fought. Come to think of it, you fought like you were coming out of a trance."

That actually made sense. Over the past few weeks, she had felt several times like memories were dropping away from her, as though they had atrophied and fallen off. Perhaps that was why her senses had seemed much more acute. "They zone out of the real world, do their thing and come back unaware," Margo said.

Fax nodded. "Yes. Maybe you were a sleeper. But you're not anymore. This is the real you, or realer than you've been, at least. We should tell Saban."

"But he'll think I'm a freak!" Margo sniffed.

"We're all freaks, dear." Fax looked over her shoulder, and so did Margo. Franklin was in the distance, running toward them and accelerating. "I prefer the word 'special,'" she added, sounding almost maternal.

Franklin arrived and appraised the scene. "Whoa! Ladies, ladies! Whud'ja do?"

"Quiet, I'm thinking." Fax resumed her emotionless facade.

"What, you want a cookie?" Franklin said, but touched his radio control. Fax touched hers, too. It looked like they were turning them off.

Margo heard the high-pitched squeal again, but this time, it wasn't through her head set, it was in front of her. They must be able to talk as fast as they could run! *Neat.* They completed several exchanges back and forth, then they both looked at her.

"Wow," said Franklin, eyeing her with new respect.

"What's the plan?" Margo asked quietly. She sniffed one more time, and she was done. Really done. *No more tears.*

More speed-speak, then Fax said, "It's whatever we wish it to be. Anni-Oakley sniped a half-dozen by herself with mercy bullets, but we can't raise her anymore on the radio. Franklin and I took out another post after you left us, but Demo and Saban are pinned down from three different positions back by the library."

Franklin continued. "Spar went all wild-thing on another half dozen, but she's trapped, too. Subnet is busy with his own one-on-one. We were supposed to extract you in about ten minutes, but Saban moved it up, because the bad guys came early to the party. Half of Charlie team is still en route. The other half is fenced in near the library. It's a mess." He counted on his fingers. "We're looking at…maybe five different pockets with two-to-four adversaries each, plus three more potential hotspots."

Fax finished. "We were tasked with getting you out of here, but now that I see you can take care of yourself, we think we have a plan…if you're game." They picked up on each other's sentences so easily; it was kind of cute despite the deadly seriousness of the situation.

"I'm game." Margo knew one thing: she was tired of feeling helpless.

"Good. I wanted you to decide before I let you hear this. It's important to make decisions based on information and not emotion." She adjusted Margo's radio set to the channel everyone else was using.

Margo heard Saban barking commands and other voices responding. She could hear the faint "pffft" of silenced gunfire in the background. No one was panicking, but they were clearly and overwhelmingly outnumbered. No matter how well Saban could work the problem, there were just too many opposing forces.

"Oh, no, I forgot!" Margo exclaimed. "I heard they're going to kill Saban if they figure out which one he is. We have to help!"

"We will," Fax and Franklin replied in unison.

Fax ushered them toward the road. "Franklin and I will run 'point.' Stay with us at first so I can explain what we're doing, then drop in behind us." As they began to run at a slow trot, she touched her radio set to activate her microphone. "Hang on, people. The cavalry is coming."

"No!" Margo heard Saban's response. "Get her out of here! We're not screwing this up!"

Margo touched her own radio set and turned on the mike. "It's already screwed up. Now it's going to get straightened out. Be ready—doof." Then she added, "Ninety-nine out."

"Oooh! Telling off the boss!" Franklin clapped his hands and rubbed them together for emphasis. "We may all get along after all."

"Let's go, Agent Ninety-nine." Fax almost chuckled. Almost.

"C'mon," Franklin said, "let's go kick butt, save the day—"

"If we live," interjected Fax almost cheerfully. "And then we're going home."

Home. Where was her home? Where was her family? Did she even have a family?

She might not know where she came from, but she was no longer powerless over where she went from here. Perhaps this family would do for now. To whom else would she go? She saw Franklin and Fax begin to pull ahead and hurried to catch up with them.

Margo had endured a lot of frustration over the past few weeks, and it was about to spill out onto the heads of someone's very unlucky private army.

CHAPTER 24: The Fine Art of Removing Oneself

Ten minutes ago, Saban had just enough time to see Margo flanked by Fax and Franklin before diving for cover. His intention had been to draw their fire after him, and it had worked almost too well. At first, Saban thought he had taken too long up in Margo's room, but most of these agents—many more than he had anticipated—had apparently been here for quite some time. They were in a neatly-drawn trap, and outnumbered perhaps five to one.

This scenario was too much of a coincidence: that the Ancient was twice out in force, and twice met up with a counter force. Either their mole was very good, or someone was playing a larger game of chess. Or both.

To make matters worse, most of their assailants were in areas where M-Sec's carefully placed cameras were not. Clearly, they had done their homework or had their homework done for them. They could have moved anytime if Margo had been the fish they wanted to catch. But they waited until Alpha showed up. Margo had been the bait. Alpha was the fish.

He scanned the field in front of him, a scene of surreal violence, like an action movie with the sound turned off. The trees swayed gently under a full moon, its tender luminescence shining over the field, the library, the surrounding buildings, and the people holding weapons aimed at him.

Their muffled fire was lost amidst the other background noises of the night. Only the sporadic shattering of tree bark and distant flicker of discharging firearms gave an indication as to what was really going on. Saban and Demo were pinned down behind a small row of trees. The few members of Charlie that had arrived were pinned down as well. Nobody was dead yet, but that might change soon.

A bullet whizzed by his helmet and exploded a branch behind him. *Focus!* At the moment, the big picture could wait. His first priority had been to get Margo out of harm's way, and that was done. Next was to extricate himself and Demo, then assist Alpha and the few Charlie members who were already engaged. If only the rest of Charlie team had arrived! If they could hold out for another ten minutes….

That was a big if. They would be lucky to last another five.

He checked in with Subnet and Spar over the radio. Still no reply from Anni, but given her position on the roof and her head cover, she was more likely concussed than dead. At least the twins had gotten Margo safely away. He fired a few more shots from his rifle, but he was not the marksman that Anni was.

He had never been in a situation this dire, but he was sure there was a way out.

From his headset, he heard the crackle of someone coming online, then Fax's voice was in his ears. "Hang on, people. The cavalry is coming." Had Charlie team arrived early? Surely she didn't mean….

His hand flew up to his radio controls. "No! Get her out of here! We're not screwing this up!" Fax and Franklin would have to travel together, so where would they put Margo to keep her safe? There was no telling where she might run off to in her state of mind.

"It's already screwed up," came Margo's voice, with an authority he hadn't heard in weeks. "Now it's going to get straightened out. Be ready—doof. Ninety-nine out."

He and Demo looked at each other. Demo shrugged. He was usually a man of no words anyway. Now Saban was, too. He was speechless.

A sudden flurry of bullets peppered the tree in front of him, jolting him back to the task at hand. The enemy was well coordinated, typically firing simultaneously from at least two different directions, so it was hard to know where to return fire. This time, he got a good idea of where one nest was and opened up. He thought he might have hit someone, but he wasn't sure. It would have to do for now. He had to address the twins.

As he raised his hand to reactivate his comm-link, he saw something—no, make that three "things"—racing towards the post at which he had just been firing. They were definitely Ancient, and inhumanly swift. The two in front had to be the twins, of course, but there was a third figure, perhaps thirty feet behind, and moving almost as fast. Margo couldn't be that fast. Could she?

The twins were on top of the post before the soldiers knew what was happening, but all the twins could do was grasp the ends of their opponents' rifles. He touched his zoom lens-adjust to get a better view.

Franklin had two barrels and Fax had one. The soldiers stood up and tried to regain control of their weapons, but they were evenly matched. Without warning, Margo was in their midst, an explosion of fists, elbows and boots. *Oh my gosh, she's destroying them!*

The twins took off for another position before the soldiers had dropped to the ground, two of them still holding onto their weapons and all of them unconscious. Margo stayed long enough to grasp the barrel of each rifle, brace her knee against it, and give each barrel a slight bend. *Unbelievable.* Saban knew she was strong, but he was stunned. Those rifles would never fire again, and this altercation would be permanently ended if she continued.

She did. Nest after nest of soldiers was visited, first by the twins, who set them up, and then by Margo, who knocked them down with brutal efficiency. It was hard for Saban not to simply stand and watch. In the end, the last group of soldiers knew what was coming, but they could not draw a bead on the twins fast enough, and only a handful of men gave Margo more than a few seconds' trouble. He was mesmerized by a violent but beautiful ballet, full of elegant evasions and bone-jarring impacts.

He and Demo stood up. He spotted Spar across the way, watching Margo with a similar sense of rapt awe. Spar was trying to rub her eyes, as if seeing a vision so beautiful it made her all misty. Figures.

No time to lose. He touched his comm-link. "That was…wow. I think you made Spar cry. Fax, did you tell her to destroy the rifles? That was genius!"

Margo's voice came on the comm-link, "She didn't. I kind of improvised that part."

"Beauty," Saban commented. "But let's not waste this; they might try something else. Spar, Subnet, Demo, form on the lift, and let's evac Anni and the rabbit's P.E." P.E. was short for "personal effects," as they all knew. "Fax, Franklin and uhm…Ninety-nine, form on me by chokepoint two. Charlie team, form on your squad leaders and follow Demo. Let's move!"

Spar got to the truck first, jumping into the bucket of the mini cherry-picker mounted near the rear. Subnet was right after her and pulled something out of the truck that looked like five or six hula hoops, sewn into a roll, with a few feet of fabric between each hoop. It was a collapsible tunnel, which he placed under one arm as he climbed into the bucket with Spar, who used the local controls to move the arm up.

When they got to Margo's window, Subnet took his end of the tunnel and climbed into her room. Spar continued moving the bucket up to the roof, where she stopped and leapt out.

"Anni is okay. Well, she's breathing," Spar reported to Saban, as he, the twins and Margo ran toward one of the campus exits. "Graze to the head from what I can see, full impact to the shoulder, no penetration. She'll be sore for a few days. She's coming 'round. I'll have her in the bucket in a few seconds."

"Ready when you are," came Subnet's voice.

"Ready," replied Demo in his booming baritone. Subnet had fastened one end of the conduit to the window and dropped the other end down to Demo, who attached it to a sunroof next to the base of the mechanical arm. At Demo's signal, Subnet began to toss all of Margo's belongings into it.

"Y'know, there's a plethora of P.E., but it's so organized. No posters to take down, no leftover foodstuffs lying about," Subnet observed. "She never struck me as a neat-freak. It's like she was ready to go."

"I was." Saban saw Margo's hand at her comm-link as they ran. "I finished packing when I saw the truck under the window."

"How did you know it was us?" Saban asked.

"I didn't," she replied. "Hey, don't throw my laptop down there."

"Roger that," came Subnet's enthusiastic response.

"We're coming down." Spar had Anni in tow.

"Affirmative. I'm done," said Subnet. He unbuckled the conduit from its mooring and let it fall on top of the SUV, where

Demo buckled it down and closed the roof. Subnet squatted in the open window, Margo's laptop in one hand, and stepped lightly into the bucket as it passed by him. When it went as far as it could go, they all stepped out, Demo helped Anni down, and all four slid into the passenger section.

The truck rumbled across the playing field, past the limp bodies of unconscious militia. Once over the curb, they drove to the nearest entrance and merged into the light traffic.

"Gone," Saban heard Demo say. And so they were.

Saban, Margo and the twins made their way on foot to the other entrance, where they convened behind a large beige van. He had heard from the missing half of Charlie team while Margo's room was being cleared out; they would arrive just in time to give Alpha a lift back to the outpost. Before then, however, Saban needed to take care of one more thing.

He rapped his knuckles on the back door of the van.

No answer. He knocked again, harder. "I know you're in there, throw your guns out first and then open up, or else I'll have one of my very strong friends rip the door from its hinges. And possibly your arms from your torsos."

Margo whispered, "I can't do that! Also, yyy-uck! That's disgusting!"

"I'm just bluffing about the torso thing, Mar," he whispered back. "Get a grip!"

"No, doofus, I mean I can't take the door off the hinges."

Saban blinked. "You can't?"

"No, I can't! I'm strong enough to bend metal, not rip it to shreds." There was more than a hint of exasperation in her voice, but she sounded so much like her old self that he didn't care.

"Well, they don't know that," he said in a hushed tone. "C'mon!" he said loudly. "I don't have all day! Last chance, or we start removing doors from hinges, guns from hands, hands from wrists…."

The door creaked open and three revolvers fell out. Some muffled but raised voices came from inside, as well as the sounds of a brief scuffle, followed by a fourth revolver. The door swung open.

Inside the van were all the sorts of electronic equipment one would expect—not state-of-the-art, not horrible—a less compact version of their own comm-car. *How can people use this sort of outdated equipment?* Sitting or standing within the somewhat cramped quarters were four men. Saban read them all in an instant. Two of them were mere hirelings, but the other two would need to be dealt with. One man was Desmond Dewitter, who Saban recognized from his intel briefings with John. The other man was Devon Ford.

* * *

The last two months had gone poorly for Devon Ford. Accosted and drafted into an international team of spooks. Placed under the direct supervision of a man who held him beneath contempt, or at least squarely at the level of contempt. That sort of treatment did not inspire loyalty.

Truth be known, Ford had spotted Margo, then Saban, in late November, but sat on the knowledge out of spite. Still, a contract was a contract. And for the longest time, he had been under two of them—honor bound to fulfill them both. And he had.

Ford sat at the console where he had watched the battle unfold between their assembled agents and the unknown faction of operatives that might possibly be the Ancient. For a time, it appeared they might take the whole group into custody with a minimum of collateral damage. Dewitter's plan had unfolded with great precision and overwhelming force.

Then those three agents came from nowhere, with one of them showcasing skills of butt-kickery to rival the kid's. And as Dewitter's mission fell apart, he had the great pleasure of watching Dewitter fall apart with it.

So the last five minutes had been no fun for the agents in the field. No fun for the snipers on the walls, or the guards by the gates. No fun for the other two schmoes in the van with him, watching the whole affair unravel from their monitors. And certainly it was no fun for Dewitter, who had been screaming orders into his headset to little avail.

But it had been great fun for Ford. He could barely keep from laughing. *Serves them right.* Though he hadn't been sure how the kid and the Ancient fit together until just now.

But when the rap came on the door and the surrender of their weapons was demanded, he knew exactly who he was dealing with.

The agent with the number "eight" on his shoulder was the kid. Ford wondered for a moment if there was any possibility that the Ancient had a dental plan, because he had just worked his way out of one job a few hours ago, and might be about to lose the other.

"So, Agent Ford," said Eight in a thick French accent, "we meet again."

Yeah, definitely the kid. "We meet again, Inspector Clouseau," he replied.

"I have to say," the kid continued in normal English, "I'm much more impressed with this bunch than the last bunch."

"Well, I can't take credit for—" Ford was interrupted by Dewitter.

Dewitter moved from the back to the front of the van, jostling Ford as he leapt to the ground. "See here, young man, you have a good deal of explaining to—"

"Shut up. I'm not talking to you, Desmond. Yeah, I know who you are, and I'm underwhelmed. Be patient. Your turn is coming."

Geez, this kid must have stones like the kind that chase Indiana Jones through caves. Ford liked that. Reminded him of…himself, when he was young. "How did you know where we would be?" Ford asked, also ignoring Dewitter.

"Well," the agent marked "A47" commented, "the satellite dish on top of the van was definitely not a complete giveaway."

"Ah. So what now?"

"That's up to you," Eight responded. "Listen, Ford. In your own strange way, I think you're an honorable man. So as one warrior to another, I'm asking you…respectfully…do not make me cross paths with you again. The endgame is coming, and I can't be responsible. Do we understand each other?" His tone was polite but firm.

Ford was taken aback. The thought of someone trying to look out for him was vaguely moving. "We understand each other." And he trusted the kid's integrity a lot more than Dewitter's empty posturing.

"Excellent. No doubt you were forced into service by this clown, Dewitter, so let me deal with him."

Ford almost felt the kid's attention turn away from him and focus on Dewitter.

"As for you," Eight said to Dewitter, and continued as if lecturing a recalcitrant student, "we have committed no crime, caused no damage, carry only weapons of self defense. We were attacked without provocation, with lethal weapons, and on private property. Does Uncle Sam know that MI-6 is leading combat assaults against US citizens on US soil?"

Dewitter was not that easily intimidated. "Who do you think loaned us the troops?" he replied snidely.

That seemed to make Eight think. "Hmm. Regardless, you have a lot more explaining to do than I will, since I'm not the one whose infantry just got the smackdown by a force less than a third its size. Incidentally, how many men did you have on the ground?"

Dewitter refused to answer.

"How many?" Eight pressed.

"Sixty," Dewitter grudgingly admitted.

"Wow," said the other male agent. "I'd lost count. You better think twice before taking us on, because the Ancient cleaned your clock today."

"Franklin," one of the female agents chided, and placed a hand on his shoulder.

Ford could almost see Eight's mental gears turning. "All this was pointless," Eight finally said. "Why don't you simply ask what you want to know?"

Ford watched Dewitter grapple with what he had just heard, as if trying to understand a word from a foreign language.

"Ask," Dewitter repeated.

"Yes, ask. We're not your enemy. I tell you what, I'll make you a deal. When we leave, don't bother us with any of your people we might have missed, and in return I'll give you sixty seconds to ask anything you want."

Again, Dewitter blinked, struggling with what was just said. "Excuse me?"

"Sixty seconds. One for each of your people that we took out. And it needs to be now, before they start waking up. Deal?"

Dewitter sighed. "Deal. Who are you?"

"I'm Saban Smith," said Eight.

Hunh. Just like his school records said.

"No, I mean who are all of you?" said Dewitter.

It was Saban/Eight's turn to sigh. He glanced at the agent named Franklin and said, "We are the Ancient, a combination paid and volunteer security team with paramilitary capabilities, deployed only to protect our varied and legitimate business interests in the United States and abroad." The answer was well-rehearsed, like literature from a brochure.

"Do those interests include the U-crystals?" Dewitter countered.

"They do, to the extent that they are not owned by anyone *per se*, and in that they represent a legitimate threat to our interests, as well as the interests of the free world."

Dewitter did not appear surprised. "So when you say security, what you mean is an unauthorized and illegal global police force."

"Illegal? Hah!" said agent Franklin. "We have a more justifiable reason for being on campus than you do. We were invited!"

Saban let out an indignant snort. "Nevertheless, we're not the ones on the verge of causing an international incident, so I would be careful throwing around terms like 'illegal' and 'unauthorized.' You are free to press suit if we're violating any laws on a national or international scale, but we're not," he glanced at his watch, then at Franklin, "though I am not at liberty to disclose the specifics. You have fifteen more seconds."

"Where is Ms. Weissmann?" asked Dewitter.

Ford thought he saw Saban turn his head almost imperceptibly toward one of the female agents, who had stood like a stone since they all had walked up. When he spoke, he did so very carefully and quietly. "Ms. Weissmann was an unfortunate civilian who was simply in the wrong place at the wrong time. You can ask Mr. Ford how much she contributed to our fracas two months ago, and I believe he will tell you she had nothing to do with it."

"It's true," Ford volunteered. "She wasn't a factor."

"Ms. Weissmann has been relocated of her own accord," Saban continued, "and will remain sequestered until a time of her choosing." Then Saban leaned forward within inches of Dewitter's face. "You never know what kind of nut job would use an innocent girl to cover his own lack of ability in legitimate intelligence gathering."

A white SUV pulled up several yards away. Saban made a fist in the air, then motioned toward the vehicle. He and his crew turned around to leave.

"Wait!" Dewitter called out. "How is it that you've been able to work behind the scenes for half a century without any other agencies knowing about you?"

"Are you sure no one knew about us, or is that just what you've been told? The truth is…oh! We've run out of time." All four of the blue-clad agents got inside except Saban, who stood near the front passenger side. "Trust me when I say that we're here to help. We're not hurting anyone. And you should stay out of our way." He waved. "Keep your head down, Ford."

"You too." There was something still nagging at Ford. He debated for a moment whether he should ask, how it would look. *What the heck.* He slipped out of the van and ran toward the car. "Hey, Smith! Eight! Hey!" he shouted.

Saban was getting into the car, but stopped, closed the door and approached Ford. "Yeah?"

"Are you giving lessons now?" Ford would have defaulted on both of his assignments for a chance to sign up under this guy. There was something irresistible about him.

"Lessons?" Saban asked.

"The females that took out so many of my guys. Aren't they your students?" Ford asked.

"No. Why?"

"Two of them fight just like you do. Except for the atomic elbow."

When Saban responded, it was very quietly. "I hadn't noticed. Two of them, not just one? You're sure about that?"

"Well, the one that was pinned down by fire, so I'm not sure about her. But the other one, Ninety-nine, I was watching her on the monitors. And I've seen you close up, so who would know better than me? Anyway, if you ever start a school or something, keep me in mind. I'm sure you could find me if you wanted to." Saban wasn't moving. "Kid?"

Saban shook his head like he was waking up. "Right. Thanks. Listen, ditch these guys, okay? They're going to get you killed for nothing. Stay frosty." Saban ducked his head into the car and they sped off, leaving Ford by the side of the road, once again weighing his options.

The thing Ford could not figure out was the point of it all. Months ago, he had been hired by some mysterious person to find a missing crystal. The mystery man provided Ford's crystal and the technology to find another. When the crystal had been lost and Ford was conscripted into Dewitter's service, the mystery man kept him on retainer, but never told him why. Ford assumed it was to make a better offer when the crystals were eventually located.

The question was, if Dewitter and his people represented a pre-existing consortium of international security interests, then who was the other person who had hired him? The American? The Russian? Could Dewitter himself be working both sides of the equation? And as Desmond might say, what was so bloody important about these crystals, anyway?

Ford made his way back to the van, deep in thought. As he approached, he looked up. Dewitter was glaring, his face crimson and his teeth actually bared.

Dewitter was hastily giving a description of the SUV to someone on the other side of his two-way, telling him to shoot the tires if the vehicle passed by their post. "What was that all about, you stupid half-wit?" he managed to spit out at Ford.

"Nothing," Ford responded coolly. "Just two warriors exchanging honorable farewells. You wouldn't understand." He took a few more steps. "Don't say I didn't warn you," he said quietly. As he walked, he scooped up one of the guns from the ground. In a single fluid motion, he turned, aimed the gun at a startled Dewitter and fired. "Oh, and by the way, Desmond, I quit."

CHAPTER 25: The Game That Was Not a Game

The ride back to the warehouse was taking forever.

As he and John talked, Saban was aware yet again that John was withholding information. Margo would be staying with Alpha, according to John, and there was to be no argument. John didn't even want them to make an attempt at hiding information from her. She was simply "in." Somehow, Saban had seen that coming, and didn't argue; he merely announced it to the other passengers as though it were a joint decision.

But the last thing John said was completely unexpected—and Saban had reached the point where he had to protest. They were not to return to the main headquarters. Not yet.

"What do you mean, we can't come back to home base? I've been in the field since the end of the summer!" Saban was trying hard to keep his voice down, but it didn't really matter, he was going to be overheard no matter what. They were all crammed into the SUV and headed toward the satellite location where he and Alpha had been staying.

Sure, there were a few things unresolved. Who was Margo Weissmann? Why did her memories go kabloo-ey and how did she get all Hong Kong Foo-ey? There was also the matter of who had hired Ford's team and where they had gotten their U-crystal. Well, John would probably figure that out, too. Or did he already know?

Finally, there was the mystery of someone taking out both sides with mercy bullets during their initial encounter with Ford's team. If there was a mole in the Ancient, it was someone who was not trying to kill anyone. Who would benefit if both teams had been taken out of the equation that night? Was there a third entity out there trying to gather the five Vulternense crystals for themselves? Or some different game?

He had assumed that, with the crystals long since retrieved, and M-Sec's security system in place, and Margo safely extracted…*well, what more is there left to do?*

"This is what I'm trying to tell you," John replied to Saban's unspoken question. "We're at a critical juncture, and you must listen to me very carefully. I mean that. Will you listen?"

"Of course. I'm listening, Six."

"Think back several months ago to the summer. You and I were finishing up as much training as I felt you could handle. In retrospect, it was probably more than you could handle."

"I remember. I've tried to make up for that."

"This isn't about you. Not entirely." John stopped talking for so long, Saban briefly wondered if the connection had been lost. "What I never told you was that during that time I was also investigating the events surrounding the accident that required you to assume a leadership position. When you began feeling the strain of leadership, I let you take over an assignment to find one crystal that had been stolen long ago and hidden somewhere at Dauphin Hill. While you were gone, I continued to go over and over the records of the day we lost so many people." John paused. "The day I lost my wife and the others. And I came to a painful conclusion."

"And what was that conclusion? I'm not sure I understand the relevance. We got the crystal and an extra. We put in the security. We pulled Margo out. Aren't we done here?"

"This game is over, Saban. But the real work has barely begun. Once you secured the crystal from the vault, do you really think we couldn't have come up with a cover story for your disappearance? Poor grades, auto accident, perhaps a sick relative…you could have been pulled out at any time. For our part, M-Sec was under no obligation to fulfill a security contract we had not yet accepted."

"But Margo—"

"—could have been protected or extracted by anyone, though you were the most logical choice. Keeping you in the field, however, also kept her in danger, since either one of you might have been identified by Devon Ford or his team, and more easily since you were together. So why did I keep you in the field? What was your true purpose?"

Saban knew why, and he didn't like the answer. "You…you…."

"Why did I keep you out in the field?" John repeated.

Saban knew the answer; he just didn't want to admit it. "Bait."

"Of course."

"I thought Margo was the bait to get us. What was I the bait for?"

"You alone were not the bait. It took me some time, but I was able make to a short list of insiders who possibly could have sabotaged our facility, and I finalized that list once you arrived at Dauphin Hill. That list has eight agents on it, several of whom are especially dear to me. I decided that if we do have a mole, the best way to draw him out was to place some pressure on each of those agents and see what happened."

"That makes sense." *Just like he taught me to do.* "So how have you been able to keep track of them all without alerting every other…agent…." He couldn't finish the thought. *It can't be.*

"I realize you're in a car full of agents, so you need to exercise caution and not respond, or at least keep your responses neutral-sounding, like 'yes' and 'no.' Do you copy?"

Saban didn't know whether to be scared or angry, but angry was winning. After being treated as a peer for so long, Saban found it irritating to be treated as a pawn.

"I repeat, do you copy?"

Saban couldn't decide if John sounded angry or desperate. "Yes."

"There was a reason why I pulled this Alpha team together at the last moment, why I chose these particular people and no more. Haven't you figured this out?"

"Yes, but I'm going to make you say it, anyway."

"Very well. The probability of being a mole was the criteria I used to assemble Alpha. You were all suspects, and most of you *still* are. I left you all out in the field to protect the Ancient, not Margo, and I was hoping to draw the mole out into the open by placing Alpha in a position of stress. That's why I hired Ford's team and outfitted them with non-lethal weapons. I gave them one of the—"

"You what?" Saban saw the familiar warehouse in the distance and readied himself to jump out of the vehicle so as to finish the conversation in private.

"Quiet. I was the person who sent them their crystal and their equipment, knowing that by the end of the evening, one team or the other would have both crystals, and perhaps our mole would be revealed. It was unfortunate that Jesse was injured. I've hired Ford on several occasions and was never sorry until then."

"You're unbelievable! Just how many times is—"

"Hold your tongue until you're alone. You're losing sight of the big picture."

The SUV was approaching the entrance to the adjoined garage. Saban opened his door, jumped out and shut it before the SUV even came to a halt. He was sure there were surprised looks going around the rest of the team. *Too bad for them.*

He rounded a corner and squatted, leaning against a wall and cradling himself. "I'm away from the others. Now, we're going to have a reckoning." His cheeks burned.

"No, we are not. This is a non-issue. I arranged a semi-controlled situation where I attempted to reveal a killer without getting anyone killed. It didn't work. What you should be focused on is that, despite my best efforts, the mole is unrevealed. That person caused an explosion that killed my dearest friends. You need to focus. I realize this is a lot to take in."

"You bet your British bum it is."

"I don't think I care for your tone, Saban."

"I don't think I care, period! You used me. You've used all of us!"

"I made a decision based on the facts at hand. I have the right to make decisions about you without asking for your permission. You would do the same thing, if the outcome were necessary—"

"I would never do that to you!"

"Thus spake Zara-Saban. Tell me you've never used your spin to ensure an outcome you felt was justified."

The resultant silence was telling to them both.

Saban's face was growing hotter and hotter as he recalled spinning the college administrator to give audience to Spar and Demo, ending an argument with James. There were other times, minor things, really. *How dare he compare what he did and what I do?*

But there were still things John needed to answer. "You said there were eight people on the list," Saban said. "There are only seven people on Alpha. Who was the eighth person?"

"You were not the first person I sent to find the crystal. I sent one of my best agents, undercover just as you were, but things did not turn out well."

"That seems to be a habit with your plans." Saban couldn't resist taking the jab.

"You have no right to question me, lad. Do you wish to know or not?"

"I'm sorry," Saban said through gritted teeth. "Please continue."

"When it was apparent this agent would not be able to complete the mission, she agreed, for personal reasons, to have her memories altered and stay in the field as a sleeper. She was given the subliminal directive to protect you whenever you were in danger. Again, something unexpected happened, and her implanted memories were overwritten by subconscious memories, which robbed her of—"

"Margo! I knew it! That's how she knew about the spin. Dammit, John, now you've crossed the line. You lied to me! You told me you knew nothing about her!"

"I most certainly did not. If you recall, I said that there was nothing I could tell you about her at that—"

"Does she know?"

"What?"

"Does she know?" Suddenly, this was the most important question Saban had ever asked. "Is she a part of this?"

"She is a part of this, ultimately. She was one of ours, and will be again when we can discover how to repair her memory. But the girl you know is every bit as honest and sincere as the Margo that I know. She currently has no idea of her past or place in all this."

"And what is her place, John? While you're at it, why don't you tell me what my role is, too!"

"Your role has not deviated. You kept the Ancient together when there was a chance it could fall apart. You were placed in a leadership role, and you have handled it better than I ever hoped you could."

"And how is it that I happened to be here to begin with? How come you've never told me that? How come there's so much you haven't shown me or told me?"

"How much of the reins did you really expect me to hand over to you, an unknown asset, with so many lives already lost? Had I given you any more, I would have destroyed you. I nearly did, and for that I do apologize." John continued when Saban remained silent. "I hired you to do a job. I assisted you in doing that job. I made you a partner, and I believe I've proven that I care what happens to you and the rest of Alpha, but you know it's 'mission first.'" John sighed loudly. "Don't you understand that I'm telling you all this because I've realized that you could not be the mole!"

"And why me? Why was I on the list at all?"

"Saban, you have the ability to alter perception, reason and memory. Why would you not be on the list? I'm not going to apologize for suspecting you or anyone else. I had to be sure. But if it will soothe your anger, I will tell you that I'm convinced the mole is not you."

"What made you sure?"

"Because you care. I see no agenda in you except doing the right thing. I confess, I never truly suspected you, and after watching you the past few weeks, especially listening to the way you tried to take care of Margo, you—"

"You were eavesdropping on me?"

"As we have eavesdropped on others. Do the rules of engagement not apply to you? Saban, we are responsible for many, many lives. I had to be sure I could trust you."

"Well, how do I know I can trust you? This isn't over, old man. You're just incredible, and I mean that in the worst possible way." Saban desperately wished he was on a regular phone instead of a cell so he could at least have the satisfaction of slamming the receiver into its holder. "I can't talk to you anymore. I have a team to take care of. I won't abandon them. Not ever. But this—is—not—over!" He pressed the "end" button to terminate the call.

How could John do this? The manipulation, the half-truths. There was no one in the world Saban admired more, no one else he fully trusted, not even Jesse. Did John arrange tonight's skirmish, too?

And one of the people on his team was a betrayer. Who could he turn to? Jesse always seemed cold, but she had it right all along. It was "mission first." Trust no one. But how was he supposed to track down the last two crystals without completely trusting his team? He would not be able to let his guard down—not for a moment—and it would be a long time before he let his guard down around John.

If ever. Damn him!

Saban walked through the garage and entered the massive warehouse where Alpha would be staying for the time being. Once past the kitchenette, he quickly and quietly locked himself into the bathroom and, for the third time since leaving home, began to cry.

CHAPTER 26: A New Family

"This will be your room," Margo heard Fax say. "Saban says you're staying with us for a while. You'd think he would be happier about it."

"Who knows what Saban wants? Probably not even Saban." Margo had already tossed her helmet onto the floor when they came in. They were in a warehouse large enough to comfortably sleep a dozen or so people. She hoped there were enough bathrooms for all of them.

"I'll have Subnet drop off your laptop. Bathroom is down the hall. You'll share with Anni, Spar and me. I thought we were to leave in the morning, but it's sounding like we're staying put. Try to get some sleep." Fax was pulling the door closed.

"Whére will you be?" Margo asked before it shut completely. She didn't want to loose track of this girl. Margo appreciated Fax's candor, like a friend who will tell you when there's spinach in your teeth.

"Well, my brother, James—we call him Franklin in the field—he's at the other end, so I'll be at this end, two doors down from you."

"You guys…don't get along?" He and Fax had bickered on the drive over, but most of it was friendly. Saban had appeared pretty steamed, however, and even more so after talking to someone named Six.

"Do we…? Oh! No, we get along fine, when he's not doing idiot things like dropping information in front of the opposition."

She must have meant that rude Englishman who was trying to capture her and Saban. "You mean when he mentioned—what are you called—the Ancient?"

"Yes, things like that. But regarding James and I, the closer we are, the more energy we have. Like microphones and speakers too close together. The feedback we generate is what makes us so fast. Great for combat—bad for rest. If we're stuck in the same room, it takes us forever to fall asleep," Fax said with a small laugh.

"That sounds like fun. How long can it keep you awake?"

"Last time we had to? About three and a half days," Fax replied.

"No way!"

"Way. Eighty-three hours, twenty-eight minutes. Roughly."

"That must have been horrible when you were kids."

"No, not really," Fax said. "We didn't meet until we were seven, and our talents didn't come in until we hit puberty, and even then it was gradual. We're still getting stronger, so we're working this out as we go." Fax shut the door, then opened it again and popped her head in. "I'm sorry; I forgot you're one of us, now. Did I mention my real name is Jessica? You can call me Jesse."

Margo smiled and extended her hand. "Pleased to meet you again, Jesse. Why do they call you Fax?"

Jesse rolled her eyes. "Ugh. That's my dumb brother's fault. I tend to be very detail-oriented, and…well, I like knowing everything I can about whatever I need to do. When we were little, James would run around mocking me, 'just the facts, ma'am, just the facts.' It stuck. When I became a field agent, I had a different code-name, but everyone kept calling me 'Facts,' like always, so I changed it a little. It's been harder to get used to people calling me 'Jesse.'"

"Huh. That's wild. What was your…you said 'code-name?' What did it used to be?"

"Oh," Jesse said quickly, "I'm sure I don't remember, it was so long ago. I was just going to say—"

Margo "saw" Jesse pause in mid-sentence. Without thinking, Margo focused her gaze slightly past her new friend. Jesse blurred around the edges, and instead Margo saw…or felt, rather…that Jesse was embarrassed about something she had just said and was gathering courage for what she would say next.

"—that I'm going to be up for a while. Saban is supposed to let us know what the plan is for getting the rest of the crystals, and we have to report to the conference area in thirty minutes, but these excursions always leave me ravenous. I burn a lot of calories. You want to get something to eat before we get debriefed? Down in the kitchen? Uhm…with me?"

This must be what Saban sees when he reads people. Margo realized right away that Jesse was not a "people person," but for some reason was trying to learn how. Jesse seemed so uncomfortable—had she never let herself get close to anyone before?

We'll have to change that! "Best thing I've heard all day. Let me peel myself out of this. I'm glowing like a pig." Margo watched relief pour over Jesse, and began to unfasten the semi-armored top piece of her suit.

"It was 'Coil,'" Jesse said abruptly.

Margo stopped and blinked. "Huh?"

"They tried to call me 'Coil.' Like a spring. That was my codename. I actually…I liked it at first, then James kept teasing that I got the name because I'm wound too tightly. I love him, I do. He was only having fun. I can't believe I let it bother me."

"Coil," Margo mused. "I like it! Can I have it? Anything is better than 'Ninety-nine.'"

She stripped off the dark blue top to reveal her old tee-shirt underneath, and threw the top onto the dresser. Her notebook fell from beneath the stiff outer garment. She picked it up and turned it over and over. As she handled her notebook, the last repository of her forgotten past, she waited for the familiar rush of despair, but it didn't come. Perhaps her whole life was not wrapped up in that notebook. Her past might be, but not her future.

"What is that?" Jesse asked.

"It's…it's just some stuff I want to hang on to."

"Are you sure you want to leave it there?"

"It'll keep," Margo answered, tossing it on the dresser, next to the rigid torso-covering garment she had just shed. "Where's the kitchen? I'm starved!"

"What are you in the mood for?"

Margo thought for a moment. "Pasta! I hope you are, too."

"Why do you say that?"

"Because I have a feeling that we're all going to Italy soon. I want to tell you about this dream I keep having."

They stood at the railing, overlooking the common area. The warehouse was filled with sounds of bustle and conversation. Fax looked at Margo. "So, we're both fast, were both smart, and I love Italian food. This could be the beginning of an interesting friendship." She smiled.

Saban entered the common area from the kitchenette, moving swiftly among the squad members as he gathered information and issued orders. Margo's eyes tracked him, and she noticed that Jesse was doing the same. "Could be," Margo said. "And who knows what else we'll find we have in common?"

Follow Alpha to the next step in the adventure, when the identity of the mole (and the purpose of the crystals) is revealed!

Saban and the Betrayer, due in late 2007.